STONEHILL
BOOK THREE

the forgotten
path

Cover design by Okay Creations
Book layout by Lori Colbeck

ISBN-13: 978-1-950348-06-0

STONEHILL
BOOK THREE

the forgotten path

MARCI
BOLDEN

PINK SAND
PRESS

CHAPTER ONE

*M*arcus barged into his boss's office. "We've got to stop meeting like this."

Annie jolted, startled by his sudden appearance. She'd taken the pins from her hair, letting her blond strands fall around her shoulders, but it was a mess from running her fingers through it. She only did that when she was stressed, proving to Marcus this intervention was most definitely needed.

She dropped her reading glasses on the desk and looked up at him with curious gray eyes. Though she tended toward more neutral colors in her clothing, he knew that she liked red lipstick that stuck out against her pale skin. When she pressed her lips together in that way she so often did where he was concerned, the red very nearly disappeared as her mouth became a thin line of disapproval. She tilted her narrow chin down as she focused on the bag in his hand. "What's that?"

He sat in his usual seat on the other side of her desk. "Meatloaf, potatoes, and green beans."

"I didn't order dinner."

"Nope. You didn't. But look at that." He dropped the bag on her desk. "I brought it anyway. I'm vying for Employee of the Year."

She smiled weakly as he tossed a packet containing plasticware and a thin napkin at her. "Why stop there?" she asked. "I'm sure you could get Real Estate Agent of the Year if you wanted."

"Nah. You've got that covered."

"I'm actually not very hungry," she said.

"It'd be rude not to eat with me, Annie. After all the trouble I went through to bring you dinner."

She scoffed the way she always did to let him know she didn't believe him. "Your sister had this delivered, didn't she?"

"She texted me earlier, and I mentioned we were working late. She knows how we are—all work, no sustenance."

"Jen is a saint."

He set a white Styrofoam container in front of Annie and eyed her as she dug in a drawer and tossed a stack of sturdier napkins on the desk. Something about her had been off all day. She'd been unusually melancholy, and he was determined to figure out why.

"Mallory graduates tomorrow," he said. "I'm surprised you aren't home getting ready for the party."

"It's all taken care of and ready to go."

"Oh."

"*Oh?*"

"Well, you've been a thousand miles away all day. I figured you were stressing about seating and finger foods."

Annie focused on her dinner and shook her head. "Nope."

Silence hung over them while he cut into his meatloaf and then chewed a big bite. "How are sales?"

"Fine. We should meet our quarterly goals."

"Good." He took another bite as the quiet lingered. Their late-night dinners didn't normally go this way. They usually spent this time summarizing the day. Taking light-hearted jabs at each other. Laughing and unwinding from work, not sitting in awkward silence. Finally, he sat forward. "Seriously, Annie. You're killing me here. What is wrong with you today?"

She lifted her brows at him. "What?"

"Something's wrong. Even Dianna noticed it. She asked me if I knew what was bugging you before she went home."

"Just because Di is about to become my sister-in-law doesn't mean she's in tune with my feelings."

"You have feelings?"

She cocked a brow at him, and he pointed a mashed-potato-topped fork at her.

"See? That right there. You let that jab go. That isn't like you."

Annie focused on her food again. "Whatever."

His amusement left him. She looked...sad. He couldn't think of a time in the last five years that he'd seen her sad. Annie

O'Connell didn't let things get to her. She wasn't a Pollyanna by any means, but when a problem came up, she tackled it and moved on. She didn't dwell, but she had *been* dwelling. "What happened?"

"Nothing."

"Look, I know when something is wrong with you, and right now, there is definitely something wrong. You can tell me to piss off if you don't want to talk about it, you can tell me I'm your subordinate and it's none of my damned business, but don't lie to me. You've been withdrawn all day. I'm concerned."

She sighed. "My kid is graduating college tomorrow, Marcus. I'm feeling old."

"Feeling old?"

"Yeah."

"You are so full of shit."

She stared at him, appearing to debate what to tell him.

"What is it?" he pushed. He wouldn't get anywhere if he didn't. The woman had never exactly been forthcoming with personal information. Marcus had worked for her for nearly a year before even knowing her birthday, and he'd only found out because her brothers, Paul and Matt, had sent her a huge bouquet. Her threats to do unseemly things with those roses had amused Marcus for days.

"Sometimes I get to thinking about things that I'd rather not think about. Mallory's graduation is stirring the memory pot a little. But I'm fine."

"Her dad?"

Mallory's "dad" hadn't been in the picture since Annie had told him she was pregnant.

"He hadn't even crossed my mind. Until this moment. Thanks for that," she said flatly.

"You're welcome."

"Can't we just enjoy dinner? Please?"

"Not when you're sulking."

"Sulking?"

"Spill it." He stabbed his meatloaf.

She pressed her full lips together when she was irritated, and he knew it also meant she was having an internal debate.

Finally, she shrugged. "I never went to college. My mom died when my brothers were young, and...well, you know this story."

He did, but it had taken him years to learn that her dad was a drunk and her mom died in a car accident. Sixteen-year-old Annie had been the closest thing her younger siblings had to a responsible adult. Her childhood ended when their mother died. Annie started working for a real estate agent before graduating high school and became the breadwinner, primary caregiver, and everything else her brothers needed.

"You're regretting that," he said quietly.

"No. Absolutely not. If I'd gone to college, Paul and Matt wouldn't have. Paul wouldn't be a successful attorney, and Matt wouldn't own his own business. They needed me to help them."

"You're wondering what life would have been like if your mother hadn't died and you'd gone to college."

Annie laughed softly. "Even if my mother hadn't died, I

wouldn't have gone to college. We couldn't afford it. The only reason I got it in my head that my brothers would earn their degrees was because I didn't want them to follow in Dad's footsteps. Working odd jobs to earn just enough to stay drunk? No. I wasn't going to let them go down that road." Pushing her green beans around, she exhaled loudly.

"You were a good sister."

She looked up and smirked at him. "Past tense?"

"*Are.* But I was referring specifically to the time between when your mother died until when you stopped financially supporting your brothers."

"You mean until I got knocked up?" she snapped.

When their dad died from liver failure, Paul had just started his career in criminal law, Matt was finishing college, and Annie got mixed up with the completely wrong kind of guy—the kind who would leave a woman pregnant and alone. Even that didn't stop her from becoming successful enough to own her own real estate agency. Annie might appear aloof and career-driven, but Marcus saw the truth. She was driven by a need for security, and her business had become her security.

She blinked several times and cleared her throat, and he wondered if she were fighting tears. He almost regretted pushing, but then she lifted her face and the grief in her eyes let him know she'd bottled this up far too long.

"I didn't mean it to sound like that. I would be lost without Mallory. Sometimes I just feel like I never had a life, you know? My own life. That's selfish—"

"No, it's not. You were a kid when your mom died, and you were *this* close to being free from the burden she left you with when Mallory was born. It's perfectly natural to feel like you missed out on something. You did, Annie. And it's okay to think about it from time to time. We all think back on our lives and wonder if we made the right decisions."

"I made the right decisions," she said firmly. He knew she wouldn't say otherwise. She wasn't prone to doubting herself. She stuck her fork in her meatloaf and pushed the container away. "Thank you for dinner."

"I owed you. You bought burgers last week. Remember?"

She nodded. "Yes. I guess we really do have to stop meeting like this."

"I actually kind of like this type of dinner over eating in the restaurant."

"Why?"

"Because when you have the menu in front of you, it takes you forever to decide what you want."

Annie cocked a brow, and he laughed.

"That's the first real go-to-hell look you've given me all day. I hadn't realized how much I missed it."

She chuckled. "You're so twisted."

"Listen, Annie—"

"This conversation is over, Marcus."

"No, it's not."

She gave him that look again, but this time it didn't have a playful edge. She really didn't want him to push this any further.

He shook his head. "You're not shutting down on me. Let it out."

"Let it out? Are you my shrink now?"

"I'm your best friend."

Wow, she mouthed as she widened her eyes. "Employee of the Year *and* my new best friend? You are really proud of yourself today."

He wanted to smile with her but managed to keep his face deadpan. "You know I'm the only person who likes you."

A giggle lightened her aura of melancholy. "That very well may be true."

He grinned. "You know better than that."

"Do I?"

"Everybody likes you."

She snorted and leaned back in her seat. "Got your eye on Liar of the Year, too?"

"I am an overachiever."

"You're something."

"Should I be offended by that?"

"Maybe."

He held her gaze until she cleared her throat and looked away. That had been happening with increasing frequency...like they somehow got lost in a moment. Those instances made his heart beat faster.

The first time they got pulled into an intense stare, he'd damn near pulled her into a kiss. Probably would have if they hadn't been setting up an open house. Annie was a great boss as long as she was happy with the work he was doing, but crossing that line would have undoubtedly gotten him fired. And probably slapped. However, he was becoming more and more convinced that he wasn't the only one feeling the underlying tension between them. Tension was a bit of an understatement, at least for Marcus. His attraction to Annie was more like an addiction he hadn't realized he'd developed until it was too late. Now that he'd recognized the attraction between them, it all but consumed him. He spent nearly as much of his workday trying to find excuses to be near her as he did actually working.

In those moments when she clearly felt the pull too, Marcus forgot how stupid it was to fall for his boss, especially when she made a second career out of keeping people at a distance. Her family and daughter were the only people she even remotely let into her heart. He liked to think he was chipping away at the wall she'd built, bit by bit, but the reality was that for every brick he knocked down, she put up two.

"Do you need help with anything tomorrow?" he asked.

"I don't think so."

"I thought I'd pick you up instead of meeting you there. If that's okay."

Her eyes widened. "What?"

"For the ceremony."

She stared at him blankly for a few moments. "You're going to Mallory's graduation ceremony?"

"She gave me a ticket. I assumed you knew."

Annie opened her mouth, and Marcus realized she hadn't had a clue that he was going to be attending the event.

"Uh. No, I didn't."

"If you don't want me to go—"

"No. It's Mallory's day. If she wants you to go…"

"But do *you* want me to go?"

She hesitated as she looked at him. "Do *you* want to?"

"Sure. She's the closest thing I'll ever get to having a kid." He hadn't thought it possible, but Annie's eyes opened even wider. He damn near chuckled. "So you want me to pick you up?"

She slowly nodded.

"About noon? I'd like to get a good parking spot."

"N-Noon is fine. Sure."

He tried not to laugh at her onset of the stutters, but it was so damned amusing when she was flustered. "Noon it is, then."

sh

"*So*," Mallory drawled as she stepped next to her mother, "still mad I invited Marcus to my graduation?"

Annie cocked a brow, silently telling her daughter where she could go. She'd called before she'd even gotten home the night before, wanting to know why Mallory had invited Marcus—or, more to the point, why she hadn't told Annie about it. Mallory had casually said about the same thing Marcus had—besides her uncles, he was the closest thing she had to a father figure. He was the only man who had been steady in her life. Marcus Callison had worked for Annie for five years, and from day one he and Mallory had hit it off.

Sure, Annie had developed a good friendship with Marcus, and because of that he and Mallory had spent some time together, but a father figure? That seemed over the top.

"I ask," Mallory said lightly, "because you've barely stopped staring at him all afternoon. I wasn't sure if that was because you were offended by his presence or because he looks so darned cute in that suit."

Before she actually could tell Mallory to go to hell, her daughter laughed and walked off.

"Why do I get the impression she just bested you?" a deep timbre asked from behind Annie.

She closed her eyes as Marcus's voice rolled through her. Heat burned up from low in her gut and settled in her face. She had no doubt that her cheeks were deep red, but short of being rude, she had no choice other than to face Marcus.

Mallory was right. He did look darned cute in his suit. The business casual dress code at the office meant they didn't dress to the nines often. Marcus's red tie and perfectly tailored black pants and coat had caught her attention. His salt-and-pepper hair was combed to the side, a perfect cut and style for his strong jawline and blue eyes.

Damn it. She was staring at him.

She tilted her head, pursed her lips, and narrowed her eyes in an attempt to get him to back off...and to get her mind off how good he looked.

Instead of slinking away, he laughed with the same enjoyment at her expense that Mallory just had. "Damn. Whatever she said must have been good. I'm sorry I missed it."

Annie started to brush past him, but he put his hand to her upper arm and stopped her retreat. She jolted a bit—not from his touch but from the way she felt the skin-on-skin contact all the way down to her toes. What the hell?

"Come on," he pleaded, "you have to share."

"She thinks she's smart."

"Well, she did just graduate college *cum laude*."

Annie's irritation faded and pride filled her. She couldn't help but smile. "Yes, she did."

He toasted her. "Congratulations."

"Oh, I can't take credit for that. She did it all on her own."

"She has your brains."

Annie shook her head. "I didn't even go to college, remember?"

His face softened, and he looked at her in that way that made her breath catch. "You would have if you hadn't been saddled with other obligations."

She didn't open up about her past often, but something about Marcus made her drop her defenses. She hadn't intended to, but she'd opened her mouth and spewed her emotional mess all over him. Who cared if she hadn't gone to college? Who cared if she'd had a rough go of it? Paul and Matt were grown and successful, and Mallory had just taken one more step along that path. But that hadn't stopped Annie from dwelling on things she shouldn't, and leave it to Marcus to dig in and make her feel all those...*feelings*.

She shrugged just the slightest bit. "It all worked out."

"Yes, it did," he said with quiet sincerity. "You've done amazingly well for yourself. And your family."

He tightened his fingers on her arm and ran this thumb over her bicep, as if to reassure her. Instead, it set her on edge, and she felt as if she were about to fall over. Damn it. What kind of voodoo was this man doing to her?

Annie's focus shifted to her daughter in an attempt to undo whatever it was that had made breathing nearly impossible. Her smile returned as Mallory squealed and hugged a friend who had just arrived at the party.

"I can't believe it," he said. "Our girl just graduated college."

Annie's attention snapped back to him. "*Our* girl?"

"I know I didn't have any part in raising her, but we've gotten close over the years. Like I said last night, she's the closest thing I'll ever have to a daughter."

Marcus smiled, and as tended to happen these days, her chest tightened and warmth spread through her. His gaze softened as he stared at her, and she sighed.

She actually freaking *sighed*.

His deep blue eyes were like an abyss that she fell into every time he looked at her like that. *Like that* meant with a tenderness he shouldn't have for his boss.

She didn't need anyone to tell her how inappropriate that was. She'd told herself a thousand times. That didn't stop her breath from catching whenever he touched her or their gazes stayed locked a few seconds too long—like they were right now.

Thankfully, an obnoxious round of laughter pulled her from his gaze. Annie glanced at her brothers. "I was, um, on my way to the kitchen. Excuse me."

She forced her feet to move her away from the tall drink of temptation in her living room. Alone in the kitchen, she shook her head and leaned against the island, where the extra chips and platters were piled. She closed her eyes and let her head drop forward like it weighed a hundred pounds.

"Get a grip," she muttered.

The door behind her opened, and she nearly laughed. She didn't have to turn around to know Marcus had followed her.

"Need help with anything?" he asked.

"No. I was just..."

Her words faded when he moved to her side, much too close, and she couldn't stop herself from looking at his clean-shaven face. She was tempted to run her fingers along his oval jaw to see if his skin was as soft as it looked. Her self-control was fading quickly. She'd used up damn near all her resolve during the graduation ceremony. He'd sat next to her, his arm resting along the back of her chair during most of the commencement. For nearly two hours, she'd sat stiffly, her hands clutched as she silently reminded herself not to lean into him. Not to put her hand on his knee. Not to smile up at him. Not to rest her head on his shoulder. And to breathe—just breathe, damn it.

Now he was that close again, and the urge to lean into him was nearly irresistible.

His smile faded, easing the deep lines around his eyes, and she did that stupid sighing thing *again*. Clearing her throat —*again*—she focused on the food.

"Chips," she said. "I was…getting more chips."

"Let me help—"

"No," she snapped but then tried to cover by softly laughing. "Go back out there. Enjoy the party."

"This is Mallory's party. *You* go enjoy it. You deserve to celebrate along with her."

Her cheeks heated. That affectionate tone struck a chord it shouldn't, and her heart picked up its pace.

She lifted the chips. "I'll just take these out and then enjoy the party."

"Wait," he said.

The warmth of his hand gently grabbing her elbow spread like wildfire through her. She'd barely gotten control after his touch a minutes ago. Was he *trying* to kill her?

"Annie, I think we should—"

The swinging door to the kitchen opened. Annie's sister-in-law, Donna, stopped in her tracks and looked from Marcus to Annie then back to Marcus.

Donna smirked a bit. "Sorry. I, um, I thought this was the bathroom."

Annie drew her eyebrows together. "That's the best you can do?"

Donna giggled and disappeared, probably to run off and tell their family all about whatever she thought she'd just walked in on.

Marcus laughed quietly as the door swung closed. "Uh-oh. The gossip wheels are turning."

Annie heaved a sigh—this time with frustration instead of whatever it was that made her exhale heavily when Marcus looked at her. "If Donna weren't gossiping, I'd be worried something was wrong with her."

"I'm sorry."

She wasn't. Okay, maybe a little, but only because she didn't want to deal with her family questioning her about her relationship with Marcus. They were convinced that just because they were all happily paired off, she should be, too. Worse, none of them saw anything wrong with Annie dating Marcus. Not that they *were* dating. Not even close. They were just co-workers—friends—who shared dinner a few nights a week. And lunch a few times a week. And attended events such as Mallory's graduation together.

And who shared a habit of staring awkwardly at each other.

She really wished her siblings hadn't started dropping not-so-subtle hints about Marcus liking her. She hadn't been this bumbling mess around him until the first time Donna and Dianna teased her about how Marcus looked at her. Hell, she hadn't even noticed he looked at her at all. Then Paul and Matt got on board, telling her what a great guy Marcus was. As if she needed them to tell her that. She knew Marcus was great. That was why she had hired him.

That and his stupid smile that made her stomach twist around itself.

She lowered her face and closed her eyes for a moment.

"Better refill the chip bowl," he said.

Annie lifted her face. "Hmm?"

He jerked his head toward the living room. "The chip bowl."

She looked at the bag in her hand for a second. "Oh. Right. Chip bowl." A strange half-laugh sound left her. "Right." She left Marcus and pushed the door open as she went back to the party. She ignored Donna and Dianna and frowned at the chip bowl that didn't need to be filled.

sh

An hour and a half later and with the last guest barely out the door, Donna planted a kiss on Annie's cheek. "Good night."

Annie pulled away. "What do you mean good night? You said you'd help clean up."

"The girls have...a thing."

Matt shrugged.

"Marcus can help," Donna offered. Marcus didn't know Donna nearly as well as he knew Paul and Dianna, but the mischief in the woman's blue eyes was plain as a sunny day.

"Marcus is a guest."

Donna creased her brow at Annie. "What am I?"

"Family."

"I don't mind," Marcus offered. He almost wished he hadn't at the look Annie gave him. Her eyes widened, and her jaw set as if he'd offended her.

"We have to run, too," Paul said, hugging his fiancée to him.

"Sorry, Annie." Dianna's pout was as fake as the *thing* Matt and Donna had to run off to do with their kids.

Annie narrowed her eyes at Paul, who smiled as he held his hand out to Marcus. Her brothers clearly weren't fooling her one bit. They were intentionally ditching her and Marcus because Donna thought she walked in on something in the kitchen. They were setting her up to be alone with Marcus. As agitated as this seemed to be making Annie, Marcus was tempted to thank them.

Paul flashed his smirk Annie's way even as he spoke to Marcus. "It was good seeing you. Thanks for helping Annie."

"No problem, Paul," Marcus said, accepting the handshake.

The door closed behind her siblings. Annie and Marcus were alone in the house.

"You don't have to stay," Annie said. "I can clean up."

He grabbed a box of big black trash bags and pulled one out. "I don't mind." He shook the bag and held it open as she collected a stack of paper plates.

"I should have stopped Mallory from sneaking out before helping with this mess."

"She was pretty eager to get home."

Annie frowned. "Yes. I reminded her she will be responsible for any damage to that house."

"I doubt she's having a party."

She gave him a look of disbelief as she added trash to the bag he was holding. "She applied for a few jobs in California."

"She's wanted to move west since I've known her. Why are you surprised?"

"I'm not," she muttered.

He caught her gaze as she shoved a handful of napkins in the bag, but to his disappointment, they didn't get trapped in a lingering stare this time. "Then what's the problem?"

"There is no problem. I just..."

He laughed softly. "You've stuttered and tripped over your words more in the last two days than you have in all the years I've known you. Just tell me what's on your mind, Annie."

She sighed as she stopped gathering trash. Facing him, she tilted her head. "I want her to go out into the world and be her own person. I've raised her to do that. But now that it's time for her to"—she flicked her hand as she searched for the words—"leave the nest..."

"You're worried?"

She closed her eyes. "Marcus, I'm terrified. And I don't know why. I don't know what to do with all this"—she waved her hand again—"stuff."

He grinned as she looked at him, as if silently pleading for him to understand. "They're called emotions, Annie, and this is normal. This is maternal, empty-nest-syndrome *stuff*."

"She hasn't lived at home for three years."

"But she's here several times a week. She's always dropping

by the office. She comes and goes," he said, reminding Annie of all the complaints she had shared about her daughter's not-quite-independent ways. "She can't do that if she's in California."

She groaned as she rolled her eyes. "Do you know how far San Diego is from Stonehill? One thousand seven hundred and fifty miles. I looked it up, Marcus. I *actually* looked it up just in case she gets a job there. I'm not that kind of mom. What is happening to me?"

He chuckled. "You *are* that kind of mom, Annie. You're the kind who loves and worries about her kid. I hate to break it to you, but just because you raised her to be independent doesn't mean you want her to leave. And do you know what is about ten miles from Stonehill? Des Moines International Airport. They have planes there that can transport people from Iowa to California in a matter of hours."

Annie frowned and went back to gathering used cups.

"She's just like you, you know."

Her steel-gray gaze snapped to his. "What does that mean?"

"She knows what she wants," he clarified. "She's going for it. She gets that from you, Annie. You aren't afraid of anything."

Her only response was a scoff and a shake of her head.

"If you hadn't been left to raise Paul and Matt after your mom died, what would you have done?"

She shoved the last handful of paper plates into the trash bag. "I've never thought about it."

"Don't lie. You were thinking about it last night. We all think about what our lives would have been like if we'd just taken that one chance we denied ourselves."

She paused with a tray of uneaten fruit in her hands. "What does it matter what I wanted, Marcus? This is what I have, and I have absolutely nothing to complain about. Except that my daughter wants to move halfway across the country because she thinks Iowa is boring."

He grinned as he followed her. "Iowa *is* boring. Some people just like that."

She stopped. "Excuse me? Is that how you sell this town to people moving here? 'If you like boring, this is the place for you'? Your job, sir, is to sell Stonehill and Des Moines *and* Iowa to new residents."

"I'm a real estate agent, Annie, not the Chamber of Commerce."

She frowned at him, and he smiled. There it was. That look of annoyance that made his soul sing. Annie's sharp wit was a never-ending source of entertainment for him. He wouldn't say he intentionally irritated her, but there was something about the fire that lit in her eyes when she was agitated that made his heart beat just a wee bit faster. He loved the spark in her. Loved the challenge she presented when he refused to back down on something insignificant at the office.

"I should fire you here and now," she said, backing into the kitchen.

They put away leftovers as she lectured him on the virtues of living in central Iowa—the parks, the growing economy, the low crime rate.

Marcus finished gathering the trash and tied the bag as she started in on the great education system. Just as Annie stepped back from the counter, he turned toward the back door with the full bag and they bumped into each other.

He instinctively reached out and grabbed her upper arm. "Sorry 'bout that."

Her cheeks turned a bright red shade that made his entire body tingle. She looked to her right arm where his hand was still resting then cocked her brow at him.

"Oh," he said and laughed awkwardly as he released her.

"Excuse me." She brushed by him.

Trash bag in hand, he watched her head into the living room as he fisted his hand, still feeling the smoothness of her skin against his palm.

When there was nothing left for him to do in the kitchen, he collapsed the folding chairs. Once those were leaning against a wall, he folded the tables and carried two at a time to his truck while Annie carried chairs.

When the furniture was loaded, he lifted the tailgate and faced her.

She brushed her palms together as if to knock away any dirt she may have gathered. "Do you want me to come to the office with you to unload?"

"No. I'll do that tomorrow."

"Well, call me. I'll come help."

"Okay."

"Thanks for sticking around, Marcus. I appreciate it. And I know Mallory appreciated you coming today."

"I was glad to be here." He shook his head. "I still can't believe she's got a college degree."

"I know."

The tinge of sadness in her voice made him want to reach out and hug her, and when she looked at him again, the urge twisted into raw desire. Standing in her driveway, the stars dim in the spring sky, the soft light from the streetlamp reflecting off her blond hair... The entire scene was the perfect setup, but he was certain if he closed the gap between them, she'd punch him in the mouth he so desperately wanted to press against hers.

She shifted on her feet as he continued to stare at her. "I'll see you tomorrow."

"Yeah. Good night, Annie."

He double-checked that the tailgate was latched, even though he'd done that already, and then climbed into the cab and sat for several moments, debating if he should just risk everything and do what he wanted. Take that opportunity he had mentioned earlier—the one that everyone always looked back on and wondered *what if*.

But he didn't. He started the ignition and pulled away, leaving another chance untaken.

"Knew it," Annie whispered at the sound of the office door opening. She leaned back in her chair and peered into the lobby.

A moment later, Marcus appeared, his lips pulled into a disapproving frown. "What are you doing here on a Sunday morning?"

"I had this sneaking suspicion that you wouldn't call for help putting the tables and chairs away. I figured I'd just be here to catch you in the act."

"I'm pretty sure I can handle this."

"I'm sure you can." She pushed herself up. "But they were used for my daughter's party, so I should at least help."

As she stepped around her desk, she sensed his eyes skimming over her body and heat coiled low in her gut. She didn't wear jeans and fitted shirts often, but she thought maybe she should reconsider that based on how he was looking at her. She cursed herself as soon as the thought occurred. Playing games of temptation with this man would be far too dangerous. She was already certain he felt as attracted to her as she was to him. The last thing either of them needed was her exacerbating this *thing*. She gestured for him to move—shooing him like she would a pesky fly—when he stood in the doorway, blocking her exit. He stepped aside, and she slid past him.

He followed her out of the building, passing her only when she stopped to wedge the door open. She reached the truck as he lowered the tailgate. They unloaded the chairs, and she carried them inside while he lifted the awkward tables from the truck bed. Annie and Marcus sidestepped each other, smiling awkwardly as they moved out of each other's way, carrying the furniture into the storage room at the back of the building. Annie focused on putting the chairs back into a neat row and tried to ignore the way discomfort filled her every time they crossed paths in the small room.

They'd been alone more times than she could count. This was nothing new, yet her nerves fired with every move he made and every time she got a whiff of his cologne. Annie silently chastised herself for being so damned aware of him, but that didn't stop her from feeling like the room was closing in on her as he leaned a table against the wall next to her.

With the chairs organized, she turned to leave the storage room, uncomfortably conscious of him walking ahead of her. When he reached the door, Marcus faced her, leaning in the doorway, just as he had when he'd stood in her office door earlier. And just as before, he blatantly lowered his gaze over her before meeting her stare. Her heart did that flippy-flop thing, and her breath caught at the look in his eyes.

She cleared her throat and dragged her palms over her denim-clad thighs. "Is that everything?" She knew it was, but what else was she going to say?

"Yeah. Thanks for the help."

"Thank you for hauling them around for me. I appreciate it."

He nodded. She laughed a bit and did that shooing motion again. He didn't move. This time, he held her gaze until she turned away from him and exhaled slowly in a futile attempt to calm her nerves.

"Annie, I've, um… I've been thinking about what I told you last night."

She creased her brow. "Remind me."

"About how it's human nature to think about the chances we let pass. How I didn't believe that you'd never considered what your life would be like if you'd made different choices."

She shook her head. "What are you getting at?"

He bit his lip hard. As if trying to stop himself from saying what he was thinking. "Annie, I've been…"

Oh, God, don't say it, she silently pleaded.

He tried again. "For the longest time…" A humorless laugh left him as he let his words trail again. Finally, he met her gaze again. "You're probably going to fire me, but—"

She gave him a forced smile. "I can't fire you, Marcus. You're invaluable. Whatever it is, I'm sure you can work it out." She took a step and tried to squeeze by him. "Just take a few days off or…" Great. Now she was the one who couldn't finish a thought.

He dropped his hand to her hip, stopping her from leaving the tension-filled room. She closed her eyes. His touch sent volts of electricity shooting through her, lighting every nerve. She wanted nothing more than to lean up and kiss the life right out of the man. For some reason, though, putting herself in a position where she could be sued for sexual harassment didn't seem like a wise business move. Not that she thought Marcus would ever go that far, but people changed. Situations got awkward and out of hand.

It was best to avoid the possibility of things going wrong between them and just ignore how much she wanted him.

"Marcus," she whispered.

"I have been attracted to you for so long, Annie. I thought I was alone in this," he said in the same hushed tone, "but lately I've started to think...you feel it, too."

She licked her lips and lowered her face. *Shit. He said it.* The elephant in the room was out there now, and neither could ignore it any longer. "I'm your boss."

"I know."

"I can't. *We* can't."

"I know. But I swear to God, I'm about to lose my mind from wanting you."

Oh, damn.

Her knees actually went weak. She leaned back against the doorjamb to stay standing.

"I think about you all the time. I know it's wrong. But all I can think about is how much I want to kiss you."

A whimpering moan left her as he closed the distance between them. He stopped a fraction of an inch from her mouth, and goddamn it, the temptation gripped her so hard she could barely breathe.

"Tell me you don't feel the same," he whispered. "Tell me to stop. And I will."

She should. She *had* to. But the words wouldn't leave her.

"Tell me to go to hell, Annie."

She wanted to, but her protest refused to form. She fought

with everything she had but then slowly gave in to need and gently pressed her hands to his face. He exhaled slowly, pressing his face against her palm and closing his eyelids, as if relishing in her touch. His heat radiated into her, burned its way down her arms, and stole her breath. Her heart pounded so hard she barely heard the heavy sigh leave him as he opened his eyes.

"You son of a bitch," she whispered, and he grinned.

She knew she shouldn't, but with her hand on his face—his skin as smooth and hot as she'd always imagined it would be—she had no choice but to brush her thumb over the lips that had been taunting her for so long. As she did, he kissed her thumb, then her palm, and then turned his face and kissed the inside of her wrist. The sensation of his lips on her flesh was more than she could resist. She'd wanted him to touch her like that for so long. She'd fantasized about it more times than she could count. Seeing him kiss her, feeling his breath tickling her skin and his lips pressing against her, was more than she'd imagined it could be. Her resolve crumbled like a sand castle in a hurricane.

He wrapped his arm around her waist and pulled her against him as he leaned back enough to search her eyes. She could read what he was thinking. This was her last chance to back away. She knew she should.

Don't do it. Don't let this happen.

But then she did. She lifted her chin and put her lips on his. Fireworks.

That was the only way she could explain what she felt in that moment. Heat erupted from their contact and engulfed her body.

She was instantly dizzy. Her muscles melted. She dug her fingers into his hair, and his mouth moved over hers as he held her so tightly she couldn't be sure he wasn't trying to crush her. A moan filled her ears, and she realized it was hers. Fisting the collar of his shirt, she held him as she parted her lips and let him delve in. The sensation of his tongue sliding over hers went straight to her groin. She clung to him, holding him as tightly as he was holding her, as he kissed her until she was breathless. She gasped as she broke the kiss. He put his forehead to hers, panting just as heavily. She couldn't recall the last time she'd been kissed so passionately or kissed someone else so passionately. The lust between them was palpable. She was certain if she asked him to make love to her right there, he would. And she would let him.

And that was a huge problem.

"Shit," she breathed, pulling away from him. "I am *so* sorry. I should *not* have done that."

He eased his hold on her. "No, I'm sorry. I instigated that." He was saying the right words, but his tone conveyed disappointment.

"I'm your boss."

"I know that."

She pushed against his chest until he stepped back. "I'm not supposed to let things like that happen. It's completely unprofessional. Goddamn it."

"Come on, Annie. You're only human. It's not like you could resist my magnetic pull forever."

She laughed softly. However, her amusement faded quickly

as her guilt returned. "I'm sorry, Marcus. If you weren't my employee…"

"I'll quit."

"No, you won't. I can't lose you. You've got connections that I don't. You carry more than your fair share around here. I'd be lost without you. You can't leave me."

"And you can't date an employee."

She sighed and looked away. "No, I can't."

"Look, Annie, I know some people would see it as disreputable—"

"Because it is."

"This isn't a large corporation where favoritism could be an issue."

"I still have standards and principles."

"I wasn't implying that you don't. I'm just saying, maybe…" He brushed his hand over her arm again. "They could slip a little."

She looked at him, licked his kiss from her lips, and then shook her head. "No. It's a risk I can't take. I can't. I'm sorry." She brushed by him and went into her office, where she grabbed her purse from the desk and left before he could convince her to break every rule she'd ever put into place.

CHAPTER TWO

*A*nnie barely glanced at the man standing in her office door as she finished typing, but that quick look was enough to send her heart into excited flutters. She *hated* that about him. How could barely acknowledging his existence send her into a tailspin? Taking a deep breath, she braced herself for that inevitable feeling of freefalling that came with hearing his voice.

"Need something, Marcus?"

"It's almost seven."

"So why are you still here?"

"I just closed the Portman deal."

"Good. They've been dragging their feet." Never in the twenty years that she'd owned her real estate business had homeowners seemed less interested in actually selling the house they'd put on the market.

He crossed the room and took his customary seat. "You should buy me a drink to celebrate."

She stopped her fingers mid-stroke on her keyboard. She'd been avoiding him all week. Ever since they'd shared a kiss in the storage room, she couldn't look at him. She shook her head and refocused on her computer monitor. "Marcus—"

"A drink, Annie. Co-workers still do that, you know. I had a drink with Dianna last night. Actually, we ate an entire meal together. And we were still able to look at each other this morning. It was quite refreshing."

Annie tried not to laugh, but a chuckle slipped through her lips. "I imagine it was." She sighed, giving up any hope she had of finishing the report. Leaning back, she tossed her reading glasses on the desk and forced herself to meet his gaze.

He stared at her as if he were analyzing her innermost thoughts. She reached for her glass of water. The cold drink did little to quench the heat that had burned low in her belly ever since she'd given in and kissed him.

"Dianna did ask if I'd be escorting you to the wedding," he said.

The idea yanked her from the memory of that kiss, a memory she relived far too frequently. Annie shook her head without taking a moment to even consider the possibility. No, he wouldn't be escorting her to her brother's wedding. "That's not a good idea."

"I accepted their invitation months ago, Annie. I'll be there, whether you're at my side or not. And just so you know, there will be plenty of room. We won't be bunking together."

Annie's mind spun. The lake house. Guests staying all weekend... She and Marcus under the same roof morning and night for an entire weekend... There would never be enough space to keep the tension between them from overflowing again.

She was going to kill her brother. And Dianna.

She wanted to close her eyes to break Marcus's intense stare, but she needed to get her point across. "We can no longer deny that there is an attraction between us, Marcus, but I can't put myself in a position that could cost me everything. I need you to understand that."

"I do. And I respect it."

"So please understand that it's best to keep some distance between us."

He opened his mouth to speak, and she lifted her hand to silence him.

"Go home, Marcus. I've got work to do."

He stared at her for another few long moments. "If you don't want me to go to the wedding, I won't." His smile returned. "I mean, if you honestly can't control yourself around me, then I'll gladly remove your temptation so you don't accidentally throw me down on the aisle and tear my clothes off."

She scowled and tossed a pencil at him. "Go home."

"Pack it up for the night. If you won't let me take you out, the least you can do is let me walk you to your car."

"Mmm, such a gentleman. I'll be done soon, and my car is about twenty yards from the door. I think I can manage."

"Spoilsport." He winked and stood. "Don't stay too late, and text me when you get home. You may not want me to, but I do worry about you."

Annie gnawed at her lip as she listened to him moving around in his office next door. A minute later, his footsteps echoed through the foyer and the front door closed. She fought the urge to peer out the window and watch him leave. She directed her attention to the monitor, but her mind kept wandering back to that damned kiss.

It'd been a long time since a man held her like that. Too long. She'd wanted nothing more than to lose herself in him. A thousand scenarios had played out in her mind since Sunday, and she could certainly imagine how easy it would be to give in to her desires after a few glasses of champagne and a couple of slow dances at the reception.

A humorless laugh left her as she realized she'd once again let Marcus distract her from her work. And he wasn't even there. With a shake of her head, she clicked to save the document and gathered her things. She'd never get anything done now. With nothing to divert her thoughts, Marcus filled her mind as she drove home.

She was disappointed when she pulled into her driveway and found it empty. Mallory moved out when she turned eighteen, but she still stopped by for dinner several nights a week. Even a twenty-one-year-old needed real food every now and then.

Tonight Annie really could have used the company. The quiet of an empty house didn't used to bother her. Actually, she normally enjoyed it. Lately, however, the silence had a bit of a sting. She blamed Marcus for that. He'd disrupted her life with his "just a quick bite" invitations that always turned into long dinners talking about everything from work to politics to their childhoods.

His had been picture-perfect; hers had been a disaster. He'd had two wonderful parents; she'd had a mother who had worked herself to death to support her children while her father drank himself to death. He'd never had kids; she'd gotten knocked up and been abandoned to raise her kid all alone. He'd had a few serious relationships; she avoided commitment like the plague.

She didn't regret that Mallory's father left before she was born. In fact, Annie was glad he had. If he'd stuck around, she suspected she would have ended up just like her mother—primary caretaker for a bushel of kids and a drunkard of a husband. Instead, Mallory had two wonderful uncles who had stepped up and filled the father-figure role without hesitation, and Annie had been able to focus on building a real life for herself and her daughter. She couldn't risk that for a man. Not even Marcus.

She dug her cell phone out of her purse and called Mallory. "Hey, kiddo. Have you had dinner?"

The door to Stonehill Café creaked as Marcus opened it, and he added oiling the hinges to his mental to-do list. When his sister had finally left her worthless-ass husband and come home to Stonehill last year, Marcus helped her buy the rundown building. It wasn't much, but it had always been Jenna's dream to own a restaurant, and she deserved for all her dreams to come true. Annie had tried to warn Marcus it wasn't a good buy, but he wanted to give his sister a reason to stand on her own, and now they were stuck with the dive—the leaky faucets, creaky door, and all. Jenna loved the place, she loved everything about it, but every time Marcus walked through the door, he was reminded how much work it needed.

Even so, the food was good, the service was better, and once Jenna could afford to do all the things she had planned, the place would look amazing.

He didn't need to read the menu, but he grabbed one so he'd have something to look at. He waved at his sister across the dining room as he sank into a table by the window. Skimming the selections, he tried to count how many times he and Annie had sat in this diner chatting about nothing for hours as Jenna refilled their coffee mugs. Too many to count.

But not as many as he'd spent sitting here alone.

Damn it.

Leave it to him to fall for his goddamned stubborn-ass boss.

"Only one thing makes a man frown that deeply," Jenna said, sliding a glass of water in front of Marcus.

He chuckled. "Oh, yeah?"

"What's happened with Annie now?"

Marcus sighed and pushed his menu toward his sister. "Got any roast beef left?"

"I do."

"Extra potatoes."

"Sure thing. Just as soon as you tell me what happened."

"She's still my boss. I'm still her subordinate. She still has more common sense than I do."

She sat down across from him and crossed her arms on the table. "We've talked about this a hundred times. You know what you have to do."

"Yeah, I know. I just haven't accepted it yet."

"If you want her as much as you say—"

"Roast beef, Jenna. Extra potatoes."

She pushed herself up. "'I quit.' Two little words. That's all you have to say."

He frowned as she walked away. In his attempt to become invaluable to Annie over the years, he'd managed to do just that. If he quit, he'd be leaving her in a terrible bind. She would lose not only an agent but someone who had become an integral part of her business.

So he had a conundrum he hadn't quite figured out how to escape. Pursue his boss in a relationship that she rightfully pointed out was inappropriate or quit his job and put the woman he was in love with in a bind. Her office was small but successful in part because when she'd brought him on board, she'd done so because he had connections that she didn't. Marcus had developed O'Connell Realty's commercial sales. If he caused her business harm, she'd likely never forgive him, but he couldn't very well push her to do something she told him she didn't want to do. Both choices left him empty-handed, and he found that increasingly unacceptable.

What was a man to do?

"Must be serious."

He looked up when Annie's daughter sat in the chair across from him. "Hey, Mal. What are you doing here?"

"Well, I thought I'd adopt a dog," she deadpanned, "but apparently the only ones they keep here are for the special."

Marcus chuckled. Damn, she was just as sarcastic as her mother.

"Are you okay?" she asked.

He shrugged. "Long day."

"Want to talk about it?"

"Not particularly."

"Mom?"

He stared at her for a moment. "Why would you say that?"

"Oh, I don't know. Maybe because I'm not an idiot."

He sighed. "No, you're not. But I'm not talking to you about your mother. She'd appreciate that about as much as she'd appreciate eating dog."

She watched him for a moment before sighing. "I'm just throwing this out there. Randomly."

"I doubt it's random, but go ahead."

Something changed in Mallory's eyes; she seemed a bit sad all of a sudden. "I know she doesn't make it easy, but don't give up on her, Marcus."

He opened his mouth, denial on the tip of his tongue, but she lifted her hand the same way Annie tended to do when she didn't want to hear what he had to say.

"Like I said. I'm not an idiot. You've looked at her like she hung the moon for years. She finally seems to have noticed. Give her time to come to terms with that. Other than my uncles, she's never had a man she could rely on. She's not exactly comfortable putting herself out there."

"She's my boss, Mallory. It has to end there."

"Says who?"

He sighed. "Your mom."

"Well. She *is* an idiot." She grinned, and he chuckled.

He turned his glass of water a few times before taking a drink.

"Mom, over here," Mallory called, and his heart tripped a bit in his chest. "Oh, did I forget to mention she was on her way?"

She smirked, and Marcus scoffed. Yeah. Just like her mother.

As he expected, when he looked up, he saw a mixture of surprise and frustration in Annie's eyes as she neared the table. She smiled, but it was forced. She stopped next to the table and looked at the chair where Mallory had deposited her purse. When Mallory didn't take the hint—intentionally, Marcus assumed—Annie sighed and sat in the vacant chair next to Marcus.

"I was here first," he muttered to expunge himself of guilt.

"I should have guessed you'd be here," she said just as quietly. She hung her purse on the back of her chair, put her elbows on the table, and looked at her daughter. "And how was your day?"

"Great. I, um"—she cleared her throat in the same way that Annie did when she got nervous—"I was actually glad you called, because I wanted to tell you... I mean... I was trying to figure out..."

Annie's eyes widened more and more with Mallory's stuttering. "Spit it out, child."

"They offered me the job in San Diego."

Marcus glanced at Annie, who was staring across the table.

"I accepted."

Mallory may have been all grown up, but the hesitant look on her face was that of a little girl seeking her mother's approval. Annie seemed stunned into silence. He gently nudged her with his elbow.

She cleared her throat. Yup, she was upset. "Um. When—when do you start?"

"Three weeks. We have so much going on with Uncle Paul and Dianna's wedding, I just didn't want to be rushed." She exhaled loudly, still looking anxiously at Annie.

"Wow," Annie said, but her voice lacked sincerity. "Congratulations."

Mallory frowned. "Mom. Go ahead. Tell me how far away it is, and how I'll be on my own, and everything else that's running through your head."

Annie shrugged. "You're a college graduate, Mallory. You

have to make these decisions for yourself. You're too old for me to lecture you."

"Am I?"

"Last I checked."

Mallory chuckled. "The misery on your face says it all."

Annie frowned at her. "Fine. I don't want you to move halfway across the country. I like having you here so I can call you up and meet you for dinner. I like that you swing by my house unannounced and eat all my food, and I like that we still go shopping on Saturday mornings. I don't want to give that up, but I'll just start dragging your aunts with me instead."

Mallory smiled mischievously. "Or you could just, you know, date *someone*"—she nodded her head toward Marcus—"who will take you to dinner and eat your food and go shopping with you."

Annie's eyes widened again. "Yes, I'm sure I could find *someone* to date. If I wanted to. Because, like you, *Mallory Jane,* I am perfectly capable of making my own decisions. And once I've made a decision, it would be nice if it were respected."

"Don't drag me into this," Marcus said.

Mallory's smile widened. "What does that mean?"

"Nothing," Annie said.

"Dianna invited me to the wedding. Your mother doesn't approve."

"I didn't say I didn't approve."

"You said you thought it was a bad idea."

"Because I do."

"This is perfect," Mallory said. "You can ride up together."

Annie's smile fell. "I thought you were riding with me?"

"I was, but I'm going early to hang out with the guys."

"What guys?" Marcus asked, feeling inexplicably protective.

She laughed. "Easy there, *Dad*."

Annie opened her mouth and creased her brow but, in another rare display, seemed speechless.

"Toby, Sean, Sam, and Jason are going early. I'm going to keep an eye on them because I don't think they can be trusted."

"Right," Annie muttered. "You just remember your cousins are underage."

Mallory frowned dramatically at her mother. "Seriously? Do I look like I'd contribute to the delinquency of a minor? Especially those minors. Sam and Sean are enough trouble without getting drunk."

"Mallory."

Marcus sat forward. "You just got a new job. Don't blow it by landing your ass in jail over a case of cheap beer."

Mallory scoffed at him. "My God, you really are in parental mode tonight. Can you believe this guy?" she asked her mother.

"Yes, I can. Listen to him."

"All right," she sighed. "This dinner has officially lost its sparkle." Grabbing her purse, she stood. "I'm going home so you two can discuss how you thought you raised me right and figure out where you went wrong. I'll give you a hint: forcing me to get braces right before the eighth-grade dance."

"What about dinner?" Annie asked.

"I only came for the pie, and my ass doesn't need it. Good night."

She left before Annie could argue.

Annie sat back and sighed. "It was the only appointment I could get."

"What?" he asked, confused.

"Her braces. That was the only time open for four months."

He chuckled. "I doubt she was serious about *that* being her moral downfall."

Annie frowned and looked at the door Mallory had just exited. "I asked her to dinner so I didn't have to eat alone."

"Well, I guess it's a good thing I'm here."

She glanced at him. "Even when I try, I can't get away from you."

"Easy now, Annie, I might start to get the impression that you like me."

"You know what I mean." She grabbed his water glass and took a drink. After returning it to the wet ring it had left on the table, she leaned forward and sighed. "She's moving to California."

"So it seems."

"I'm not ready for that. But at least she's not pregnant. Because I'm even *less* ready for that, and I was fairly certain that was where she was headed when she couldn't get the words out." She dropped her forehead into her palm. "*California*? Shit."

Though he knew he shouldn't, he put his hand on her knee and squeezed it reassuringly. She tolerated his touch for a good five seconds before turning her face to him. Her lips were drawn tight and her eyes looked sad. She shook her head at him. However, he couldn't really say if the sorrow on her face was over the idea of her daughter branching out on her own or reminding him of their personal space agreement.

He frowned, pulling his hand away and lacing his fingers together to stop from touching her. Looking out the window, he sighed heavily.

"I should go," she said quietly.

He wanted to argue, but he didn't.

Her chair scraped across the floor as she stood.

"Hey, Annie," Jenna said cheerfully. "You leaving already?"

"Yeah. I need to check on some things. Night."

Jenna set a plate in front of Marcus, and he looked up at her.

"Go ahead," he said.

"Two words," she whispered, and then she, too, left him alone.

CHAPTER THREE

*A*nnie let a string of curse words rip through her lips as she finally accepted that she was not going to sleep. Kicking the blankets off, she dragged herself into the kitchen and started a pot of coffee. Her mind had been racing all night. First, she thought of Mallory living on her own in a big city and all the horrors mothers think of when a child really leaves home. Then she thought of Marcus. *Everything* about Marcus. His voice. His soothing touch at the café. His caring eyes. His tender smile. His gentle laugh. That damned kiss.

After calling Mallory to make sure she wasn't angry, Annie had eaten leftovers in front of the television and wondered why she had left Marcus sitting alone. Why hadn't she just stayed? Eaten dinner? Chatted with him like they used to?

Was it really her concern about dating a subordinate or something else? Marcus wasn't the type to sue her if things ended badly. He wasn't the type to expect special treatment, and she wasn't the type to give it. So what the hell was stopping her from just going for what she so badly wanted?

She took her time in the shower as her coffee brewed and then sipped a cup before heading to the office way too early. By the time everyone else started to roll in, she had finalized several contracts, updated the spreadsheet she used to monitor clients, and stared out her window thinking about Marcus far more than she should have. That went to the wayside the moment heavy footsteps crossed the tiled lobby and entered the office next to hers.

"Morning," Marcus called.

She closed her eyes and shook her head harshly as his voice awakened her nerves. "Good morning."

He appeared in her door a few minutes later. "Early start today?"

He'd dressed casually today, in slacks and a dark blue golf shirt. She licked her lips. "What makes you ask?"

"Half the pot of coffee is gone already."

She gave him a halfhearted smile. "I couldn't sleep."

His face turned serious. "Mallory?"

She nodded, not willing to share the other issue that had kept her awake.

"Want to talk about it?"

She shrugged. "What's there to say?"

"Plenty, apparently."

She drew a breath and let it out slowly. "No. Not really. My daughter has grown up to be the fierce, independent woman I wanted her to be. Now I have to deal with that."

He sat across from her in the seat he so frequently occupied. "You've raised her right, Annie. She knows how to take care of herself. She'll be fine."

"I know," she said softly.

They both jolted when the front door slammed. Marcus turned, and Annie looked out her door toward the lobby.

"You can't do this," Dianna was saying. "I'm getting married in less than three weeks."

"Uh-oh," Marcus muttered, turning back to Annie. "That sounds like trouble."

Annie pushed herself up and walked around her desk. By the time she reached Dianna's office, her brother's fiancée was gripping her dark auburn hair in both hands and staring at Annie with wide eyes.

"My florist is going out of business."

"Okay," Annie said soothingly. "So we find another one."

Dianna looked up, and the tears in her eyes nearly set Annie in a panic. "It just seems like everything I've planned for this wedding is falling apart."

The sound of Dianna's voice cracking was more than Annie could handle. Tears. She hated tears. "Stop. Right there. Breathe. I will make it my mission—*today*—to find you flowers. Just don't do that crying thing."

Dianna's lip trembled. "I can't help it. It won't stop."

"Stress," Marcus diagnosed. "If Annie had human emotions, she'd know this."

Annie jutted her elbow into his ribs, and Dianna laughed. "I'll start making calls now. You call Kara. I bet she can harvest some roses under a grow light in her basement if necessary."

Dianna's best friend was sweet but too eccentric for Annie's taste. However, Annie did respect that the woman knew how to get things done.

Dianna playfully frowned. "Kara doesn't smoke pot, Annie."

"You keep telling yourself that," she said with a wink. "I'll make some calls. You'll have flowers ordered by the end of the day. You," she said, looking up at Marcus, "keep your sarcasm to yourself, huh?"

"You love my sarcasm," he said as they left Dianna's office.

Annie couldn't help but smile. He smiled in return, and she'd be damned if she didn't let out another of those stupid girly sighs.

Marcus couldn't quite believe he was doing it, but without another chance to talk himself out of it, he clicked the mouse and sent his résumé to the Canton Company. Annie mentioning Kara Canton had sparked an idea in Marcus. Not long ago, at one of the many dinner parties Paul and Dianna held, Kara's husband, Harry, had been complaining about how difficult it was to find good sales reps for his marketing firm. It wasn't quite the same as real estate, but if Harry hired Marcus, Marcus would have a new job that didn't put him in direct competition with Annie. She would be hurt enough by his decision to quit and by the likely loss to her commercial sales his leaving would mean. If he took business from her by selling real estate elsewhere, he might as well put all the nails in the coffin of their relationship. She'd never give him a chance.

As it stood now, he had no idea how long it'd take for her to get over the sense of betrayal she was likely to feel if he quit, but maybe if he had the chance to actually date her, he could convince her his quitting was the best thing for them.

"Everything okay?"

He looked up and smiled at the woman in question. "Yeah. Fine."

"You look a bit perplexed."

He drew a breath and closed the window he'd had open. "Just following a lead. Are you okay? You've stuck pretty close to your desk all day."

"Catching up on paperwork." She bit her lip and sighed. "And avoiding you."

He lifted his brows, surprised by her honesty. "Oh?"

"I'm sorry about running out on dinner last night. I guess Mallory's announcement hit me harder than I wanted to admit."

"Which bit? Moving across the country or the likelihood that she'll be binge-drinking with her underage cousins?"

She laughed softly. "Both, I suppose."

"She's a big girl, Annie. She's got to make her own choices and her own mistakes."

She nodded. "I know. I'm trying to let her."

"It's not easy, I suppose."

She shook her head. "No, it's not. The O'Connell women aren't the wisest lot around. We tend to screw up our lives on stupendous levels when left to our own devices."

"You seem to be doing okay."

Her smile looked sad. "Says you."

His face sagged a bit as she left. He looked at the monitor again before pushing himself up and following her. She turned into the break room and poured the hours-old coffee down the sink before rinsing the pot.

He found it impossible to look away when her gray pencil skirt and fitted blouse stretched tight across her body as she put the coffee pot back on the burner and grabbed a towel to wipe the counter clean. "Why don't you let the cleaning service do that?"

"Because I can't stand to see a mess. You know that."

"I do. That's why you're really avoiding me."

She paused just for a moment before she started scrubbing with more diligence.

"Isn't it?" he pushed.

"I didn't sleep well last night. I'm tired."

"Annie."

She stopped wiping and faced him. Leaning her slender hip against the countertop, she frowned. "You know, part of me says,

'To hell with it. Jump his bones.' The other part of me says, 'Show a little class, lady.'"

"I like the first part better."

"Me too. But the other part isn't so easily discounted. I can't believe I let things get this mixed up. I'm sorry, Marcus. What happened the other day was so unprofessional."

"Don't apologize to me," he said firmly as he came into the room. "If you weren't as confused as I am, I'd really be upset with you."

"I've never been in this position before," she said quietly.

"Good. I'd hate to think this is something you regularly do."

"Tell me what to do," she whispered.

He lifted his brows. "Annie O'Connell is giving me control?"

She smirked. "I didn't say I would listen. I just need to hear you tell me what you want me to do."

He closed the space between them and could swear the air lit with electricity as he neared her. He stopped within a respectable distance but couldn't resist brushing her hair behind her ear. Her lips parted as she took a breath, tempting him to kiss her, but he somehow controlled the urge. That wouldn't be fair to either of them—kissing her now would only complicate things more.

"Have dinner with me," he said softly. "Talk to me about your day. About Mallory. About all the things we used to talk about before things got awkward. I miss you, Annie. I miss being with you."

She exhaled slowly, as if what he'd said was the last thing she expected to hear. And it may well have been. She licked her lips and nodded. "Give me a few minutes to wrap things up?"

"Sure. Come get me when you're ready."

She started around him, but he wrapped his arm around her, resting his hand on her hip to stop her. She hesitantly looked up at him.

"Don't take too long," he said. "I'm starving."

A smile slowly touched her lips. "Then let me pass, you fool."

He grinned to match hers. "I just wanted a reason to touch you."

"I know."

He slowly lowered his hand, and she brushed by him. Swallowing hard, he inhaled. Her scent—lilac—still lingered in the air. He exhaled heavily and closed his eyes, trying to get control of himself before he did something really stupid. Like follow her into her office and shut the door behind him.

sh

Annie secured her seat belt. "What's the special at the café tonight?"

"The café? We had the café last night. Well, I did. You ran out before ordering."

She cocked an eyebrow at him as she pressed her lips together.

"The café it is," he muttered and started the engine.

"Really? Not even an argument? Not even a challenge? Clearly you don't want the café."

"What do you want me to do, Annie? You gave me that look."

"What look?"

"The one that melts my heart. And scares small children."

She laughed as he backed out of his parking spot. "You're an ass."

"You've told me that so often, I'm starting to believe it."

Her smile softened. "What would you like for dinner, Marcus?"

He pulled out of the parking lot and headed toward the town square. "I think I'd like to go to my sister's café, Annie. We haven't seen Jenna in about twenty-four hours. I'm sure she's quite concerned about us."

She smirked at his sarcasm. "We should support her. It isn't easy making a business successful."

"Well, we've certainly given her the best chance possible. If we ever stopped eating there, she'd go under in a week."

Annie rolled her eyes and shook her head, though he wasn't completely off the mark. Annie felt obligated to eat at Jenna's place as much as she could stand.

She both loved and hated how contentment filled her. She couldn't remember before Marcus ever feeling so at ease with herself or her life. He seemed to have filled a void that she hadn't known existed. And she hated that. Hated that she'd had a void.

Hated that he filled it. Even more than that, she hated that she had noticed.

But she loved that he did that for her when no one else could.

He stopped for a red light and glanced at her. "Where does your mind keep going lately?"

"Hmm?"

"Your wheels. They are a-turnin'."

"Actually, I was trying to figure out what to order."

"Liar."

"I went through the paperwork for the Portman deal today. How did you get them to finally accept an offer?"

"I threatened to turn their sale over to you."

"Oh, you monster."

He chuckled as the light turned green. "What were you thinking about?"

"Nothing."

"Back to that, huh?"

They were quiet until he parked in front of the restaurant. She released her seat belt and dropped her head against the headrest, looking at him looking at her. He had that look again—the one that clearly told her all she had to do was say yes and he'd make her forget every workplace boundary she'd ever used as an excuse not to let him love her. "Feed me, Marcus."

"Be honest with me, Annie. Where has your mind been going?"

"Fine. I was thinking how much I enjoy this."

"This?"

She bit her lip for a moment. "Us. Bantering. Teasing. Unwinding after a long day."

He nodded. "I enjoy it, too."

"I don't want to lose this, but..."

"I know," he breathed. He smiled sadly. "Things are complicated now."

"To say the least."

He looked out the windshield for a few moments. "If they weren't complicated?"

"They are."

"But if they weren't?" he asked, meeting her gaze again. "Would you still come up with reasons not to be with me?"

She swallowed hard. This was the type of situation she always did her best to avoid. This kind of open, honest conversation about how messed up she was always made her uncomfortable. "I'm not good at this, Marcus."

"At what?"

She sighed as she did what he'd just done—diverted her gaze out the window. "Whenever I get too close to someone, I tend to shut down. I panic. I get scared. Then I push them away. Not because I don't care but because I do. Does that make sense?"

He nodded. "You're scared of getting hurt."

"No. I'm scared of hurting you because I'm incapable of being what you need me to be." She climbed from the car and started for the restaurant. She was almost to the door when he dropped his hand to her shoulder and fell in step with her. "You're in my bubble," she said teasingly, hoping he'd let the more serious side of their conversation drop.

"I know. I can't help myself. Blame it on that skirt."

She smiled, pleased that he'd followed her lead into more comfortable, though equally inappropriate, territory. "Blatant sexual harassment, Mr. Callison."

"Apologies, Ms. O'Connell. Sometimes I forget myself." He reached around her and opened the door to the café.

"*Jen*," he called as if he hadn't seen his little sister for years. "How *are* you?"

She looked beyond him to Annie. "What's wrong with him?"

"He was trying to tell me we eat here too often and should broaden our horizons."

Jenna's brown eyes widened. "Marcus. I am offended."

He put his hand to his heart. "I was just trying to get the old girl out of a rut."

Annie gasped. "What?"

Jenna laughed. "You two sit wherever. I'll be with you in a minute."

They took a table by the door, and Annie immediately wadded up a napkin and threw it at him. "Old girl?"

She joined in as he laughed heartily, and again silently thanked him for not pushing her. "You're a royal pain in my ass, Marcus. You know that, right?"

"That's the sweetest thing you've ever said to me, Annie."

sh

One of the perks of applying for a job with an acquaintance was the quick response. One of the downsides? The quick response. Jenna had just slid plates onto the table when Marcus's phone rang.

Since they both received evening phone calls from clients, Marcus didn't think it would be inappropriate to check the caller ID and answer.

"Marcus Callison."

"Marcus. This is Harrison Canton. From the Canton Company."

Marcus's mouth fell open as he looked at his dinner companion. "Wow, you're fast."

"Well, I'm impressed with your résumé, and Dianna speaks very highly of you. If you have time tomorrow, can you swing by the office?"

Marcus forced a smile as his heart skipped a few beats. Annie creased her brow, clearly sensing something off with the call.

"That shouldn't be a problem. I don't have my schedule right in front of me. Can I call you back in the morning and set up a time?"

"Of course. You have my number?"

"Yes, I do. Thanks for the call."

"Thank you. I'm looking forward to meeting with you."

Marcus returned the sentiment and hung up.

"What was that?" Annie asked, a forkful of chicken inches from her mouth.

He sighed as he looked at her. The moment of truth. Did he

love her enough to leave her? Or should he stay and hope that eventually they'd find a way to be together despite the unethical aspect of their relationship?

"Marcus?" She put the fork down. "What is it?"

"I don't want you to get upset."

She stared at him, and he wavered for a moment.

"I've applied for a job elsewhere."

"Marcus—"

"Hey," he said firmly enough that she stopped before she could object. "It's not right of me to expect you to put your business on the line for a relationship that may or may not work, and I think we both know that this thing between us isn't going to just go away."

She was shaking her head before he finished speaking. "You can't do this. I need you."

"And I need you. Just not the same way. I've been thinking about this a lot. Weighing my options—*our* options. This is the only one that makes sense."

She sagged back in her seat, no longer smiling at him. She looked upset. Frustrated. "I just told you—"

"That you're going to push me away. I heard you." He nudged his plate away and sighed. "I never thought for a moment that being with you would be easy. You don't know how to make things easy, Annie. But you're worth it. To me you're worth it."

Her lip trembled for the briefest of moments before she clenched her jaw and pursed her lips together. Reaching into her purse, she pulled out some cash and dropped it on the table.

"Annie," he called as she slid from the booth.

He started to follow her, but she turned and glared at him. He sat back and lifted his hands. "At least take my car back to the office."

"I'd rather walk."

sh

As expected, the lights were shining from Annie's office when Marcus pulled into the parking lot. He'd explained the situation to his sister, sat through her unwanted advice, then had what was left of their dinner packed into to-go containers. He grabbed a bottle of wine—a gift from a client—from his office and braced himself for the impending confrontation. He hadn't expected Annie to march out on him like that, but he didn't know why he was surprised. He knew she would feel betrayed by his decision to apply elsewhere and cornered by his declaration that he intended to pursue her.

If he got the job at the marketing firm and she still opted not to date him, then he'd know that she didn't care about him nearly as much as he wanted her to. That would hurt like hell, but it couldn't be any worse than being so damn close to the woman he wanted to be with while she kept him at arm's length. Seeing her every day, having dinner several times a week, teasing each other like they did was hell, and he couldn't stand it anymore.

He needed more.

Carrying their dinner and the wine with him, he walked into

her office. She was pounding on the keyboard, looking pissed as hell.

"If you're typing an e-mail, I'd strongly suggest you let it sit until morning before hitting send."

"I appreciate your suggestion," she muttered before moving the mouse and slamming a button, which he could only assume meant she'd sent it anyway. She pulled her reading glasses off and carelessly tossed them aside. "What do you want, Judas?"

He winced dramatically for effect. "Oh, that's a little harsh." He held up a bag from the café. "You didn't finish your dinner. Jenna packed it up and added a slice of chocolate cake. She says that will help soften you up so you'll forgive me."

She scoffed. "Go home."

"No." Crossing her office, he put the food on her desk, sat across from her, and went to work twisting the cap off the bottle of wine. "This might be working for you, but it isn't for me. I want more than just looking at you and thinking about what we *could* have. I want to actually have it."

Other than a slight softening of her hard stare, she didn't respond.

He removed the cap and sniffed the wine. Setting the bottle down, he frowned as he looked at her. "Despite our mutual dislike of bullshit and dancing around the truth, we've been doing that for far too long. I can't keep lying to you or myself. I love you, Annie. Despite your bad temperament and lack of tolerance for everyone and everything around you."

"Oh, that's some profession of love, you bastard."

"It's not my fault you're moody."

She scowled, and he looked into her coffee cup. Confident the mug was clean and empty, he filled it with wine.

"This is the part where you tell me how you feel."

"Betrayed."

He grinned. "Fair enough. But do you love me?" Her face paled a shade or two, and he chuckled flatly. "You can say no."

"Marcus..." She closed her eyes. "Don't put me on the spot like this."

He nodded. "Okay. You don't love me."

She creased her brow and stared at him. "I didn't say that."

"So you do love me. You're just too scared to admit it because you're terrified to put yourself out there. Despite the fact that you know I'd never intentionally hurt you, you can't let go of the past and believe in me even though you know—and you damned well better know—that I'm not your dad, and I'm not that jerk who walked out without a care for you *or* Mallory."

"Stop right there."

He took a drink and made a face. "That's terrible."

"Well, look at the label. It practically begs you not to drink it."

He turned the bottle and had to agree with her assessment. Pushing the wine aside, he met her gaze. "Every time I look at you, I'm reminded that there is a chasm between us. I don't want you to be my boss, Annie. I want you to be my...whatever. Girlfriend."

"Don't ever call me your girlfriend."

"Significant other?"

She scrunched up her nose and shook her head.

"The fact is, it's getting to me, Annie. I think that became pretty damn clear the other day. I can't stay here and not be with you."

"So you're leaving me?"

"No. I'm removing your excuse. If not dating an employee was just that, just an excuse, then at least I'm saving myself some misery. If it was a legitimate reason and you really were concerned that somewhere down the road it will make things too awkward at work, then I'm opening the door for our future. The next move is yours."

"Well, I don't think I'll have time for any kind of relationship, Marcus. I'm about to lose my best agent."

"Don't let Dianna hear you say that."

"I rely on you for more than just sales. You are my right arm around this place, and you know people. You have connections and bring in commercial business that Dianna can't."

"I have to do this. For me. For us. If there's ever going to be an us." Focusing on pulling their food from the bag, he set a container in front of her. "I haven't gotten the job yet, Annie, but if I don't, I'm going to apply somewhere else. This is the right thing for both of us. You'd know that if you weren't so scared of what it means."

"That you're ditching me?"

"That I want to be in a relationship with you. Listen, you

have to let go of the past, sweetheart. I'm not your dad, and I'm definitely not Mallory's dad."

"Why do you keep bringing up that jerk?"

"Which one?"

"Either. *Both*."

"Because whether you want to admit it or not, I know how your mind works. This isn't me abandoning you, Annie. This isn't me walking away and never looking back. This isn't me dumping my responsibilities, forcing you to pick up my slack."

"Sure feels like you're dumping your responsibilities and leaving me with the slack."

"No, I'm taking the lead here. I know I'm putting you in a bit of a bind at the office, but you will find another salesperson. You'll be fine. It's time for us to decide what we are to each other. If we're anything at all. All I want is for you to stop making excuses as to why you can't love me back."

"I hate you," she said softly and without an ounce of conviction. "How about that as an excuse?"

"Now if that were true, none of this would be an issue, would it? You don't have to say that you love me. You don't even have to love me. I love you, and I can't be here day in and day out and not have you in my life the way I want you in my life. I've done it for too long. I'm at a crossroads, Annie. I have to make a choice. I'm choosing you. It may not feel like it to you, but I am choosing you."

She lowered her gaze and shook her head slightly.

"You'll find another agent, Annie. You'll find someone who

can fill my shoes. But I'll never find another woman who makes my heart race and my palms sweat."

She looked up at him for a moment but then snorted. "You're so full of shit."

He grinned. "I'm not lying. One look from you turns me into a puddle."

Her smile fell a bit as she sighed. "I know that feeling. And I love you, too," she whispered. "Despite you being egotistical, stubborn as hell, and impossible to deal with most days."

The smile that broke on his face was so wide it made his cheeks hurt. She loved him. She'd actually said that she loved him. He knew she meant it. Annie didn't say things just to appease people. If she said it, she felt it.

He was tempted to round her desk and kiss her again. This time slowly and sensually so she would feel every ounce of love he had for her. But she'd probably lose her mind if he tried to cross the lines of decency at work yet again. Instead, he held out a plastic fork to her. "Eat your dinner, darling. Before it gets as cold as your heart."

Marcus hadn't stopped feeling like he was floating on a cloud since Annie had admitted that she felt the same about him, and that feeling intensified when Harrison Canton called to offer him a job. Two weeks. In *two weeks*, he'd no longer be Annie's employee. The first thing he was going to do, five p.m. on the dot, was pull her into his arms and kiss her with everything he'd been bottling up.

"That's some smile," Dianna said from his doorway.

He chuckled. "I just got a job at the Canton Company."

Dianna's face sagged a bit. "Annie said you'd met with Harry. Are you sure you want to leave, Marcus?"

He nodded.

She sat across from him, as if waiting for an explanation. Finally, a light went off in her eyes. "She gave in?"

He chuckled and rapped his knuckles on the desk. "I'll be escorting her to your wedding, as a friend. But once I'm no longer her employee, Annie and I will... Well, I guess we'll see where this is going. If anywhere."

"Congratulations."

"Thanks."

"You know she's going to need a lot of patience."

"I've been patient for five years, Di. I think I got this."

"Good. Are you busy? I have a client who hasn't been in to fill out the identification forms yet. I'm sure he's perfectly fine, but you know how Annie is. She'll have a conniption if I meet him alone before verifying his identity."

Marcus would have a conniption, too. Being an agent presented dangers, and Annie's insistence that every client fill out a form with proof of identity and employment had skirted off more than one person who might or might not have been looking for a target to mug. If a client couldn't be verified before the first meeting, the agent was to cancel or partner up with a co-worker.

"Give me five." When he finished filling out the paperwork for the deal he was negotiating, he set it aside to be signed by the buyer later in the day and called out to Dianna. She met him in the lobby, and they headed out to meet her new client.

Marcus was in such a good mood, he didn't even mind her nonstop rambling about the weather report. Having an outdoor wedding in April was risky, but she and Paul had decided to go for it. And she'd been afraid rain would ruin her wedding ever since. Now that the day was actually showing in the televised forecast, and with a twenty percent chance of precipitation, she was on the verge of having a panic attack.

She had played it cool, she said, for Paul's sake, but the truth was, she didn't know what they'd do if it rained on Saturday.

"Twenty percent chance of rain means eighty percent chance of it not raining. And if it does rain, you can always move things inside. I know it isn't ideal, but it's the ceremony that counts, not the location," Marcus offered.

She sighed and looked at him. "I know. But I've been planning this since Paul proposed Christmas morning, and Murphy's Law has done nothing but mock me."

He chuckled. "You've handled it like a champ."

He parked in front of a house with a for-sale sign in the yard. A man was already standing in the driveway looking up at the house.

Marcus climbed out and walked ahead of Dianna. "Hi. Marcus Callison."

The man glanced past him at Dianna. "Brad Schafer."

"I hope you don't mind my tagging along. I haven't seen this place yet and thought this was the perfect opportunity."

"Not at all," he said.

Dianna gestured toward the house, and Marcus followed behind, thinking how much he was going to miss being part of the O'Connell Realty team. It was going to be worth it, though. Being with Annie would be worth it.

CHAPTER FOUR

*A*nnie had just finished filling her coffee mug when two large hands gripped her hips. She sighed loudly but couldn't quite stop herself from smiling. She and Marcus had arrived later than most of the wedding guests—he'd insisted on stopping for dinner at some dinky sandwich shop along the way —but even so, she'd been the first one awake. She thought she'd have some peace and quiet before the hubbub of wedding preparations started, but it wasn't to be.

She didn't actually mind that he was touching her, but for the sake of continuity in their relationship, she said, "You're in my bubble again."

"I like your bubble," Marcus said over her shoulder. "I'd like it more if it came with coffee."

She reached into the cabinet and grabbed another mug, filling it for him as he advanced his invasion by sliding his arms around her waist and pressing his cheek to her head.

"What are you doing?"

He exhaled slowly. "Imagining what our mornings are going to be like after I move in with you."

She pulled away enough to look over her shoulder. "*What?*"

"Your house is much too nice to rent. Mine is better suited for that."

She turned and faced him in the small amount of space he was allotting between his body and the counter. "Are you insane?"

"Yes. I'm also teasing you. Maybe." Reaching around her, he grabbed his mug. "In one week, I'll no longer be on your staff. If you think I'm wasting one more minute—"

A throat clearing behind them made Marcus take a step back.

Paul pointed over Annie's head. "If I can just get two cups of coffee to go, you can get back to...whatever."

"Oh, we're done with *whatever*." Annie slid around Marcus and sat at the table, where she'd left her toast and fresh fruit before her space had been so temptingly invaded.

"Everything ready for today?" Marcus sat beside Annie and snagged an apple slice from her plate.

She merely cocked a brow at him. He was certainly getting comfortable with their relationship. They weren't even dating, and he was talking about moving in? And stealing food off her plate? Brave man.

"As ready as can be," Paul said.

"How are your nerves?"

"None to speak of." He poured creamer into his coffee and

stirred his drink. "I'm marrying an incredible woman. We'll be surrounded by our family. And the forecast finally cleared so my bride can stop stressing about rain. It's going to be perfect."

With that he disappeared from the kitchen, and Marcus smiled at Annie. "He's incredibly calm."

"He's internalizing his fear."

"How can you tell?"

"He fixed two cups of coffee and then walked away without them." She nodded toward the mugs still sitting by the pot. She grinned when Paul came back in, grabbed the cups, and left again, muttering about wedding rings and vows and hoping he didn't forget anything else.

Marcus chuckled. "We should definitely just elope. Skip out on all this."

Annie stopped lifting her cup to her lips so abruptly, liquid sloshed over the side and splattered on the table. "*Elope?*"

"Unless you want a big wedding. I didn't think you'd be the type for all this fuss."

"Who says we're getting married?"

"Well, after I move in with you, eventually the next step will be marriage. Don't you think? We want to set a good example for Mallory."

His deadpan face cracked a bit, and his smile shone through, but she shook her head at him anyway.

"You need to leave my daughter out of your delusions."

"She's the one who brought it up."

She let her jaw go slack as he stood and got a paper towel. "When did you talk to Mallory about us?"

"Oh, we had lunch Thursday after you blew her off, even though she drove all the way to the office."

"I didn't blow her off. A deal almost fell through at the last minute. I couldn't back out of the meeting I was in." She took the towel from him to clean up her mess. "What has gotten into you?"

He crossed his arms and rested them on the table, and all signs of teasing faded. "We're not exactly teenagers anymore. We have to take our happiness while we can."

"We're not exactly ready for the nursing home yet, either. Jumping into conversations about moving in and getting married feels a bit premature."

"You're right. It is. I'm just teasing you. Maybe. But to be honest, we've danced around this thing between us for too long, Annie. One more week, and I'm all in. And I'm dragging you in with me."

She couldn't help but smile at him. "Do you think we could maybe have at least one real date before jumping all in? Maybe get to know each other on that level before deciding when and how we're getting married."

"Oh, I'm going to get to know you on *every* level."

He leaned close but didn't kiss her. She was surprised how deep her disappointment ran. She wanted him to. It seemed like the perfect moment. But she'd drawn lines, and while he might nudge them, Marcus wasn't going to outright disrespect her wishes. Damn it.

She closed her eyes and moaned quietly as she looked away. "I can't decide if your cockiness turns me on or annoys me."

"Oh, it annoys you. But being annoyed turns you on, so it works out well for me."

Cupping her mug in her hands, she stared at him. "Did Mallory really talk about us getting married?"

"Yes, but she was just teasing me. She learned that from you."

She drew a slow breath. "You love when I tease you."

"I love everything about you. Well. Almost."

He smirked, and she glared playfully.

"She just wants to see you happy."

"And she thinks I need a man to be happy?"

"No." He ran his hand over her hair. "No, you most certainly don't. But I do like to think you need *me*."

Swallowing as that familiar anxiety—the one that warned her against putting too much faith in anyone but herself—started to rise, Annie leaned away and pulled his hand from her. He clutched on to hers, though, refusing to be dismissed.

"You sure want to put the cart before the horse, don't you?"

He smirked. "Not as much as you want to shoot the horse before the journey even begins."

She laughed, mostly because she couldn't argue. Patting his hand, she pulled free as she stood and slid her uneaten breakfast toward him. "I'm going to get ready for the wedding before you decide which retirement community we should move into."

"Stonehill Senior Village," he called as she left the kitchen. "They have an indoor pool *and* shuffleboard."

The sun shone high in the sky, only a few white clouds peppering the perfect blue. The lakefront air was a bit chilly but not as cold as it could have been in April. Marcus chuckled as the ceremony started with Kara's granddaughter tossing white petals like the professional flower girl she insisted she was. Her brown hair was swept up in a bun, and her fancy dress flowed as she walked dramatically down the makeshift aisle.

Sean and Toby, Paul's sons, stood next to their father, and he beamed with happiness as Dianna's sons, Jason and Sam, walked at her sides. With their four college-aged boys standing around them and family and friends looking on, Paul and Dianna became husband and wife.

Annie sniffed as Paul slipped a ring on Dianna's finger. Marcus imagined if Annie weren't feeling so sentimental, she would have put an elbow into his ribs when he wrapped his arm around her shoulders and held a handkerchief out. Instead, she snatched the cloth and dabbed her eyes as her brother kissed his wife.

"Okay," Sam sang out after a several seconds, "your children don't need to see this."

The couple parted as everyone laughed. A moment later, Paul was hugging Annie tightly. Marcus envied how close Annie was to her siblings. He was determined that eventually she'd be that free with her affection for him, but jealousy still unreasonably bit at his gut at how willing she was to hug and kiss her family.

"I'm so happy for you," she said and then hugged her new sister while Marcus and Paul shook hands.

"How are you doing?" Marcus asked Annie as the newlyweds moved on to embrace other members of their family.

"I have all these…things going on inside me."

He nodded with understanding. "Those are called feelings, sweetheart."

She wiped her cheeks dry again. "My eyes won't stop leaking. I think they're broken."

He laughed and put his arm around her again. He expected her to remind him of her bubble—the personal space that she preferred to keep intact—but she actually leaned into him and rested her head on his shoulder.

"What's wrong with me?"

Marcus chuckled. "I think you could be happy."

"I don't like it. I don't like it at all."

Wrapping his other arm around her, he used this unusual moment of vulnerability to hold her. "You might want to get used to it. I plan on making you all kinds of happy."

She shook her head. "Please don't. I can't handle this. I need bickering and opposition."

"There will be plenty of that, too."

She tried to pull away as Mallory approached them, but

Marcus kept one arm around Annie and put the other around her daughter. Annie looked up at him. Something in her eyes told him she wasn't exactly comfortable, but he felt her body relax a bit and she didn't pull away.

"That was a lovely wedding, don't you think?" he asked Mallory.

She grinned at Annie. "There is something *very* lovely about small weddings."

Annie's mouth fell open, probably to tell them both where to stick it, as the photographer approached.

"Smile," said the kid, who didn't look like he was even out of high school.

Marcus pulled his girls closer to him and smiled. When the photographer walked off, he chuckled at the look on Annie's face. "That'll look good on the mantel, don't you think?"

"She's going to kill you." Mallory laughed and walked off.

Annie gave him a side-eye glance and then pulled away and joined in a conversation with her sisters-in-law. Marcus followed her lead and starting mingling. When dinner was served, however, he moved to Annie's side and sat at a table with her and Mallory.

"So, you two," Annie said, cutting her chicken. "Let's clear this up right now. If I decide to get married, it'll be on my terms."

"And Marcus's, I assume," Mallory said innocently.

Annie stabbed at her lunch. "Who says I'd marry Marcus? Maybe I have better options."

Mallory smirked. "I hear Oscar the Grouch is taken, but Grumpy Cat may still be available."

Annie narrowed her eyes, but Marcus howled with laughter. He loved when Mallory and Annie engaged in their native language of sarcasm. Few bounced quick wit off Annie as well as her daughter.

Annie turned her glare to him. "You two are just like peas in a pod these days, huh?"

Mallory smiled at Marcus. "I happen to like him. Not only does he tolerate you, but he seems to actually enjoy your company. Two pluses in my book."

"What book is that? 'How to Marry Off Your Mother'?"

Marcus tried to hide his grin when Annie glared at him, but he knew he wasn't doing a good job. "Your mother hasn't quite come to terms with this change in our relationship. She still thinks she has the power to resist me."

"Oh, I have the power."

"Come on, Mom. Look at his dimples."

Annie snorted and picked her fork up again. "Those aren't dimples, Mallory. Those are potholes on the road to hell."

sh

"Good day?" Marcus asked, startling Annie.

She gasped and looked over her shoulder as he stepped into the living room. "Damn it. You scared me."

"Whatever it takes to get that stone-cold heart of yours to go pitter-patter."

She returned her focus to the view outside the big window. It was dark, but the moon was reflecting off the water, creating a mesmerizing view. "It's late. Why are you still up?"

"Why are *you* still up?"

"Thinking."

He sat on the couch next to her and looked at the lake as well. "About?"

She took a deep breath when his knee bumped hers and an unexpected thrill made her stomach clench. "I just... I hate change, and everything is changing so fast."

Putting his hand on her knee, he waited for her to look at him. "Are you really happy with the way things were between us, Annie?"

"Yes."

"Really?"

"Really."

"Working late every night, ignoring how we felt, going home to an empty house. Getting up the next day and doing it again. That made you happy?"

She pressed her lips together and focused on the night sky again. "If you're going to psychoanalyze me, I'm going to bed."

"I'm not trying to psychoanalyze you. I'm trying to have a conversation that we've been avoiding for too long. You can't keep going through life bottling things up, Annie. It isn't healthy."

She frowned. "This certainly feels more like an analysis than a conversation."

"It's time to let go of a little of that control and let someone take care of you for a change."

"And you're the one to do that, huh?"

"Yeah, I *am* the one. I'm the one who can see right through that cold façade of yours. You use sarcasm and frigid interaction hoping no one will see that you're lonely, and you're tired, and you're ready for your chance to have what Matt and Paul have. But you know what? I'll see your sarcasm and raise you some cold hard truth. You have used taking care of Paul and Matt and Mallory as an excuse to not let anyone in. You've kept me at arm's length for years because you're scared."

"Because you were my employee."

"Because you think if you let me in, I would hurt you, so it's easier to be aloof and act like you don't need me and that you don't love me. But you do."

Tears stung her eyes without warning. She swallowed hard, but it was useless. They sat on her bottom lids, threatening to spill over. Looking out the window to avoid his piercing gaze, she shook her head.

He tightened his hold on her knee. "I see through you, Annie. I'm not intimidated by your bitterness. Hell, you've earned it. You have every right to think that you can't rely on anyone but yourself. You've yet to find someone to prove you wrong. But you *can* rely on me. I'm not going to leave you holding the bag while I drown myself in a bottle of tequila."

She laughed quietly as she wiped a tear from her cheek. "Well, we're pushing fifty, Marcus, so I'm not too concerned about you leaving me with nothing but a fetus and a late rent payment."

"But you do think I'll leave you. Don't you?"

Her lip trembled, betraying her determination not to cry. "I like where we're at. I can trust where we're at. Even though you were joking, once you start throwing in things like living together and...marriage..." She sighed and bit her lip.

"Then things feel real and that's frightening."

"I don't need romance to care about you, Marcus."

"I don't need either, Annie. I already care about you. I *love* you. But it sure as hell would be nice to hold you now and then." He exhaled loudly and looked down at where his hand was resting on her leg. "Here's the thing. When I go home at night, and my house is quiet and my bed is empty, my heart aches for you." He put his free hand to his chest. "I physically hurt because you aren't in my life in all the places I want you to be."

She swallowed hard. Damn him and his emotional confessions. "Maybe it's just indigestion."

He smiled. "Maybe. Or maybe I'm so goddamned in love with you, the fear that you don't feel the same is tearing me apart inside."

That did it. She creased her brow as her tears overflowed. "You know, when I was younger, I had all these plans for how my life was going to go. I had this path planned out: college, career— I wanted to be the first female CEO of some huge corporation and have a big family with all these kids and a great husband. A white picket fence and a mansion." She laughed flatly. "After Mom died, I kept saying to myself I'd see Paul and Matt off to college because Dad sure as hell wasn't going to take care of them. I decided I'd work as hard as I had to, and then it would be my turn. Then I got mixed up with Mal's dad, and he bailed. So I told myself, I'd work hard and see Mallory grow up, and *then* it would be my turn. Eventually, I just forgot about me. About that path I wanted to take. I look at my life now, and it's nothing like what I wanted. I don't just mean the career and the kids, Marcus. I mean *me*. Donna and Dianna are so domestic and maternal and warm, and I just... I can't be like that. That's not me."

"Hey," he said gently. "Just because you didn't bake cookies and run the PTA doesn't make you any less maternal. Mallory never had to ask you to be there for her, Annie. You are now, and you always have been with her. Every step of the way."

"But I keep things in. I hide myself. I get moody when things get too real. You deserve better. You deserve someone who can be warm and open."

He scooted closer, so close she had to lift her bent leg off the cushion to make room for him. Cupping the back of her head, he met her gaze. "If I wanted sweet and sugary, I would be with someone like Donna or Dianna."

"So you want someone bitter?"

He grinned. "I prefer tart with just enough bite to let me know I'm alive."

"How long before you realize tart is just a nice word for unpleasant?"

"Oh, honey, I already know you're unpleasant. I just don't mind as much as you seem to think I should. I don't want you to change. I don't want you to try to be something you're not or something you think I want, because the only thing I want is you."

"You can find someone better than me," she whispered.

"I don't want someone better than you," he said just as quietly.

"And if you change your mind?"

"Annie, I can sit here and make you heartfelt promises all night long with every intention of living up to them, but we both know life happens. Paths change. People change. But right now, you are the only tart for me."

She smiled softly, and he put his hand to her face.

"Just give us a chance," he said. "Give me a chance, a *real* chance. I can't promise you forever, but I can promise you the near future. And it will be amazing if you'll just let it be. Maybe it isn't the path you wanted when you were a kid, but that doesn't mean it isn't the right path for you to take now."

She put her fingertips to his cheek as she looked into his eyes. Heat shot down her fingers and right through the wall of ice she tried to keep around her heart. Everything inside her melted as she pressed her lips to his.

The last time they'd kissed, the exchange exploded from

tentative to intense in just a few seconds, and this was no different.

One moment her lips were just meeting his, the next his hands were digging into her hair as he pulled her closer. The moment after that, she turned as he simultaneously lifted her. Straddling his hips, she sat on his lap and wrapped her arms around his neck as his arm slid around her waist. His tongue pressed at her lips, and she parted them to accept him. She moaned as he pulled her even closer—so close she could feel his body responding to their passionate kiss. The thin material of their respective pajama pants did little to hide his erection or her heat.

She was about as far from wanton as a woman could get, but instinct took over and she ground her body against his, desperate to feel every part of him. Threading her fingers into his hair, she kissed him as he pressed up to meet her.

Her determination to remain platonic until he was officially no longer her employee was forgotten.

She moaned deep in her throat and broke away from his mouth to take a breath. Apparently he had gills, because he went straight for her neck, delving in with an open mouth and gently nipping the skin without taking the time to catch his breath. She moaned again. For some reason, moaning and grinding were the only responses she could make. They seemed to be sufficient, because after thoroughly attacking her neck, Marcus shifted their bodies until she was on her back on the sofa. She found his mouth with hers again and arched up to meet his roaming hands.

His palm covered her breast, his tongue moved over hers, and he pressed the most intimate parts of their bodies together. If they were naked, there would be no stopping him from taking her right there on the couch of her brother's vacation home. The thought gave her pause. When he lowered his hand and skimmed the hem of her shirt, she grabbed his wrist.

Fear struck her. Everything was suddenly very real. "Marcus," she panted. "I'm sorry. I—we can't do this. We can't. I'm sorry."

He moved from between her legs and stretched out beside her. "No. I got carried away."

"Me too."

He laughed quietly. "I've just wanted this for so long."

"I know." She took a breath. She had wanted this, too. She could no longer deny that. Even now, her body was demanding release that only making love to Marcus could give. Part of her wanted to roll on top of him and finish what she'd just stopped. But she didn't. She lay there silently, feeling him next to her, wondering why the hell she couldn't just take what she damn well knew she wanted.

He leaned up onto his elbow and brushed her hair behind her ear before kissing her. "I don't want to bid you a good night, but if I don't, I'm probably going to turn into a teenage boy and beg you to let me at least make it to third base."

She giggled and bit her lip. "I'd hate to see you act any more immaturely than you already do."

"I'd be offended by that if I could think about anything other than the fact that I just squeezed your boob."

Her giggle turned into an outright laugh.

"Are you okay?" he asked softly.

"Yeah, I'm fine. Really."

Rolling onto her, he put a soft kiss on her lips. "I love you, Annie."

She sighed. "I love you."

"Get some sleep."

She nodded, and he kissed her one more time before pushing himself up and disappearing into the darkness.

CHAPTER FIVE

"What'd you think?" Marcus asked as he and Annie left the restaurant he'd chosen for lunch.

She made a face. "I think Greek isn't for me."

"No?"

"Nope."

He grabbed her hand and tugged her closer to him. She started toward his car, but he pulled her farther along the sidewalk. She gave him a quizzical look, and he nodded toward the quaint downtown.

"This is my first time visiting the lake house. Let's explore the town. Unless you're in a hurry to get home and sit alone."

She fell in step with him. Even though it was still off-season, the sidewalks were crowded with kids eating oversized cookies and men and women carrying disposable coffee cups. They wandered into a small shop, looked over souvenirs they had no intention of buying, and then followed the sticky lead of other tourists and bought cookies and coffee.

Annie blew into her latte. "What was your path?"

He looked at her, pausing just a moment before his chocolate-chip cookie touched his lips. "What?"

"Last night." Her face turned red, and she glanced away as if looking at something to her left. "I told you my path—white picket fence and all that. What was your path?"

He stuttered for a moment. It was not often—if ever—that Annie instigated real, deep conversation. She usually skimmed the surface, making him dig if he wanted any actual insight into her. This was not the norm, and it took a moment for him to catch up.

"I was going to be a teacher."

"A teacher?"

"Yeah. I thought I'd change the world, you know. I'd reach the unreachable. Break the unbreakable. I'd be the teacher all the kids looked back on and said, 'That's the guy who finally got through to me.'"

She chuckled. "You still have that determination. Only now you use it on me."

He smiled. "I try. You've been a pretty tough case."

"So what happened? How did you get from teacher to real estate agent?"

"I started school. I hated it. I hated everything about it, which is kind of ironic, don't you think? I wanted to teach but hated the process of *learning* to teach. I just wanted to be out there. You know, in the world. So I switched majors. Thought I'd be a historian. Then I thought I'd be an architect. Then I realized I didn't know what I wanted to do, so I just dropped out altogether."

"Why didn't you ever get married and have a family and white fences and all that?"

"After dropping out of college, I was just a bit lost, I guess. I had jobs here and there, and then I decided to travel. I lived in London for a few years. Did you know that?"

"No," she said, clearly surprised. "Why'd you leave?"

"I met this lovely girl named Isabel. Thought I loved her. Thought we'd get married someday. She met a man named Thomas. Married him instead. I came home with my tail between my legs and my heart in a thousand pieces."

Annie gave him a sad smile. "Aw. I'm sorry."

"Don't be. It wasn't meant to be. I hated London. It was crowded and damp. Anyway, after I finally recovered from that betrayal, I met Charlene. A Southern belle almost as saucy as you but not nearly as beautiful and charming. One day, after about four years of dealing with her bad attitude, she said the worst thing a woman can ever say to a man."

Annie gasped dramatically. "She questioned your manhood."

"No. She said 'marry me or leave me.' I chose the latter."

She threw her head back and laughed. "Oh, Marcus, you really do have terrible taste in women."

He shrugged. "I don't know about that. I kind of like you. Most days."

She nudged him in his side with her elbow. "Which only proves my point. So those horrid women turned you against marriage?"

"No, not completely. I was just waiting for the right tart to come along."

She giggled as she shook her head, but then she grew serious as she looked around them.

"After you went to bed last night, I still couldn't sleep. I couldn't turn my brain off. All my life, I've treated change as just something to get through, one more challenge to tackle and overcome. My daughter is grown now, Marcus. My brothers haven't needed me to take care of them for years. My job with them is done. And here I am desperately clinging to a role they don't need me to play anymore. I know," she said before he could speak, "Mom and big sister are always needed, but not like when they couldn't fend for themselves. Not like when they were kids." She sipped her drink. And then she sighed and looked at him. "Maybe I'm not so far off my path as I thought I was. I own a business. I own a home. I have an incredible daughter. The only thing missing…is you."

His heart lifted. "I'm right here."

"And you've been incredibly patient with me, Marcus. I know I'm not the easiest person to love."

"Don't put yourself down."

"The truth isn't a put-down. I'm crass. I'm temperamental. I'm stubborn. And…I'm terrified of…"

"Being abandoned."

"It's much easier to be alone than to be rejected by someone you care about."

He couldn't see through her sunglasses, but he suspected there were tears in her eyes by the way her lip quivered as she turned away.

"If I were brave enough to be honest, with you and myself, the truth is that I don't want to be alone anymore. I thought what we had would be enough. You know, office banter and non-obligatory dinner a couple times a week was wonderful. For a while. Then it wasn't enough, for either of us. I knew that, I knew you were feeling this just as strongly as I was and we had to either move forward or stop. I just kept ignoring that like I ignore everything that makes me uncomfortable. But the truth is, I do want what Paul and Matt have." She took a deep breath. "I want that with you, but every time I look over the edge, I get terrified. I just can't make myself jump."

Marcus very nearly threw his fist in the air and let out a victory cheer. He'd finally broken through to her. His heart melted as he put his hand to her cheek and she ever so slightly pressed her face into his light touch. "You don't have to jump, honey. There is no jumping. There's just that path that we've both wanted to take and somehow kept missing. We just have to take it. I wish I could promise you it will be smooth, but it won't be, Annie. Life never is. There will be ups and downs and twists and turns, but we're going to be taking them together. That makes it worth the trouble. I'm standing right here waiting. All you have to do is take my hand and take the path with me."

A slow but brilliant smile spread across her face. She put her hand over his hand and sighed. "Okay. Let's take it."

"Yeah?"

"Yeah."

Sliding his hand to the back of her head, he pulled her to him and kissed her right there on the sidewalk for everyone to see.

And she didn't even stop him.

Annie hadn't intended to get home so late, but Marcus had wanted to explore the little lakeside town and then they'd walked along the beach. When it was dinnertime, they tried a lakefront burger joint. She thought the food was much better than the Greek he had picked for lunch, but Marcus passionately disagreed. The debate took up quite a bit of their drive home, but that eventually turned to talk about Mallory and figuring out what to do with her things. She'd be leaving in a week, and as far as Marcus and Annie could tell, she hadn't put much thought in what to do with the things she wasn't taking to California.

Annie could have a cleaner in and be ready to rent the house in no time, unless the closets were filled with Mallory's junk. Part of Annie suspected one of her guest rooms—Mallory's old bedroom—was about to turn into a storage unit.

As Marcus took the exit off the highway for Stonehill, Annie rested her head on the seat and watched him. She'd had an amazing weekend. And not just because Paul had married a woman who deserved him and all he would give to her. She'd finally let go of her fears and accepted that she and Marcus could give this thing between them a go. She felt a strange sense of freedom that she wasn't sure she'd ever felt before. She suspected if she analyzed it too much, she'd realize he was right—she was actually happy.

He grinned after a moment of her scrutiny. "What are you thinking about, Ms. O'Connell?"

"I was just thinking that I am very lucky to have you. I love you."

"I love you."

She held her breath for a moment. "Would you be opposed to, um..."

"What?"

"Staying with me tonight?" she asked quietly. Maybe if he didn't want to, he would pretend he hadn't heard her.

Instead, his smile widened. "Oh, let me think about that."

"I don't know what I'm asking exactly. Maybe just wine and conversation." She ran her hand over the back of his neck. "I can't promise more, but I...I'm not ready for you to go home yet."

"I would never expect you to promise me anything, Annie." He brought her hand to his mouth and kissed it. "Although I'll have to get up early and get home for clothes. My boss will turn into a bear if I'm late."

"Good thing you've only got to work with her for one more week."

"It's a damn good thing."

He kissed her hand one more time before pressing it over his heart. She couldn't help but smile.

A few minutes later, he pulled into her driveway and got their bags from the trunk as she unlocked the door. Walking into her home somehow felt different with Marcus behind her. She held the door and let him enter before locking it behind him. She led him to the bedroom, and tension lingered in the air as he put the bags at the foot of her bed.

Annie glanced at the clock. It was just after nine thirty. "Wine?"

He nodded and followed her to the kitchen. He knew his way around well enough that he grabbed two glasses while she selected a bottle. He stood next to her as she poured. She set the bottle aside and handed him a glass. He toasted her before drinking.

"Much better than the gas-station wine I brought to the office last week."

She smiled at the memory. "Very much so. Are you hungry or…"

He shook his head.

She took another drink from her wine—a large swallow rather than a subtle sip—and sighed heavily. She felt as though a big neon sign was flashing S-E-X in the room.

"This is awkward, isn't it?" Annie asked.

"Not too much."

"Liar." She lowered her face and drew a breath before

pushing her wine glass away and taking his from his hand. She set it next to hers and faced him.

"Annie, I don't—"

"Don't argue with me right now."

"But...if—"

She cocked a brow at him, and he stopped talking. "Look, I'm sure you had some great romantic evening playing out in your mind, and I thought I could do that, but...that's not me." She frowned. "I don't really know how to be seductive, so..."

Reaching out, he grabbed her by her hips and pulled her to him. "You silly woman. You seduce me every time you look at me." Brushing her hair behind her ear, he looked into her eyes as if he could see inside her mind. "I want you, Annie. Just standing here like this, I want you. You don't have to try. You don't have to do anything. Having you near me is more temptation than I can take. You have no idea how lucky you are that I can control myself around you."

She grinned as she slowly slid her hands up his arms and around his neck. "There's this part of me that would like to see how far I can push my luck. And another part of me that wants to take your self-control and shatter it."

Slipping his arms around her waist, he pulled her against him. She gasped quietly at the feel of his body responding to her.

He brushed his nose against hers. "I'd take it either way."

Leaning into him, she kissed him tenderly. Unlike with their other kisses, she held back even when he tried to deepen it.

She leaned back, lightly traced his lips with her fingertips, and smirked. "I'm pressing my luck here. I can't do that if you don't play along."

He exhaled a shaky breath. "This just might kill me."

"So be it," she whispered and then kissed him again.

Instead of crazy heat engulfing them, a slow simmer started low in her stomach and spread through her, leaving tingles in its wake. His hands moved lightly over her, caressing instead of groping as he'd done the night before.

After several soft kisses, she took his hand and led him from the kitchen. Inside the bedroom, she closed the door behind them. It was dark in her room, darker than it'd been in the living room the night before. Annie almost regretted that she couldn't see his face, but she was also relieved that it eliminated the element of him seeing her when she wasn't quite as confident as she was letting on.

She pressed her lips against his one more time before lifting his shirt up. He helped her remove it, carelessly tossing the material aside before his hands fell on her hips again. She touched his bare chest. His skin was so warm, it reminded her of how he'd felt as the sun beat down on them as they'd walked along the beach earlier in the day. Even though it had been chilly, he'd looked sun-warmed and sexy as hell as the breeze mussed his hair. Leaning in, she gingerly put her hands on his waist and rested her forehead to his chest. She was more than familiar with his cologne by now, but inhaling it directly from his skin made the spicy scent even more alluring. Breathing him in soothed her, quieted the few lingering doubts in the back of her mind, and made her heart beat harder and faster.

She never knew that simply smelling a man could twist her insides around so tightly. Brushing her nose over his chest, she placed light kisses on his skin as she slipped her hands from his sides, found the button of his shorts, and released it with trembling fingers. The sound of his zipper opening filled her ears, and she had to remind herself to breathe.

This was happening. Really happening. Marcus was in her bedroom. Ready and willing to love her, and she was actually going to let it happen. The thought was frightening and thrilling all at the same time. She couldn't quite grasp the reality of it.

Then his shorts fell, and he lifted the hem of her shirt. She swallowed hard as, a moment later, her bra dropped away and then the remainder of their clothes. They stood in the dark, naked with nothing but his hands on her, and her mind finally let go of any remaining reservations.

He ran his hands down her sides, over her hips, and to her thighs. She gasped when he lifted her, one leg on either side of him, and then he sat on the edge of the bed—her straddling his lap, chest to chest, with her legs around his waist and his body pressing against hers. Heat and desire chased her fears and her breath away. He was there—right there—just waiting for her to take him.

She pressed her mouth to his and raked her fingers through his hair as she rubbed her body over his. Rolling her head back, she silently begged for him to kiss her neck. He did and then leaned her back farther and kissed lower. She nearly exploded as he cupped her breast and sucked her nipple into his mouth. He licked for a moment before moving his kisses back to her lips.

She shifted her pelvis, bit her lip, and whimpered as he entered her. Dear God, he felt like he was made to be inside her. He put his hands to her hips but simply held on while she moved —a slow rock that gradually quickened as instinct took over.

Finding his mouth, she kissed him hard and deep as her body tensed around his. His arms wrapped around her and a moment later, he had them flipped over, her on her back with him on top, without even leaving her body. It wasn't the most graceful move, but it was efficient.

She dug her heels into the mattress, pressing up to meet him thrust for thrust as he gripped her hair and gently nipped her shoulder. She fisted the blankets in her hands and cried out as an orgasm crashed through her. She was still reeling from the sensation when Marcus leaned back, pulled her hips off the mattress, and rammed into her until he, too, made a primal sound and then fell onto the bed beside her.

Marcus was looking forward to waking up next to Annie, but when the alarm rang out, scaring him from a dead sleep, he was alone in her queen-sized bed. Damn it. He'd set his alarm early, making sure he had enough time to get home and shower before work. For some reason, he thought that would ensure she'd still be asleep. He rolled onto his side, swiped his phone to turn off the annoying buzzing, and then sighed and dropped his head on the pillow as his eyes closed again.

"Well, that was obnoxious."

He lifted his head and found Annie crossing the room, wearing a long lilac-colored satin robe and carrying two cups—presumably filled with coffee. If she really loved him as much as he hoped she did, it would be coffee. Morning had come way too soon, and the disappointment of waking up without her was all he could take this early.

Sitting next to him, she set the mugs on the nightstand. "You should at least have a soothing sound to wake up to. It would ruin my day if I woke up to that screeching every morning."

"That screech makes sure I actually wake up to turn it off. Tell me that's coffee."

She leaned down and kissed his cheek as she ran her hand down his back. "Freshly brewed."

"I love you," he said on a long exhale.

She kissed him again. "Did I keep you up too late last night?"

"I'm just not a morning person." Pulling her down to him, he wrapped his arms around her and kissed her satin-covered shoulder. "I should have warned you about that when you begged me to shack up with you."

She chuckled. "You also should have warned me that you have dragon breath in the morning."

He laughed as she buried her face in his chest. "I bet if you hadn't already had a cup of coffee, you would, too."

She leaned her head back and grinned. "I've slayed many a knight the morning after."

"I don't want to hear about them."

They shared a quick kiss before she pulled away. He sat up, leaning against the headboard. He sipped from one of the mugs she'd set down as he watched her walk to her closet and disappear inside. She reappeared a moment later with white slacks and a yellow top. She held them against her, clearly debating.

He swallowed a bit more of the coffee. "Have you showered yet?"

"Yes."

"Well, that's a damn shame and a waste of my perfectly good morning."

She smirked. "I suppose you thought we'd be doing that together?"

"I had high hopes."

"That's what you get for sleeping in."

"Sleeping in? It's"—he looked at his phone—"quarter till six."

She grabbed some underclothes and carried them with her to the bathroom then closed the door behind her. He took another drink of his coffee before tossing the covers aside and joining her, not bothering to knock.

Pulling her robe closed, she gawked at him. "What are you doing?"

"We had sex last night. Remember?"

She diverted her eyes, looking adorably embarrassed. "Yes."

He yanked her to him and then kissed her firmly on the mouth as he lifted her up and sat her on the bathroom counter, all while she held the front of her robe closed. She grunted, leaned to one side, and pulled a tube of toothpaste from beneath her.

She held it up to him. "You need to use this."

"Don't move."

She sighed loudly and looked away when he walked to the toilet. "When did we get comfortable enough to pee in front of each other?"

"I'm more than comfortable enough, and I really have to pee. Apparently it's your comfort level we need to work on. You don't even want me to see you naked. *Don't move*," he said when she started to get off the counter. To his surprise, she actually stayed put.

She didn't look at him again, though, until he had flushed the toilet and was washing his hands.

Stepping to her, he held her gaze. "Are you trying to hide your body from me?"

"I'm not twenty anymore."

"Neither am I."

"Well, *my* not being twenty and *your* not being twenty are two completely different things. Your body hasn't..." Her words faded as she gestured aimlessly with her hand.

"Don't ever become a mime. You are terrible at it." He grinned when she playfully swatted his arm. Stepping away, he grabbed the toothbrush he'd left sitting out the night before and the tube of mint-flavored paste. "My body has changed plenty in the last thirty years." He stuck toothpaste-covered bristles into his mouth.

"I'd rather you imagined me…perkier."

He chuckled as he scrubbed the coffee and morning breath from his mouth. A quick rinse and he was patting his hands and mouth dry on a towel then moving back between her legs. He pushed her satin robe aside at the knees and pulled her to the edge so their bodies were nestled against each other.

"Marcus," she softly chastised even as she slipped one arm around his neck.

"Never, for one moment, have I ever considered anything about you to be perky."

She laughed as she shook her head at him. "You are in a mood this morning. Is this what having sex does to you?"

He kissed her firmly on the lips. Now that he had fresh breath, she didn't pull away from him.

After breaking the kiss, he put his forehead to hers. "Are you really planning to spend the rest of our lives hiding your body from me?"

"Maybe."

"That seems silly," he whispered. "I think you're beautiful. I think everything about you is amazing. Including your body. *Especially* your body," he breathed. He dipped his head and kissed her deeply as she dug her fingers into his hair. He pushed his underwear down and lifted her thighs around his hips. One thrust and he was inside her.

She rolled her head back, exposing the sinful temptation that was her neck. He didn't think he'd ever pass on a chance to taste her there. He dragged his tongue along her jaw and then pushed it between her lips. She kissed him back, just as hot and wet and demanding. He moved his hand from her hip to her breast, squeezing the plump flesh and rolling her nipple between his fingers until it stood out.

"Open your robe," he breathed. "Let me see you."

She held his gaze for several long seconds before finally slipping the satin off her shoulders, letting it fall around her waist. He moaned his approval and grabbed her breast again. She leaned back until her head and shoulders were against the mirror. Eyes closed tight, she panted as he moved in and out of her.

"Look at me, Annie."

She grinned slightly. "Don't push your luck, Marcus."

He leaned forward, capturing her mouth with his. Resting his forehead to hers, he gripped her thighs again, holding her as he loved her. "Open your eyes," he whispered.

She slowly lifted her eyelids.

"You're beautiful. You're absolutely lovely. Every inch of you."

She kissed him as they finished together.

CHAPTER SIX

"So," Donna drawled out with a stupid know-it-all grin on her face as she looked at Annie over the rim of her iced tea. "Did you and Marcus...you know?"

Annie dropped the lemon into her cup and looked around the café, trying to find Jenna. "What makes you think this is your business?"

"I'm your sister-in-law."

"How, exactly, does that give you the right to know what is happening to my vagina?"

Donna started to speak and then stopped and watched as two clearly shocked women stared as they passed their table. The women moved on, and Donna looked at Annie. "Did you have sex with Marcus?"

She immediately flashed to an image of him taking her on her bathroom counter that morning. God, she couldn't believe she'd let him do that. That was *not* normal lovemaking for her. What had she been thinking? She didn't know, but she actually didn't really regret it. In fact, thinking about it made her stomach flutter with a strange kind of longing. "I'm not talking to you about this."

She gasped and opened her mouth wide. "Annie O'Connell, you jezebel. You did."

Annie's eyes widened as well. "Did you just—"

Donna was so excited about this turn of events, she practically squealed as she leaned forward. "How was it?"

"Excuse me. Do I ask about your sex life?"

"*I* am married to your brother. Asking me about my sex life would be icky."

"Trust me, so is this. Some things are meant to be private, even between sisters. I'm not having this conversation."

Donna giggled and sat back. "Fine. Don't tell me. The fact that your face is as red as the ketchup bottle says all I need to know. I'm so happy for you."

"Because you presume I had sex?"

"Because it's about damn time you let that man have sex. Can you at least admit you are a couple now? As if you haven't been since the day he started working for you."

"We haven't been."

"Please. You have dinner several nights a week, lunch on the days you don't have dinner—"

"We both have hectic schedules. Dining out is a much easier option most nights."

"Oh, and he just happens to be there in the office, so why not dine together? Every day."

"Why not?"

Donna smirked. "Whatever. Besides all that, he tolerates you."

"I hear that a lot."

"Because it's a *huge* deal. It takes a special kind of affection to be able to put up with all your bullshit."

Annie finally caught Jenna's attention and gestured for her to come take their order. "I hope sometime in between asking about my sex life and analyzing my dining habits you decided what you want. I'm in a hurry."

"Have an appointment?"

"No. I'm just really hating our conversation today."

"What would you rather talk about?"

Annie ordered a chicken sandwich while Donna requested a burger. After passing off her menu to Jenna, Annie sighed. "It was a lovely wedding. I'm happy to see Paul and Dianna married. Once they get home from the honeymoon, they can get settled into their life together. Everything has fallen into place for them. It's wonderful."

"Yes, it's good to see two of the three O'Connell siblings happy."

Annie stared at Donna. "Why is everyone giving me such a hard time lately?"

"Because it's fun."

Using a straw to stab at a lemon slice sitting at the bottom of her glass, Annie sighed. "Marcus..." She drew a breath and looked at Donna, who had her eyebrows raised, impatiently waiting. "He was just joking but...he said we should elope."

"*What?*"

"He's just kidding," Annie insisted. "But it..." She frowned deeply. "I gave up thinking I'd ever get married a long time ago. And I was fine with that. I've always been so focused on taking care of my brothers and Mallory. Even after Marcus and I started...whatever we were doing...marriage wasn't on my radar."

"And now?"

She stabbed the lemon harder. "Now, all of a sudden, I'm... God. What's wrong with me, Donna?"

Her face sagged. "Nothing."

"No. *Something.* It shouldn't be this hard to admit that I want things like a relationship with Marcus and marriage and a normal life. But I just... There are women who had it way worse than I ever did. So my dad was worthless. Mallory's dad was worthless. That doesn't justify this absolute terror I have at the thought of intimacy. And I don't mean physical intimacy," she said before Donna could get confused. "I mean love. Why the hell am I so scared of loving him? I don't get it. He's a great guy. He's perfect for me. When I'm with him, I don't feel so... emotionally disconnected. But then he pushes, and my defenses go up before I even know it."

"Why are you scared?"

"I don't know." She closed her eyes and exhaled. "You know

how I am. I like things to go as planned, and Marcus is a huge monkey wrench in my life."

She smiled. "You need a monkey wrench, Annie. You need something to shake you up."

"I don't like it. I had my life figured out."

"And it was a great plan. On paper. Work sixty hours a week until you retire. Sell the business. Sell the house. Downsize to one of your rental homes. Travel. It's all nice when you spell it out. But what about you? What about your emotional needs?"

She rolled her eyes and scoffed. "Emotional needs?"

"Yeah, honey. Everybody has those. Even the ever-practical Annie O'Connell. You dumped that energy into Mallory for so long, but she's grown now and about to move away. You have to redirect it somewhere."

"I should get a dog," she muttered.

"You could. But I bet Marcus would be more fun."

Annie smiled slightly, but it didn't last. "I can't imagine what he sees in me that has kept him trying to break through my defenses for so long."

"Stop cutting yourself down, Annie. There is plenty to see in you. You are funny and strong and courageous. Maybe you are careful who you give your love to, but when you do, your love is fierce and it runs deep. I don't think it's wrong that you are wary of who you let in, because when you let someone in, you do so completely. You are not as tough or as cold as you keep trying to pretend to be. You just hold back until you know someone deserves your love. There is nothing wrong with that."

She sagged in her seat. "Look at what Dianna went through. Her husband cheated on her, left her broken, and she jumped right into a relationship with Paul without hesitation."

"Well, that's not true. They both danced around things for a long time."

"Not five years."

"No. Not five years, but just because you don't move at the same pace doesn't mean there's something wrong with you. Listen, Matt was younger when your parents passed. He was a bit more resilient. But Paul had issues. You know he did. He blew through two marriages before figuring himself out, and he probably wouldn't have done that if he hadn't met Dianna. They straightened each other out. You have to give yourself a break here. Give yourself and Marcus a chance."

"I'm just worried that..."

"What?"

"What if it was all about the chase? What if he gets bored now that I'm not running? What if he gets tired of me and leaves?"

Donna smiled. "Honey, that man is insanely in love with you. We've all seen it practically since the day you hired him. There has always been something between you. *Always*. When you two first started having dinner and seeing each other outside of the office, we were thrilled for you because it was a huge step for you. It's taken a long time, but you both finally see what we've seen all along. He's not going to get bored. He's not going to change his mind. And I'd bet all that teasing about running off to elope wasn't teasing at all. I bet he'd put a ring on your finger this very minute if he thought you'd say yes."

"God," she said on a sigh, "he really is an idiot, isn't he? I thought it was just a phase."

Donna laughed. "Do you love him?"

Annie closed her eyes and rubbed her temple for a moment. "Yes. As terrifying as it is to admit, yes, I do love him."

"Then embrace this. There is always a chance that it won't work out, but there's also a chance that it will."

Annie inhaled slowly and then let a grin spread across her lips. "Well, I guess if I'm stuck with him for the rest of my life, at least he's really great in bed."

Donna gasped before throwing her head back and laughing.

A window popped up in the bottom-right-hand corner of Marcus's computer monitor, notifying him of a new e-mail from Matthew O'Connell. Clicking on the notification, he skimmed the text letting him know a photo was attached. Marcus opened it and was greeted by three smiling faces—his in between Annie's and Mallory's.

It frightened him how much he wanted to belong in that picture. He'd slowly integrated himself into the O'Connell family unit, and it felt so right to be there. He'd become friends with Matt and Paul. He felt as close to Donna and Dianna as he did to his own sister. Over the years he'd developed a good rapport with Mallory. Now that he'd finally gotten Annie to admit she loved him, he felt like his life was almost complete.

The picture encompassed everything he wanted. In the image, Annie stood next to him, smiling as he draped his arm over her shoulder with her palm resting casually on his chest. On the other side, Mallory smiled brightly. He was in between them, beaming proudly. Like a man who had everything he ever needed.

While he pushed Annie to get over her fear, he had to admit he had a bit of his own. She'd warned him that she had a tendency of freezing up and pushing people away. He knew better than most that was true. She'd kept him as far away from her heart as she could for as long as he'd been subtly trying to find his way in. She said she could hurt him, but she had no idea. Hurt him? No. She'd *obliterate* him if she turned away from him now.

As determined as he was that he wasn't going to let her, if Annie decided to end things, there'd be no changing her mind. He'd been gently nudging her into opening up to him for years. If she shut down on him now, who knew how long it'd take to pry her heart open again.

That terrified him about as much as he suspected she was terrified of him leaving her. But he wasn't going to leave her. She'd have to find a way to trust him. And he'd have to find a way to believe that she wouldn't panic and go running as far and fast away from him as she could. Trust and faith in each other. That was all they needed. Too bad neither came easily.

"How's it going?"

He turned his attention to his office door, where Annie had appeared. "Come here. Look at this."

She moved around his desk and put one hand on the back of his chair, the other on his desk. Her light perfume surrounded him, and he instinctively inhaled to get more. He'd watched, that very morning, as she spritzed it on her wrists. The memory reminded him of more than that: of making love to her so unabashedly in the bathroom. Of the shower they took after. Of watching her dress while she reminded him that he had to get home to dress himself if he expected to get to work on time.

He couldn't deny that he had hoped the weekend away would end with them in bed together, but he hadn't actually expected it to happen. The most he expected was to chip away another brick from Annie's defenses. He was so happy at the moment, it took all his strength not to pull her into his lap and nuzzle her neck all damn day long.

"Wow," Annie said, distracting him from his thoughts. "Good picture."

"It really is." He twisted his head so he could look up at her and try to gauge her reaction.

She looked thoughtful, like she was weighing all that the photo could mean. She bit her lip, her eyes moving slowly, as if absorbing every pixel, one at a time. "You're right," she said quietly. "We do make a great family."

His heart rolled over in his chest. He started to speak but didn't know what to say.

"I'm sorry it took me so long to see that."

His excitement instantly turned to worry. He spun his chair so he could see her face more clearly. "Everything okay?"

She nodded, took another few seconds to stare at the photo, and then leaned back. She took a step back, like she were going to leave, but he reached out and grabbed her wrist. "Donna and I had a...*strange* lunch. That's all."

"Strange how?"

She glanced to the reception desk and then whispered, "She asked inappropriate questions. I evaded."

"Questions about us?"

"It wasn't exactly difficult for her to realize things have changed between us. I couldn't stop blushing."

His smile widened. "Good."

She playfully narrowed her eyes at him. "You're a terrible influence on me," she whispered.

"Oh yeah?"

"Yeah," she confirmed, stepping away from him.

Clearing his throat, he tried to tame his body's reaction to her. "Is it too soon for me to ask if I can come over tonight with take-out?"

She exhaled, and he'd swear her breath trembled. "I'm meeting a client at six. We're only looking at one place, so I shouldn't be late. Shall I text you when I'm done?"

"I'd like that."

She licked her lip. "Okay." She started for the door then

turned. "Marcus, that photo *will* look perfect on the mantel. I'll ask for a few copies for us."

His chest filled to the point of nearly bursting. "That'd be great. Thanks."

She hesitated, as if she wanted to say something else, but then left him with his heart singing and his body tingling.

8h

Annie reached for an eggroll. "I've never done this before."

"What?"

"Had Chinese food in bed." Covered by nothing but a sheet, she took a huge bite, starved from the late hour of their dinner. Marcus hadn't shown up with a bag of Chinese until after seven, and when he did, food ended up being the last thing on her mind. He'd changed from his work clothes to jeans and a T-shirt, and something in her snapped. She hadn't intended to, but he had barely set the bag down before she stepped behind him and wrapped her arms around his waist. He turned to greet her, and the quick kiss somehow ended up with them stripping as they made their way to her bedroom.

After yet another toe-curling round in her bed, she had reheated the food and carried it to her room. Now, she couldn't seem to stop eating. Everything tasted so wonderful. She *felt* so wonderful. Sitting there with him like this brought a sense of peace and belonging that she wasn't sure she'd ever felt before. She'd had lovers in the past, but that was all they were—men who were passing through, and they had both known it. She'd never tried to pretend they were more, and they'd never tried to be more. But being with Marcus was different.

He did want more. So did she. And the fear that thought had carried for the last few years was quickly fading. Somehow the idea of giving her heart over to this man wasn't emotionally crippling her. Loving him was actually starting to feel right. She smiled as he wrangled a piece of broccoli between his chopsticks, only to drop the veggie before he made the complete journey to his mouth.

"Do you think..." Her words trailed off before she finished.

He looked at her curiously. After a moment, he grinned. "Oh, honey. I know I am irresistible as hell, but I am merely a mortal man. You've got to let me rest before round two."

"Not that, you fiend." She nudged him with her elbow, and he laughed. "Do you think we would still do things like this if...if we ever did get married?"

His smile sank a bit and took her heart with it.

She shook her head and looked down at her eggroll. "Don't answer that. That was stupid."

"Yes," he said, and she looked at him again. "I think we would definitely do these things if we got married. Moments like this would be the best part of being married."

She imagined the grin that spread across her face was as giddy and girly as she felt inside. And then that old familiar fear kicked in. She looked once again at the eggroll in her hand. Suddenly it wasn't as appetizing. "I told her that I don't know why this is so hard for me." Her good mood darkened, and she dropped the food back on her plate. "I love you, Marcus. If I ever found a way to be honest with myself, I would admit that I've loved you for a long time. But it's like I have an emotional blockage somewhere that I can't get past. I'd given up the idea of ever getting married, but when you said it, it was like a light bulb went off inside me, illuminating what it is that I've been missing. I don't understand why I can't see myself like you do. That's not how other people go through life, is it?"

He put his chopsticks down. "You know, I've wanted this relationship a lot longer than you have. I've had more time to think about all the things we could mean to each other. But as soon as Mallory teased me about us getting married, I had the same kind of light-going-off feeling. Sure, I'd thought in the back of my mind, maybe someday you and I could make things official, but hearing her say it somehow made it seem like a viable option. She was kidding when she said it, and I was kidding when I said it. But then again, maybe neither of us was really joking at all. Maybe it is something we should consider down the road. Honestly, there's no reason why we shouldn't. It's on the table. Let's just both acknowledge that marriage is on the table, sometime, and let that be enough for now."

She sighed. "Is it? Enough for you. Is *this* enough for you?"

He leaned over and kissed her. "We've been doing *this* for all of forty-eight hours, sweetheart. This is perfect for now. And when we're ready for more, we'll take more."

She swallowed and reached for her eggroll again. "For the

first time in a very long time, I want to share my life with someone. That terrifies me. You know that, right?"

"I know, but we're in this thing together, so just hang on to me, and we'll figure out the rest together."

"Together, hmm?"

"Yes. Together. Which means you don't get to be in complete control of everything."

She drew a slow breath. "I may have to reconsider this." She smiled when he laughed and put her hand on his knee. "Do me one favor?"

"What's that?"

"Don't give up on me."

He grinned as he leaned in for a kiss. "Not going to happen."

CHAPTER SEVEN

*A*nnie dropped a pile of empty, flattened boxes on Mallory's living room floor. "You haven't packed anything."

"I know," she said dramatically. "I just don't know where to start."

Annie looked around the house her daughter had rented for the last three years. Mallory had accumulated far too many knickknacks while in college.

Picking up a tiny figurine of Spider-Man, Annie sighed. "Are you taking all this with you to San Diego?"

"Well, I was thinking that I'd pack all this up, put it in my old bedroom at your house—"

"I knew that was coming," Annie said.

"—and *then*, when you and Marcus come for your first visit, you could bring a moving truck with the rest of my stuff."

"Okay, I didn't know *that* was coming. *What?*"

"Which part? You and Marcus coming to visit or bringing my belongings with you?"

Annie didn't answer. "We're together now, Mallory. You can stop dropping hints about how I should date him."

Mallory clapped her hands and giggled like a schoolgirl. "I knew it. I could tell at the wedding you were giving in."

"Why am I the only one who understands how unprofessional it is to date my employee?"

"Come on, Mom. It's not like you coerced him into your bed in exchange for a promotion. He's—"

"Loved me forever. I know." She picked up a box and assembled it before taping the bottom shut. "So what do you plan to actually take with you?"

"Clothes. Toiletries. Blankets and pillows."

"Have you booked a hotel for your first few nights there?"

"Yes, and appointments to look at the apartments Marcus helped me pick out. He found a really nice real estate agent to show me around."

"Good. I'm glad he was able to do that."

Mallory stopped unwrapping the packing paper Annie had brought. "Really? Because I thought you'd be pissed that he butted into our business."

"It's your business," Annie said. "You can let anyone you want butt in." She glanced to her daughter when Mallory snorted. "Fine. I was a bit put off at first, but I trust Marcus to look out for your best interests. He cares about you, too."

"I wish you'd met him a long time ago."

Annie took a few sheets of packing paper and started wrapping up Mallory's collectables. "I wouldn't have given him a chance a long time ago."

"Why?"

"Because I was focused on you."

Mallory stopped wrapping a ceramic pony and frowned at her mother.

"Don't look at me like that. I was happy with my life then. I'm happy with my life *now*," she quickly corrected.

"Are you?"

"Yes."

Silence fell between them as they focused on emptying the shelf of sculpted plastic comic book heroes. "I always felt guilty. Like you didn't date because of me."

"I did date, Mallory."

"No, you didn't."

Annie put her hand on her hip and tilted her head. "Just because I didn't rotate father figures in and out of your life didn't mean I wasn't dating. I never was with anyone long enough to introduce you, but I *did* date."

"When?"

"Plenty of those sleepovers with your uncles were nights out for Mom. I just wasn't going to tell my kid that. Look, I may not be one to cling to men or jump in and out of relationships, but I haven't exactly been sitting on a shelf for the last twenty years, Mallory."

She frowned. "How did I not know this?"

"Because associating your parents with dating is creepy? Did you see how Toby and Sean were cringing the first time they came to a family dinner with Paul and Dianna? Every time Paul put his arm around Di, they both looked like they were going to be sick. Parents and sex don't commingle in kids' minds. Besides, I've never been serious enough about anyone to include them in our family."

"Until Marcus."

"Well, the two of you aren't giving me much choice, are you?"

"That's the plan." She smiled and added another wrapped breakable to the box. "I just need to know that you're taken care of so I can enjoy California."

"I can take care of myself."

"Not as well as I can. Or Marcus can."

Annie frowned as she tucked a strand of hair behind Mallory's ear. "Who is going to come over and eat all my ice cream on her lunch break, hmm?"

"I can probably find someone. I'll ask my friends to take turns raiding your fridge while you aren't home. Meg thinks you're awesome. I'll have her drop in unexpectedly so it feels like I'm still here."

She smiled. "Do you remember your fourteenth birthday party?"

Mallory moaned and pulled away from her mother. "Don't."

"You and six of your closest friends camped out stuffing

every piece of junk food you could find down your throats. Then Amber got sick. Which made you sick."

"*Mom.*"

"Before it was all said and done, each and every one of you had vomited. Uncle Matt had to come over and hose off the back porch because I couldn't stomach it."

"Why are you bringing this up?"

"Because, honey, I don't want your friends coming to my house to eat junk food. They throw up."

Mallory laughed before hugging Annie. Leaning back, Annie frowned as her heart grew heavy.

"Marcus is about to start his new job. I don't know when we can come out, but I bet he'll work it out somehow. He wouldn't miss a chance to come see you."

"Or to be with you. I hope you give him a chance, Mom. A real chance. He's earned it."

"Maybe if we run off to elope, we'll do it in San Diego."

Mallory's face split into a huge smile. "That would be *awesome*."

"I was kidding."

"I'm telling him you said that."

Annie grabbed Mallory's cell phone before she could and held it out of her daughter's reach. "I don't care if you are about to move, Mallory Jane, I will ground you."

Marcus looked at Matt with a frown. "All this is supposed to fit in Annie's guest room?"

"Annie said to leave the living and dining room furniture. She's going to help Mal buy new when you guys take her stuff out."

Marcus's chest puffed a bit at Matt's comment. For the first time ever, Annie had asked for his help instead of her brothers'. She said she'd understand if he couldn't take the time from work to drive to California with her. She said she could always get Matt or Paul to help. She said she'd hire movers if she had to. But Marcus was having none of that. He didn't care if he had to quit his new job and find another when they returned. He was not letting this opportunity to step up for Annie and Mallory pass him by.

He was even excited about the idea of moving her stuff into an apartment, helping her unpack, and the possibility of carrying a new couch up however many flights of stairs it might be. Wasn't that what parents did? Moved their kids wherever their new lives were starting?

Matt chuckled and patted him on the back. "Come on. Let's get started. I'd rather not spend my entire Friday night moving boxes."

"We're going to have to make several trips to get all this stuff out of here."

"I hope Annie holds up her end of the bargain. I'm starving."

"She was pattying up the burgers when I left."

Matt glanced at him. "When you left?"

Marcus grabbed a box and grunted at the unexpected heft of it. "Her place is closer than mine. I swung by and changed after work. Moving boxes in khakis didn't seem like a good idea."

"You could have changed here. Or at the office."

Marcus ignored the logic of Matt's comment.

"Donna says you two are official now?"

Marcus put the box in the back of Matt's truck. "Yup. That okay?"

"Not my business."

He laughed. "If there is one thing I've learned about your family, it's that everybody's business is everybody's business. You O'Connell siblings don't know how to keep your noses to yourselves."

"Learned it from Annie."

"No doubt." They headed inside to get more boxes. "Yes. We're official."

"Does Annie know that?"

"Yes, she knows that. I practically had to beat her over the head with it, but she's finally accepted that we're dating."

Matt shook his head. "You are a brave man."

"She's not nearly as scary as she tries to be."

"I don't mean her. I mean Paul and me." He stopped with two stacked boxes in his arms. "We both trust you. We think you're good for her. But if you hurt our sister, they won't find your body."

"I would expect no less."

They managed to empty most of Mallory's belongings from

the house in two trips. Everything else, she was taking with her in her car or Annie was leaving in the house to rent as partially furnished.

Exhausted, Matt and Marcus sat at the table with Annie and Mallory, who had put together the promised moving fee of burgers, homemade potato salad, and beer.

"You all set, kiddo?" Matt asked his niece.

"I think so."

Marcus piled two tomatoes on top of his burger. "When do you leave?"

"I was planning to leave tomorrow morning, but we decided to have a big dinner to welcome Paul and Dianna home."

"They'll want to see you before you go," Matt said.

Annie looked at Marcus as she grabbed a bottle of pickles. "Donna is making reservations somewhere. She said she'll let us know when and where. I let her know it had to be after seven since we have an open house."

"My last one," Marcus said with exaggerated disappointment.

"Doubtful," Annie commented. "I'm sure you'll be keeping me company at plenty of those things in the future."

"But I won't be working them."

She snorted. "If you think quitting your job means I'm not putting you to work, you are in for a rude awakening."

"I know all about how to stage an open house, and I'm not even a real estate agent," Matt said. "You can't escape."

"If you aren't at open houses, you'll be mowing lawns," Mallory said.

"That's not necessarily true." Annie held her burger inches from her mouth. "I've finally found a decent landscaper."

"Who found a decent landscaper?" Marcus asked.

She playfully narrowed her eyes at him. "My knight in rusted armor found a company who actually knows how to follow a schedule without being harassed to do their job. I just keep them up-to-date on the places that need care, and they do it. It is amazing."

Marcus creased his brow as he looked at her over his sandwich. "Rusted armor? Tarnished, maybe. But rusted?"

She grinned. "Trust me. It's rusted."

"You are so mean to me."

"You obviously like it."

He winked at her. "You have no idea."

"Are you staying at the house tomorrow night, or do you want to stay here?" Annie asked, returning her focus to Mallory.

"I had thought about staying here, but maybe you two would rather I didn't."

Marcus chuckled, and Annie cut her gaze in his direction.

"Of course you're welcome to stay here," Annie said. "I want you to. We can have breakfast before you head out."

"Sounds good," Mallory said.

Marcus nodded. "I'll make the bacon, though. Your mom is terrible at making bacon."

"Hey," Annie chastised. "My bacon is fine."

"If you say so."

"Who said you were invited anyway?"

He swallowed the bite in his mouth. "Oh. I just assumed since you've asked me to stay here every night this week that you had no intention of ever letting me go home again." He grinned at her as she lifted her brows, clearly stunned by his comment.

"*Mom*," Mallory teased. "You ho."

Matt laughed and shook his head. "Forget what I said, Marcus. You don't need Paul and me threatening to kill you. Annie's going to rip you to shreds."

CHAPTER EIGHT

"Y ou know," Marcus said, leaning against Annie's office door, "considering today is my last day, you could have bought cookies or something."

Annie smiled. She couldn't help it. This sappy feeling was annoying as hell but completely out of her control. Every time she saw him, her cheeks warmed and her heart did that crazy flip thing.

She cleared her throat and sat back in her office chair. "I did."

"Because you're dragging me to an open house. Not because you are trying to show me how much you've appreciated my service."

She smirked. "I've shown you that plenty in the last week."

He grinned as he crossed the room. "That you have."

"Don't do it," she warned as he rounded her desk.

"We're the only two here," he reminded her in that low tone he used in the bedroom. As always, he left her breathless.

"We're at work."

Leaning down, he pressed his lips to her neck and whispered, "Do you have any idea how many times I've wanted to take you right here in this office?"

She wanted to be shocked, but she'd had plenty of those thoughts herself. Heat rushed through her, and for a moment, she considered how much time they had before having to rush off to the open house. She couldn't believe she'd entertained the idea, even for a moment. That wasn't like her. He was such a bad influence on her. Even so, she smiled as he kissed just below her ear.

"You're terrible," she said.

"You love it."

As he nipped at her neck, she saved the document she was working on and then turned her chair to face him. "We should go."

"We have plenty of time."

Putting her hand to his chest, she gently pushed him away. He grabbed her wrist and pulled her to her feet and right into his arms. She didn't struggle. She simply wrapped her arms around his neck and let him kiss her. His tongue pressed into her mouth and a moan rumbled in his throat. Breaking the kiss, he met her gaze, and Annie's heart swelled with the way he was looking at her.

His hands slid down her body, and she shook her head. He ignored her and lifted her onto her desk.

"Mr. Callison, this is highly inappropriate."

He sighed. "Oh, Ms. O'Connell, I'm aware." Stepping between her knees, he traced her lips. "If you only knew how many times I've wanted to do this, you'd allow me this one moment as a reward for all the times you made it out of this office unscathed."

She giggled. "I should reward you for not seducing me sooner?"

"Yes," he whispered and kissed her neck again. "Yes, you should." He smiled when she gripped his hips and pulled him closer to her. "I've had more than my fair share of fantasies about you and this desk."

She inhaled and slid her arms around his neck then whispered in his ear, "Me too."

Marcus's body instantly reacted.

"I'll tell you sometime."

"Now?"

She leaned back and shook her head. "Just because I'm unethical enough to have sex with my employee doesn't mean I'm unethical enough to have sex in the office, and we both know where this little show of yours is headed if I don't put an end to it now."

"I love you so much," he whispered. "But I don't love this set of ethics you keep throwing at me."

She ran her hand over his hair. "Thank you."

"For kissing you?"

"For not giving up on me."

"You keep saying that, Annie, but I'm never going to give up on you. You're stuck with me."

"I hope so. I probably won't make your life easy."

"I don't expect you to." He grinned as he lowered his hands and cupped her bottom. "I enjoy the challenge, and my persistence *always* pays off. It may have taken me years, but not only have I gotten you to admit I'm the best thing that's ever happened to you, I finally got you to cross the lines of decency right here in your office. That has been my goal for the last five years."

"Well"—she pressed her torso into his—"it is your last day, and I do want you to know how much I appreciate your years of service. I thought you deserved more than a store-bought cookie."

He smiled as she threw his words back at him. "Are you absolutely certain we have to go to this open house?"

"I am. Unfortunately."

He started to pull away, but she held on to him. "I'm going to miss having you here. You really have been an invaluable asset to me. I hate that you're leaving."

"Reconsider your no-sex-with-employees stance, and I'll consider staying."

"I'll have you know, I've thought about it a time or ten this week."

He lifted his brows, clearly surprised. "Really?"

She nodded. "Here's the problem, though. Things are great with us now. But what if in a year or two, they aren't so great.

And I'm your boss, your roommate, and whatever other titles get thrown in there. There would be no escaping each other, and things at the office could get very ugly. I can't allow that to happen."

"I get that. I respect it." He caressed her cheek. "I'm happy to move on to this new job, if you feel it's best to keep our professional lives separate."

"I hate losing you here, but I really do think we shouldn't work together if we're going to *be* together."

"Then that's how it will be." He kissed her softly and stepped away. "Get your things and let's go. If we stay in here alone too much longer, I'm going to have my way with you right there on the desk."

She laughed softly. "My sweet-talking man."

"You know it."

She watched him leave before reaching into her desk drawer. She dug in her purse, removing her sunglasses, driver's license, and credit card to pay for dinner. Shaking the gloom from her mind, Annie dropped her purse back in the drawer, locked it, and left to meet Marcus. He already had the cookies and a stack of papers.

She settled into the passenger seat as he drove the short distance to the house they were showing. A hint of depression hovered over her heart as they prepared for the open house with perfect synchronization that reminded her of the day they'd shared their first kiss after putting chairs away. She knew he would attend open houses with her in the future—whenever

other agents weren't available, she would ask friends to step in—
but it wouldn't be the same.

"You okay?"

She looked over to where he'd finished staging the
countertop with flyers and her business cards. "Mm-hmm."

Stepping to her, he kissed her forehead. "I'm going to miss
this, too."

She grinned. "Get out of my head."

"I love your head." He kissed her again and looked at his
watch. "I'm going to get the sign up and the door open. It's about
time to start."

"Hey." She put her hand on his waist, catching him as he
walked around her. She grinned slowly as he looked at her
curiously. "One more inappropriate kiss before the open house
closes and you're officially out of my employ?"

He smiled and pulled her to him. "I love it when you're
naughty." Dipping his head, he covered her mouth with his, and
her toes practically curled.

The hair on the back of Annie's neck stood up the moment the
young man walked into the house. She smiled graciously even
though something inside her wanted to tell him to leave.
Though he was dressed nicely enough, in jeans and a button-
down shirt, he wasn't old enough to have a job that would afford
him a house in this neighborhood. She wasn't stereotyping the

kid; it was simply a fact. Even with the baseball cap pulled down low, she could tell he wasn't more than nineteen.

All the valuables in the house had been locked away before they opened the doors to the public, so he couldn't steal anything of value, but she was concerned he might be there to case the house and come back another time. She glanced toward the kitchen, where Marcus was chatting with a couple who looked like they could actually afford a mortgage. She silently hoped to see them coming through the doors so the kid knew she wasn't there alone, but the short hallway remained empty.

She smiled from across the room, not wanting to get too close until she could determine what he was up to. "Hi, I'm Annie."

He nodded in response but didn't give her a name.

She gestured toward the guestbook as she considered whether she should excuse herself to go get Marcus. "There's a guestbook on the table by the door, and I'll need to see your ID before I can let you look at the house. Don't worry. We won't contact you. It's just so we can keep track of who's been here." Usually that deterred anyone who wasn't really interested in the house, but he reached behind him, as if going for his wallet.

Her nerves lit, sizzling like a thousand water droplets hitting a hot griddle. Over the years, she'd always advised agents to go with their intuition. Her intuition was telling her this kid was trouble. Something was off about him. Something was *very* off about him. She took a step back as her breath hitched anxiously.

He struggled for a moment before pulling out a handgun and

aiming it at her. Annie's heart dropped like a boulder rolling off a cliff and hit the bottom of her stomach just as hard.

Goddamn it. All the conferences she'd attended over the years came at her in a barrage of unintelligible information. Move slowly. Don't surprise or scare him. Give him what he wants.

She struggled to swallow as she stared at the gun and took another step back.

Shit. This was happening. This was really happening. He was really standing there, looking like he was going to be sick as he held a weapon on her. She wasn't sure whose hands were shaking more—hers or the idiot kid's. The difference was that his finger was on the trigger of a presumably loaded gun.

She scanned his face, which was partially hidden by the baseball cap. Caucasian. Seventeen to twenty. Brown hair. Dark eyes. Sharp nose. Square jaw. Maybe five-seven, but no taller than five-ten.

"Did you hear me?" he demanded, pulling her attention to what he was saying instead of memorizing his appearance. "I said give me your purse." Even his voice was trembling.

His lack of confidence made her think he was an inexperienced criminal, but that brought little comfort at the moment. If anything, it made her more nervous. If he was jumpy, he was more likely to do something stupid.

She lifted her hands to show him she was no threat. "I-I don't carry one to open houses."

"Don't fuckin' lie to me."

"I'm not lying."

He hesitated before shoving the gun in her direction to emphasize his point. "Give me the damn purse, lady."

She drew a breath, held it, exhaled, and tried again. "I *don't* carry one."

"Then empty your pockets."

She lowered her hands slowly and turned her pockets out, holding up her phone in her left hand. Her license and credit card were in Marcus's glove box along with his wallet. Just in case something like this ever happened.

"Don't fuck with me!"

"I'm not," she said in her best soothing tone.

"Where's your cash?"

"It's not..." She licked her lip and swallowed. "It's not safe for real estate agents to carry cash."

He put his free hand to his head. He looked like he was starting to panic, which made her heart race even faster.

"Fuck!" Turning, he kicked the stand where the guestbook was resting. The wooden structure toppled over, and the crash of it echoed through the room as papers and pens scattered across the wood floor.

Fear gripped her and made it nearly impossible to breathe. Her stomach churned with anxiety, and she suddenly regretted the two cookies she'd snuck in between potential buyers touring the house. A stupid kid holding a gun was one thing; a stupid, angry, and empty-handed thief was another.

He faced her and once again lifted the gun in her direction. "You're lying to me!"

Annie's breath caught when footsteps fell heavy behind her. *Don't come in here, Marcus. Please. Please. Please.*

Too late.

"Annie," he said from behind her, "is everything—"

A loud popping noise slammed her eardrums, followed by high-pitched ringing. The kid stared at her, his eyes wide and his mouth hanging open. An eternity seemed to pass—staring into each other's eyes—before he turned and bolted for the door. As he did, Annie felt like the ground was spinning out from underneath her. Her equilibrium shifted, and she grew dizzier than she'd ever felt before.

For a moment, she recalled being a teenager on a ride at the county fair. She was with her brothers, screaming as they spun the seat they were in as fast as they could. She could hear their laughter—Paul's and Matt's. Smell the fried foods. Then gravity pulled at her so strongly, she couldn't help but fall back.

Instead of leaning into the seat of the ride, she felt the memory slip away, and she was on the floor, staring up as Marcus leaned over her, his blue eyes wide and his face pale. His mouth moved, but Annie couldn't hear anything over the shrill sound reverberating in her ears.

Something had happened. Something was happening. She didn't know what. Couldn't seem to think.

Confusion grew heavier, thicker, clouding her mind. Darkness, starting in her peripheral vision, filled her eyes, and she stopped trying to think, stopped trying to understand what was going on, stopped trying to hear Marcus's voice through the ringing.

Whatever was happening around her—*to her*—didn't matter. Whatever Marcus was saying didn't matter.

Nothing mattered.

Except the sense of peace enfolding her.

Marcus pictured Annie's face. Her smile. Heard the sarcastic bite that he loved so much. No comment ever went unanswered with her. At least not until she was lying on the floor, her eyes glazed over as she stared at the ceiling, not responding. He'd caught her as she crumpled, eased her down, pressed his hand to her forehead as blood oozed from the hole half an inch or so above the arch of her left eyebrow. He'd talked to her, begged her to stay with him while the frantic couple called 911.

He'd told the medics everything he could. He'd talked to the police several times. He'd relayed the events over and over as her family rushed in. He'd done everything right. He'd done everything he was supposed to.

But as the hours ticked by while she was in surgery, his mind started making him doubt himself.

What if he hadn't barged in? What if he'd let Annie talk to the couple instead of allowing her to pass them off to him?

"One last sale," she'd whispered and winked at him as he followed them to the kitchen.

He hadn't seen the kid for more than a split second, but it was enough to realize that he hadn't intended to shoot Annie. He looked just as shocked by his actions as Marcus had.

And in the split second, why didn't he take more notice of the kid's appearance? He'd had on a nice shirt. Jeans. A baseball cap. That was it. That was all he could tell the police. It wasn't much, but he'd never forget what little he had seen.

But that didn't matter. None of that mattered.

Annie was lying in an operating room as a bullet was removed from her brain.

Her *brain*.

Jesus.

If it'd been her stomach or her shoulder or just about anywhere else, Marcus might have some sense of hope. But the punk shot her in the head.

Marcus didn't snap out of his internal debate until Mallory called his name. She'd been packing up her car, preparing to drive to California in the morning, when he'd called her. She'd answered, the excitement evident in her voice as she prepared to set out on her own. Then he'd told her to rush to Stonehill Hospital. Her mother had been hurt.

Giving her a soft smile, he accepted the cup she held out to him even though the last thing he wanted was more coffee. Jenna had shown up with thermoses filled with "decent" coffee and platters of food. She and Mallory took up playing waiting-room hostesses, offering drinks and snacks, which seemed to stop them both from falling apart.

Even so, Marcus took Mallory's hand and pulled her to the chair next to him. "Sit for a few minutes, kid. You're wearing out the linoleum."

They gave each other sad smiles as she eased into the hard plastic chair next to him. He thought for the thousandth time in the last five years how much Mallory looked like her mother. This time, though, the thought was like a fist clenching his heart. His stomach tightened as the vision of Annie lying on the floor, staring blankly through him, flashed through his mind again. He tried to contain it, but a sob ripped through him.

Mallory squeezed his hand.

"I'm sorry," he said quietly and dragged his free hand under his eyes. "I just keep seeing her lying there."

"I'm sorry," she whispered. "I can't imagine how horrible that was."

He shook his head to stop himself from saying more. She didn't need to hear this. The poor kid was going through enough. Sniffing, he looked at his watch. Annie had been in surgery for over eight hours. What the hell was taking so long?

As if on cue, a woman walked in wearing scrubs. She was immediately crowded by O'Connells.

The look she gave them wasn't encouraging.

Marcus's breath caught as he stepped into the ICU. Paul and Matt had warned him, but he still wasn't prepared for what he saw. Annie's face was barely visible for the layers of gauze and all the tubes running from her bruised face and head.

Coma.

The word kept running through his mind, but it didn't really sink in until he saw her.

Annie was in a coma, and they didn't know how deep or how long or if she'd ever wake up. They really didn't know anything.

Except that at this moment, right now, she was alive and that, in and of itself, was more than the surgical team had expected.

He tried to block the memory from filling his mind, but it rushed in. The sound of the shot. The smell of the gunpowder. The sight of Annie stumbling back, falling into his arms, her eyes staring at nothing as he called out to her.

"Jesus," he choked out. "Oh, God." Moving to the bed, he sank down in the hard chair and took her hand. He kissed it, closed his eyes, and cried.

CHAPTER NINE

*A*nnie licked her parched lips. Damn, she was thirsty. A moment later, something cool and wet pressed against her lips. She sucked at it, pulling as much water as she could. She managed to get enough to barely count as a sip, but she swallowed the liquid gratefully.

"Annie?"

The man sounded like he was at the other end of a long tunnel. She tried to call out, but her own voice didn't sound right.

"Annie, can you open your eyes?" someone else asked. This voice, thick with an accent—Polish, maybe—and quivering like an elderly man's, said her name again as cold fingers settled on her forehead. Suddenly, her left eye filled with a light that was so bright it hurt. She winced and tried to fight the pressure keeping her eyelid open. Blessedly, he released his hold on her and the light faded, leaving starbursts behind her eyelid. But then the bastard did it again with her other eye.

"Annie," the old Polish man said again, "can you squeeze my hand?"

The cold hand grabbed hers. She tried to pull away, but his cool skin still rested on hers. What the hell was going on?

"Annie, squeeze my hand. She's moving." He sounded far too excited about her achievement.

Of course she was moving. What was he talking about?

She wanted to look at him, but her damn eyes wouldn't cooperate. She didn't know how long she'd struggled before she finally was able to lift her eyelids, but it was long enough that she was tired of hearing the chatter around her. The voices were talking over each other, mixing and bouncing around in her brain. She couldn't quite decipher one from another to understand what they were saying.

Her vision wasn't much better. The figures looming over her were blurry and the room was so damned bright, but slowly she was able to focus. Marcus smiled like a goofball and looked as excited as the Polish man had sounded.

She tried to speak, but her mouth was so damned dry, like she'd eaten a pack of crackers without a drop of water to wash them down. And her body was so heavy, as if something were weighing her down.

What. The. Hell.

Panic washed over her like a tsunami. It came out of nowhere, and she was suddenly drowning in it.

What was happening? What was wrong with her? She looked around her until she spotted a man. He was blurred, but she could tell he was wearing a white coat as he talked to a woman in pink scrubs.

Was she in the hospital? Breathing became more difficult as fear started to overtake her confusion. She was in the hospital. Something had happened. She gripped the hand that was holding hers as hard as she could.

"Annie," Marcus said with a sickeningly patronizing tone, "you're safe. You're okay."

She must have appeared as scared as she felt. He kissed her forehead and hugged her as much as it seemed he could with her lying in a bed.

"You're okay. You're just fine."

Clearly she wasn't. People didn't insist that someone was okay that many times unless they weren't. She scanned the room again. Her brothers? Mallory? She closed her eyes with frustration when she again failed to form the words she wanted to say.

Her confusion was heavy, like a blanket, as it pressed down on her. The more she tried to figure out what was going on, the foggier her mind became. She closed her eyes and welcomed the soothing darkness that surrounded her.

The next time Annie heard voices calling out to her, they came to her more clearly. Closer. Her mouth was still that sticky dry that reminded her of waking up after a night of too much drinking. She considered her eyelids for a few moments. They felt like bricks. Heavy and rough. Lifting them seemed impossible, but she finally managed. When she did, Marcus was standing over her.

It seemed that they'd gone through this before. This routine seemed familiar. Her waking up from what felt like a dead sleep with Marcus hovering, smiling like she'd done something amazing. She wanted to ask, but her parched mouth wouldn't cooperate.

"Hey, Mal," he said quietly. "Look who's awake."

And then Mallory was staring at her.

"Mom? Mom, can you hear me?"

Finally, Annie was able to make a garbled noise—not exactly what she had intended. Mallory sobbed and dropped her face. Marcus put his hand on Mallory's shoulder.

"Why don't you go find your uncles? I'm sure they'll want to see your mom."

Mallory sniffed and stood, still crying as she disappeared from Annie's field of vision.

"She's okay," Marcus said, running his hand over Annie's head. "So are you."

But she wasn't okay. She didn't understand why but did understand that she was *not* okay, and that terrified her.

He must have been able to see the panic on her face, because he stroked her face and kissed her head. "You're okay, Annie."

Why did he keep saying that?

Another unrecognizable noise left her.

"Here," he whispered as he put a damp rag to her mouth.

She pulled water from it, enough to wet her mouth, and closed her eyes as she struggled to swallow. Her muscles didn't quite seem to know how. Finally, she managed to push the meager drink down and opened her mouth. He understood what she meant and put the cloth to her lips again.

Why was everything so confusing? She felt as if some barrier were keeping her from completely engaging in what was going on around her. Medicine head. That's what it reminded her of. She felt like she'd had too much cold medicine on an empty stomach. Her brain just wasn't connecting to reality properly.

Marcus glanced over his shoulder. "There're some people here who want to see you."

"Hey, you," Matt said from Annie's other side.

It took effort—too much effort—to find him. He took her hand, and she finally felt some measure of consolation. Having Marcus with her was comforting, but he wasn't her brother. The O'Connell siblings were a unit. They were an unbreakable trio. Having Matt there made her feel one step closer to being whole. But where was Paul?

Another foreign noise left her.

She opened her mouth. Paul. His name was right there, in her throat, but it was stuck somehow. The word wouldn't leave her. But then he said her name. Her gaze finally found him next to Matt.

"I can't tell you how good it is to see you," Paul said.

She tried again. Paul. Matt. Marcus. Why couldn't she say their names? The warmth of tears trickled from her eyes and down her temples. Dear God, what was happening? She was trapped inside her own body—unable to speak, to move.

Her eyes slowly turned to Marcus, because, damn it, they couldn't seem to move faster. She pleaded with him, as much as she could manage without speaking, to tell her what was happening.

He gave her that stupid reassuring look that they all seemed to be wearing. "You got hurt, Annie," he said softly.

Hurt?

"But you're okay," Marcus said. "You're safe now. Just take a few deep breaths, honey."

She tried, but her heart was pounding and everything was so heavy, even her chest. She wanted to get up. Get out. Get away from whatever was happening. She tried, but her body didn't do what she demanded. Looking at Marcus again, she made another of those stupid fucking noises.

"Sweetheart, I know you're scared," he said soothingly, "but I *promise* you are okay. Just try to relax. I'm here. Your brothers are here. We're with you."

She wanted to scream. Demand the truth. She just needed the truth. She wasn't okay. She most definitely was *not* okay. And nobody, not even Marcus, was going to convince her otherwise. She turned her attention to the other side of the bed. Matt was looking down as Paul put his hand on his shoulder. They both looked upset. Which confirmed, in her mind, that she should be upset, too.

Paul leaned close to her. "Do you hear that beeping?"

She listened until she could focus enough to hear the rhythmic *ping-ping* of a machine.

"That's your heart monitor." He laughed softly. "It's going a little bit crazy right now, Annie. If you don't calm down, your nurse is going to come in here and kick us out for upsetting you. I know you're scared. You have every right to be, but you're not alone, and you're not in any kind of danger. We're all right here, and we are going to take care of you, so just take some breaths and do your best to calm down."

She looked beyond him to her youngest brother. Matt nodded. Marcus agreed as well.

He lifted her hand and kissed her knuckles. At first, her attention fell on the scruff of his unshaved face as it brushed over her skin, and then she noticed how pale he was, how red his eyes were. How aged he looked. His hair was longer than she remembered—not scraggly, just longer.

He looked unkempt. Marcus never looked unkempt.

Taking in her brothers' appearances, she saw they were clearly tired. Stressed. Whatever was going on was bad. It was very bad.

Closing her eyes, she inhaled slowly, deeply, and let herself fall away.

Marcus stroked the hair from Annie's face, smiling when she

looked up at him. She licked her lips and visibly struggled to swallow.

"Thirsty?"

She nodded just enough for him to understand, and he grabbed the cup of ice chips a nurse had brought in. Most of them had melted, but he managed to fish out a few. She parted her lips, and he slipped the ice in her mouth. "Better?"

"Yeah."

His movements stopped. Returning the cup to the table was no longer important.

She'd just spoken to him. Her whispered answer was barely discernible, but it was a word. A real word, not a grunt.

Hearing her voice lifted his spirits higher than anything else could have. The doctor continually cautioned Marcus and her family about getting too excited—the odds of her coming out of this unscathed were very slim—but he didn't know Annie. Annie was a fighter, and there was no way she was going to just lie back and not do her damnedest to get better.

"The nurse went to get the doctor. He'll be here in a few minutes."

Confusion filled her eyes. "Doctor?"

Each time she woke, she seemed to be more aware, but each time was also the same. Confusion. Fear. Panic. Sleep. That was her cycle, but he hoped it was broken now that she was actually speaking. He tried not to get his hopes up too high—he didn't want them crushed—but she seemed to be there. To be seeing him, hearing him, communicating with him. That was more than the doctors thought they'd ever see from her again.

He traced his thumb lightly over the mark left from her surgery. "You got hurt, honey."

"Hurt?"

"Yeah, but you're on the road to recovery now."

Her eyes drifted closed. He wanted to beg her to stay awake, to keep looking at him, but he didn't have to. She blinked a few times, and he was certain that some of the fog in her mind cleared a little as she looked at him.

"Mal?"

"She's home right now, but I'm going to call her in just a minute." He grinned. "She's going to lose her mind when she sees you."

"My brothers."

"Matt's here. He's getting coffee. I can go get him."

She lightly squeezed his hand. "Wait."

He glanced back when the door to her room opened. "This is Doctor Oritz. He's been taking care of you."

She moved her eyes around until she focused on the elderly man standing on the other side of her bed.

"Well, look at you," he said in his thick accent. "How are you feeling, Annie?"

"Tired."

He smiled and patted her hand. "I bet you are."

Per the ritual, Oritz moved around Annie's body, asking if she felt this and that as he poked and pressed on her, asking questions about her and her family and Marcus, and doing it all over again. This time, however, Annie was much more alert throughout the exam. She actually answered with words instead of sounds and nods.

Marcus's heart was damn near the point of exploding with happiness by the time the doctor finished.

"You're doing great, Annie," he reassured her. "You're doing just great."

She turned her eyes toward Marcus. She looked uncertain, but she didn't look terrified like she had so many times before as her mind was coming alive again. She slowly lifted her hand, reaching for Marcus. He sighed with relief as he slid his palm against hers. Leaning down, he kissed her knuckles and tried not to let his emotions show. He didn't want to frighten her or upset her in any way, but he honestly had begun to wonder if she'd ever fully wake up. As she'd slowly started regaining consciousness, the doctors continually warned her family about getting too excited or expecting too much. But seeing her reach for him—it was more than he had dared to hope.

He lowered his face so she couldn't see the tears that were burning in his eyes.

She moved her hand in his. "Marcus?"

He laughed softly. Hearing his name on her lips—even though her voice was thick and hard to understand—made the tears run. "Give me just a second." He sniffed, trying to control his emotions.

"Marcus and your family have been waiting for you for a long time," Oritz said in his cheery voice.

"What?" she asked weakly.

"You've been in a coma, Annie."

"What?" she asked again.

Marcus looked up, no longer caring that she was going to see him crying. "Three months, honey. You've been gone for three very long months."

sh

Annie couldn't quite grasp what everyone kept telling her. She'd been in a coma. For three months. Three months of her life was gone. She'd missed it. In what felt like the blink of an eye.

She'd been at work. She remembered that. When she closed her eyes, she remembered being at the office. She remembered the car ride, or at least parts of it, to the house. Marcus had laughed at something she'd said. He'd put his hand on her knee and told her that he loved her.

Then she awoke in the hospital and was told she'd lost three months.

She didn't believe it initially, but a nurse had opened the blinds in her room, and the trees, which had been just starting to blossom, were filled with green leaves. Spring had passed, and summer had arrived.

She couldn't make sense of that. She couldn't make sense of a lot of things.

Her family talked to her, but she couldn't focus long enough for a conversation. Her mind kind of went blank until someone would touch her hand or say her name and draw her back. Sometimes they looked at her when she was talking. They didn't have to say that they couldn't understand her. She read the confusion on their faces.

She'd have to swallow, take a breath, and try again. She felt like her tongue would get too fat for her mouth sometimes. Or maybe like she'd had three too many margaritas. She had yet to ask, but when Donna and Dianna finished catching her up on all the gossip they mistakenly thought she cared about, she finally ventured into territory she'd been too scared to ask about.

"What's wrong with me?"

Her sisters-in-law stared at her.

Annie sighed. "Please. Tell me."

Donna smiled. "Honey, you're fine."

"Liar." She looked from one in-law to the other. "Tell me."

They cast anxious glances between them, and Annie knew, undoubtedly, that whatever it was that was causing her to space out and trip over her words wasn't something minor. She wasn't looking at something that could be resolved with rest or medication. There really was something wrong with her.

No one had told her what had happened. Just that she'd been hurt. No one had told her the extent of her injury. Just that she'd been hurt. And no one would tell her about her recovery. They'd just again remind her that she'd been hurt.

"Annie," Dianna started, "you were hurt."

Something reminiscent of a laugh pushed through Annie's throat, but she wasn't amused. "Someone talk to me."

"We've been talking to you."

Annie slammed her hand down as hard as she could and glared at them. "About me. Tell me about me. What is wrong with *me*?"

Donna hesitated. "You've been in a coma, Annie. You can't expect—"

Annie wasn't a crier, she never had been, but tears stung her eyes as her irritation built inside her, and she couldn't find the words to let it out. "Goddamn it."

"Please don't get upset," Dianna said soothingly. "Annie, it's just that...we're not the ones who should talk to you about this."

"But nobody talks to me." She swallowed hard. Her anger and frustration were exacerbating her confusion and the heaviness in her voice. She put her hand to her head. "You just say I got hurt, but you don't say how or why or what it means. Someone tell me. Now."

"Honey," Donna pleaded.

Closing her eyes, Annie sighed. "Get out."

"Ann—"

"Get. Out. Now."

Donna stared at her for a moment. "Listen—"

"Get. Out," she said angrily.

"Ladies?" Marcus asked from the door. "What's going on?"

Donna and Dianna stood, both looking shocked, but it was Dianna who spoke. "She's a little agitated." She smiled down at

Annie, but it lacked that condescending sweetness from before. "We'll see you later."

Annie exhaled harshly. She wanted to tell them not to bother if they couldn't tell her the truth, but she didn't have enough energy to waste on the rant.

"What happened?" Marcus asked quietly, as if Annie couldn't hear.

She was right there. Yes, she was in a hospital bed, but she wasn't deaf. And she wasn't stupid. And she was damned tired of everyone handling her with kid gloves.

"She was asking about her condition," Donna said just as softly.

"You have to talk to her," Dianna said.

He nodded as he looked at Annie. "See if you can find her doctor. Ask him to join us."

Annie sighed when they left, and Marcus sat in the chair Dianna had just vacated.

He took her hand. "You okay?"

Once again, her words got jumbled. Grinding her teeth, she closed her eyes and took a moment. "What's wrong? With me?"

"Your doctor wanted you to start feeling a bit stronger before we got into all this. We told him that was a bad idea, but we took his advice. We should have gone with our instincts and told you. I'm sorry."

"Just tell me."

"We were at an open house. Some kid came in, we think to mug you. He shot you."

Annie widened her eyes. "What?"

"Right here." He ran his finger along her forehead.

She gasped.

In the head? She'd been shot in the head?

"The doctors told us you probably weren't going to survive. But you did. You held on. You were in a coma, but you held on. And then little by little you started coming back. Sometimes you'd move your hand or open your eyes. They said it didn't mean anything, but we stayed with you, and we talked to you." He smiled. "And look at you now."

She swallowed as another stupid tear fell from her eyes. "Broken."

"No," he whispered.

Putting her hand to her head, she drew a ragged breath. "I'm in a fog. All the time. Can't think."

"That will get better. It will. You got shot in the head and then spent three months playing Sleeping Beauty. Do you really think you can just wake up from that and everything will be perfect?"

She stared at him for a moment. Yes, that was what she'd thought. Apparently, that was wrong.

He stroked her hair, and his smile fell. "I'm probably going to get in trouble with Doctor Oritz for talking to you without his consent, but I'd rather face his fury than yours. He wants you to get some strength back before they do any testing, so right now, we don't know the extent of the damage done to your brain."

Damage? To her brain? This couldn't be happening.

"A lot of the symptoms you're displaying are going to get better with time and physical therapy, including that fog you mentioned, but we don't know how much or how quickly."

"Symptoms?"

There was that supportive, condescending smile she hated so much.

"Some of the things you noticed: how it's hard to speak sometimes, and you can't move quite right. Your speech is slurred," he said. "Sometimes it's hard to understand you. Doctor Oritz doesn't seem concerned about recovering full use of your legs, but he is worried that you've permanently lost some ability in your hands. He's very happy that you are moving your fingers, but doing so isn't a sign of how much you'll recover. Some of the confusion you're feeling may not clear up as much as we're hoping. That short fuse you had might be a little shorter—which may or may not have just shown itself when you kicked your sisters-in-law out of the room."

Annie swallowed as she tried to process what he was saying. She wasn't going to be able to talk, use her hands, or think clearly, and she'd be even bitchier than normal.

Great.

She turned her face away, but Marcus put his fingers to her cheek and pulled her back. He ran his thumb over her lips as they trembled with her attempt not to cry.

"Hey," he said softly but firmly. "We're going to do everything we can to get you back to being just as strong as before. It's going to take some time and a lot of work, but we're all here to help you through this."

She shook her head and a sound left her—was that a sob?

He held her face and put a long, lingering kiss on her head. "Do you know how lucky we are that you're alive?"

"Not like this."

"Oh, honey, this is so much more than they told us to hope for." Leaning back, he wiped her tears away. "I know you don't remember what happened, but I do. I was there. I didn't think you were going to make it." His brow creased and he blinked, but he couldn't hide how his eyes shimmered with the sudden onset of unshed tears. "I honestly thought you were going to die before help even got there. But you didn't. You held on, and you made it through surgery, and you pulled out of your coma. And, yes, there are some side effects to all of that. I'm not going to lie to you; this is going to be difficult. You've got a battle ahead of you, but you are here to fight it. And that, sweetheart, is so much more than any of us—including your doctors—expected."

Her heart ached. "You don't have to—"

"I swear to God, woman, if you even attempt to tell me that I don't have to stick by you through this, you'll also be recovering from having my foot shoved up your ass."

She laughed as much as she could manage. "There's therapy for that?"

"They'll have to come up with something." He kissed her hand. "I was so scared that I'd lost you forever. I don't care if you never fully recover, Annie. I don't care if I have to listen a little more closely or help you with the little things for the rest of our lives, because you're still here to share our lives. And I'm not going to put up with your stubborn, overly proud bullshit this time. I'm here, and I'm going to help you, and you're going to just have to deal with that. Got it?"

She reached out for him, and he leaned in to her. She kissed him, or at least tried, closed her eyes, and sighed as he put his forehead to hers.

"I love you," he whispered, and she let out another of those sobbing sounds. He hushed her, tried to soothe her, but all she could focus on was how far from herself she was. "It's okay," he breathed, hugging her. "We're going to work this out, sweetheart. You're going to be okay." He put his hands on her cheeks and dragged his thumbs across them before he kissed her again.

This time she knew she kissed him back. Maybe not as gracefully as before she'd been shot, but she figured it was better than sleeping through it.

"Who knew the first step to recovery was PDA?" Oritz teased, coming into the room.

Annie grinned slightly as Marcus leaned back.

"I've filled her in a little bit," Marcus said as he stood. "But I'm sure she'd like to hear the whole story from you."

Doctor Oritz pulled a chair next to her bed and settled in to tell her all about her injuries and impending recovery.

The last thing Marcus wanted was to leave Annie's side, but Paul and Matt practically kicked him out. He didn't want to miss a moment of Annie being awake. What if she slipped back into her coma? What if she slipped away, and he wasn't there when she needed him?

But her brothers twisted his arm and his guilt. Someone needed to take Mallory home and make sure she actually got some rest. She'd been sitting in the hospital just as much as Marcus had since Annie had come back. The O'Connell brothers put the responsibility of taking care of Mallory squarely on Marcus. Unfair, he thought, but effective.

"I'm so tired," Mallory said as they left the hospital where Annie had been for the first few weeks of her coma. After she'd recovered sufficiently from the surgery, with still no signs of waking, she'd been moved to the long-term care facility. But after she'd started to come to, they'd moved her back to the ICU. Only two visitors were allowed at a time, and Marcus and Mallory did their best to monopolize visiting hours.

"It's probably a good thing they bullied us out," he agreed.

"I can't decide if I want real food or to sleep in a real bed first."

"Food," Marcus said. "Or at least as real as it gets going through a drive-through." He put his arm around her shoulder as they sleepily made their way toward the parking lot. "My treat?"

"Sounds fair."

They climbed into his car and debated which burger place was most appealing. If Marcus were honest, he could go for a good home-cooked meal. Dianna and Donna did their best to keep Sunday dinners going, but they all admitted that it wasn't the same without Annie. More often than not these days, dinner was skipped in favor of rotating through her room.

Jenna regularly stocked his fridge with leftovers, but Marcus had stopped frequenting her café. Sitting in the small restaurant reminded him of every meal they'd shared there and had been like a knife in his heart. Now that she was awake, he'd have to give it a try again. He hated not seeing his sister as often, but emotionally it had been the best choice for him. Maybe now it wouldn't be so bad.

Finally, with the scent of burgers and fries filling the car, Marcus and Mallory headed for Annie's house.

"I think we need to start thinking about when she comes home," Mallory said.

"That's going to be a while yet."

"I know, but... Okay, I'm going to be honest. I'm a little terrified of being solely responsible for her care. I think we need a nurse."

"You're jumping the..." He sighed, stopping himself before the everyday phrase could slip through his lips. "You're getting ahead of yourself here, Mal. She may not need a nurse, and there are plenty of O'Connells to keep up with her. You won't have to go it alone."

"I think you should move in."

He glanced at her.

"At least temporarily."

He pondered her words for a minute. "I'm not opposed to that. I'd like it actually. I want to be there for her. But given her condition, I think we have to talk to Paul and Matt about it, too."

"You and Mom are a couple."

"We are. But we weren't for very long before... Well, they may not feel that it's appropriate."

"You've barely left her side. They know how much you love her. We all do."

"I just don't want to overstep here."

She nodded. "I get that. And I think it's great that you are concerned about my uncles, but the truth is, I'm her next of kin, and if I want you there to help me, then you'll be there to help me. My uncles can have their say, but I get the final word, and the final word is I want you to move in with Mom and me to help take care of her."

Marcus glanced at her again and smiled. "You sound just like her sometimes."

Mallory grinned. "Yeah, I know." Her smile didn't last long; just a moment later, it had turned back into that frown that was so familiar these days. "She's going to be okay, right?"

"She's got a long road ahead of her, Mallory, but it seems that she's getting stronger every day—little by little."

"You know what I mean."

He exhaled slowly. "Doctor Oritz continues to caution that we shouldn't expect too much. With physical and speech therapy, she'll improve, but—"

"Cut the bullshit, please," Mallory said.

He laughed softly. "Okay. No bullshit. She's never going to fully recover and be the mom you remember. She's probably always going to have issues. But she's still Mom. She's alive. We still have her, and that's more than enough for me. It needs to be enough for you, too. She's going to have a hard enough time coming to terms with the changes she's facing. She doesn't need to know how hard it is on us, too." He sighed when she choked out a broken little sound that tugged at his heart. Reaching over, he patted her knee. "Sorry, kiddo."

She sniffed. "No. I knew what you were going to say. Just hearing it…"

"I know." He parked his car in Annie's driveway, turned off the ignition, and looked at Mallory. "I'm here for you. Just like I have been. If you need anything, just call me. Anytime."

"I know. Thanks, Marcus." They walked quietly into the house, but once they were inside and situated at the island in Annie's kitchen, Mallory said, "I once told Mom that you were the closest thing I ever had to a dad." She smiled sadly. "She looked like she was about to fall over. But it's true. You know?"

She looked at him tentatively, as if expecting him to reject her. Again, she looked just like her mother. Annie had given him that look so many times.

Marcus smiled as he put his hand on her head. "And you're the closest thing I'll ever have to a daughter, Mal. I love you, kid."

Her lip trembled, but she held herself together. "Love you, too."

"We're going to be okay."

"Mom's right. You do keep saying that."

He shrugged and let his hand fall. "What else am I supposed to say?"

"I don't know."

He didn't either, so he focused on his dinner. After wrapping up her trash, Mallory went to her room, and Marcus went to Annie's.

Walking into the bedroom hit him like a punch to the gut that he hadn't anticipated. It wasn't the first time that he'd crashed at her house since she'd slipped into a coma. The first time had nearly killed him. Her scent was still on the sheets. A blouse she'd tried on the morning of the shooting had still been lying across the foot of the bed. Her robe, the one she'd been wearing when they'd made love in the bathroom, was hanging on the back of the bedroom door. Everywhere he'd turned had been a reminder that her life was hanging on by a thread.

But those things had slowly disappeared. He'd hung her blouse and robe in the closet. He'd put away a size-seven pair of heels. He'd used what was left of her toothpaste, shampoo, and body wash. They'd been replaced with his own. Her perfume still sat on the dresser, though. Her makeup drawer still held varying shades of lipsticks and eye shadows.

But the sheets no longer smelled like her. Her side of the couch was now Mallory's. Her favorite coffee mug was rarely taken out of the cabinet. It was like she'd slowly disappeared from the house.

So standing there now, in her room, in the room they'd shared for such a brief time, hit Marcus hard. She'd be coming home soon. She'd be in this bed again. She'd want her shampoo and wash and toothpaste. She'd use her mug. She'd spritz her perfume.

But it wouldn't be the same.

Nothing would ever be the same. And that terrified him as much as it seemed to have Mallory. He hadn't admitted it, not even to himself, but he was scared to death of what was to come. Would Annie still want him? Would she still believe in him? It'd taken him so long to break through to her. Would she shut him out again? What if she wanted to focus on her family and her recovery and decided she didn't have time for him?

What if she didn't love him anymore?

He ran his fingers through his hair and cursed himself for being so selfish.

So what if she kicked him out of her life? At least she had a life. At least she was still alive. At least she was awake. Even if she wasn't exactly the same. Even if she did decide she couldn't give part of herself to him any longer. She was alive, and he had to embrace that.

Moving to the dresser, he lifted her perfume and sniffed the top. It wasn't as he remembered without it being on the warmth of her neck, but the scent brought back a flood of memories. Holding her. Loving her. Sitting in her bed eating Chinese food and promising that nothing would change if they got married.

He swallowed the lump that rose in his throat. Kicking his

shoes off, he stretched out on her side of the bed and thought of all the ways he was going to make sure that even though everything was different, nothing that mattered would change. He'd make sure she still loved him, still wanted him. He'd serve her Chinese in bed and argue just to get a rise out of her. He'd still make her smile, make her feel safe, and goddamn it, he'd never let anything ever hurt her again.

Marcus let his mind wander and apparently dozed off, because he woke with a start, sweat soaking his forehead as he gasped for breath. Staring into the darkness, he listened to the pounding of his heart in his ears. *Boom-boom-boom.* Finally it started to slow and he could breathe easier. He'd slowly started getting a handle on his nightmares, but ever since Annie had woken up they'd started taunting him again.

"One final sale," Annie had whispered with a smile and a wink. He'd smiled and winked in return and then disappeared into the kitchen.

That was the last time he'd seen her. The last time she'd looked at him like that. The last moment when his life had felt complete.

Then the sound hit him, and he woke terrified.

Sitting up, Marcus choked on the cry that erupted from his throat as he wiped a hand over his face. Looking at the clock, he frowned when he realized it wasn't even midnight. He knew from experience he'd never get back to sleep. He'd simply lie there and relive every moment of that day again and again.

Rather than torture himself, he stumbled into the bathroom to take a shower and rinse the sweat from his body.

That was a mistake. Memories of being with Annie in that room flooded him. Dropping his head against the doorjamb, he stared at the bathroom vanity. He could still hear her teasing about his breath and him teasing about how they were going to live together.

Damn it, he missed that. He hadn't had enough of that. He needed more, and he was terrified that she wasn't going to be able to give him that. He'd take what he could, of course he would. He'd love her no matter what. But he wished to hell it could be what it was.

Shaking his head, he turned from the bathroom and headed for the kitchen. Thankfully, Mallory had beer in the fridge. He cracked one open and leaned against the counter as more recollections pecked away at his sanity.

Mallory walked in, yawning as she headed for the fridge. "Can't sleep?"

"No."

"Me either." She grabbed a beer and sat at the small table in the corner. "What's keeping you awake?"

He eased into a chair, debating what to say. "She would hate that you quit your job before you even started to stay here with her."

"Hey, so did you."

"That's completely different, Mallory."

She looked at her beer and frowned. "Growing up, she was

always so busy with work. We'd go on vacation, and she'd always have a stack of paperwork with her. I remember when I was about ten, we were at the lake. I was building a sandcastle while she was reading contracts. I kept trying to get her to help me, but she said I could play while she worked. I got so mad, I threw sand all over her papers. She sat me down and told me the only reason we had a nice house, and I was in gymnastics, and we could go on vacation was because she worked so hard. I didn't get it then. But I do now. Helping you guys out made me realize what she gave up to provide for me. Helping her now is right. It's the right thing. I know she'd rather I just went on living life like nothing had changed, but everything changed. In that moment, the moment she was shot, everything changed."

Once again thinking of the dinner he'd shared with Annie, he nodded. "Yes, it did."

She took a long drink from the beer in her hand. "One thing is still the same, though."

"What's that?"

"We still make a great family."

Marcus smiled as he put his hand on hers. "Yes, we do."

"We'll be okay," she said quietly. "We'll find a way to be okay."

Marcus nodded and forced a smile. "Yes, we will," he said, though he wasn't sure he believed it at the moment.

CHAPTER TEN

*M*arcus walked into Annie's hospital room and crossed his arms over his chest. "What did you tell the nurse?"

She frowned at him. Her disapproving looks weren't as scary as they used to be. He was quite certain that was because he was so happy she was awake that it didn't matter that she was frustrated with him. It was a million times better than her just lying there unmoving.

"No visitors. Not until I'm better."

"Until you're better?"

"Yes."

"You realize that could be months and months and maybe never, right?"

She looked away.

"You sent Mallory away."

"She hovers."

"She's worried."

"She hovers because I'm not normal."

He shrugged. "You've never been normal."

She looked at him, a flicker of hurt in her eyes instead of the amusement he was hoping to get. He softened his approach as he sat in the chair next to her bed. "Her mother almost died, Annie. She's a little bit traumatized."

"She should stay away. Until I'm better."

"No, she shouldn't."

"She should go back. To work. In California."

"Honey, she never went to California."

Annie creased her brow as that now-familiar confusion filled her eyes.

"You were shot before she left. She quit her job so she could stay here with you."

"To watch me…hibernate?"

"It's what she needed to do. For herself. She can always go to California or somewhere else when she's ready, but right now, she wants to be with you. So don't send her away anymore. She may not know what to say or do, but she needs to be here with you. Okay?"

She nodded slowly.

"As for your sisters-in-law, they've spent months taking care of you and your family. Show a little gratitude."

She frowned. "They cry. Always."

"Listen"—he took her hand—"we're all emotional right now, and sometimes it's difficult for us to keep it together. We have all had our moments, our breakdowns. The guys are just better at holding it in so you don't see."

She closed her eyes and exhaled slowly. "Hate this."

"I know this is difficult for you," he whispered. "I wish I could make it easier. As frustrating as it is for you that we're all hanging out staring at you with amazement and tripping over ourselves to make sure you're okay, you know damn well that we aren't doing anything for you that you wouldn't do for us. For three months, someone was here with you. Talking to you, reading to you, holding your hand."

"No wonder I woke up exhausted. You never let me rest."

He smirked. "Because we love you, and you are everything to us. So I don't care if you have a hard time talking, or if you've lost some use of your hand, or anything else. You are here. You are awake. You are alive. And we're not leaving, so just suck it up and for once in your life, be nice."

She frowned. "I hate how they look at me. So sad."

"I'll talk to them."

She shook her head. "I'll work on my tolerance."

"No, you have enough things to work on." He swiped a tear from her cheek. He'd never seen the woman cry as much in five years as she had in the last week. "They don't mean it, Annie. You know they love you."

"Makes me feel...weak."

He nodded. "I get that. They need to stop. I'll tell them to stop."

She said something, and frustration lit in her eyes when she realized he didn't understand her. Taking a breath, she let it out slowly. "I want to go home."

"I know. You've got some work to do first. Doctor Oritz says you're set to start physical therapy tomorrow."

She moaned and dropped her head back. "I don't..."

"What?"

"I don't know how to do this."

"Do what?"

"Not...not be me."

"Aw, baby," he breathed as he put his hand to her cheek. "We're all a little lost right now, but we're in this together. We're going to figure this out together. Would it help you to know that I am scared to the bone right now?"

She creased her brow.

"I stayed at your place last night. Slept in your bed. And I just kept remembering us there together, and there was this fear in the back of my mind that maybe..."

"What?"

"Maybe you won't want me now," he whispered. "I'm scared you're going to decide to leave me."

Annie frowned. "I'm scared. That you'll leave me. Because..." She sighed and gestured limply. "I'm not me anymore."

"That's the second time you've said that today," he whispered. "And you know, I said it to Mallory last night. You're not going to be the Annie that we remember. But you know what? I'm not the Marcus you remember. And she's not the Mallory that you remember. These last few months have changed us all. But one thing hasn't changed, will never change."

"What?"

"We're family, Annie, and I love you so much." He grabbed her hand and brought it to his lips. "I'm not going anywhere."

"Me either," she said quietly. "I can't."

Marcus lifted his gaze to her, shocked at her joke, but then laughed when she chuckled. Standing, he moved to the bed and sat on the edge. "Can you scoot?"

She wriggled, doing her best to make room for him. He stretched out beside her and helped her turn onto her side, careful of the few IVs and wires that had yet to be removed. Propping his head up, he smiled as he brushed his hand over her hair.

She sighed. "Oh, yeah. What happened to my hair?"

"They shaved it before surgery. It's growing out."

"Can't talk. Can't move. Can't think. And I'm bald?"

"Stop looking at the downside."

"What's the upside?"

"Less arguing. No more running away. Less sarcasm. No bad hair days."

Her frown deepened. "How did I get stuck with an optimist?"

"Someone has to counter your dark side."

She chuckled. "I needed this."

Sighing, he lowered his head onto her pillow. "Me too."

CHAPTER ELEVEN

"You ou will not believe how hard it is to smuggle carry-out into this joint," Marcus said, closing the door to Annie's room.

She wiped her face with her stupid hand that didn't work right. She couldn't open her fingers all the way, nor could she make a fist. They were just stuck in limbo, barely moving no matter how hard she tried.

She'd had a bad day—a worse than bad day.

Physical therapy was not for the faint of heart. She had managed to delude herself about the extent of her injuries and how *she* could recover. How *she* could overcome. Today, however, had been a great big wake-up call. Her hands were weak and unresponsive. Her speech patterns were not so easily fixed; her mind and her mouth were not getting along. She could think the words, but they just didn't form properly. And walking? When had that become so damn complicated? Her feet flopped, her knees buckled, and if she hadn't been leaning on her therapist, she would have fallen flat on her face.

"Not hungry," she said as Marcus deposited the sneaked-in bag onto the table.

"Well. I guess you get to watch me eat, then, because I'm starving."

She shook her head at his inability to take a hint. "Marcus, I'd like to be alone."

"Sulking isn't going to help."

"Sulking?"

He set a white Chinese food carton on the stand next to her bed. "This isn't going to be easy, Annie. Nobody said it would be easy."

"You weren't there."

"I know, but Paul and I did talk to your therapist. We know you had a rough go of things today."

A rough go of things? Understatement of the year. "I can't walk."

"You were in a coma—"

"For three fucking months. I know."

He stared at her for a moment before smirking. "Well, you still know how to cuss like a sailor, so there's that."

"Not funny," she snapped.

"Today was disappointing. I get that. I really do. I wish I could take this burden from you. All I can do, all any of us can do, is try to help you get through it."

"With Chinese food?"

He lifted one shoulder and let if fall casually. "Why not? You like Chinese food, don't you?"

She lifted her head off the pillow then dropped it back. It was the closest she could get to banging her head against a wall. "I just need to be alone."

"To feel sorry for yourself?"

She gestured aimlessly. "You go. You leave this place, and I'm here. All day. All night. Broken."

"You want me to move in with you?"

The sting of tears bit her eyes. "I want to go home. I want to leave."

"You think going home is going to make this go away?" Sitting on her bed, he frowned at her. "You are an incredibly stubborn woman, Annie O'Connell."

She opened her mouth, but he pressed his finger to her lips.

"That is one of your endearing qualities, believe it or not. You are strong. You are independent. I have no doubt that the level of frustration you are feeling right now is about as high as it has ever been. I know you are used to busting through and coming out on the other side, but this isn't something that you are going to tackle and conquer. This is something that is going to get better little by little, day by day. There will be no miracle turnaround here. You will only go as far down this road as you take yourself. I'll help you, with Chinese food or whatever else I can, but this is on you. And sulking is not going to help."

"I hate you sometimes."

"I know. But I did bring eggrolls."

She didn't want to smile, but she couldn't help herself. "Chinese food in bed."

"Yes. Chinese food in bed. That's our thing now. Whenever life gets to be too much, we're taking a break from reality with rangoons and mattresses."

She chuckled. "Sounds like a terrible novel. *Rangoons and Mattresses.*"

"Maybe you can write it with all this downtime you're taking."

He held out a container with two perfectly fried eggrolls inside. She started to reach with her right hand but then dropped it.

"I keep forgetting," she said and used her left hand instead. "This one works better. Do you know how hard it's going to be to retrain myself to use my left hand for everything?"

"Not as hard as it's going to be to regain the muscle tone in your legs so you can walk again."

She sighed as she stared at the food in her hand. "The last time we did this, everything seemed so complicated. Nothing compared to today."

"In a few weeks, you're going to be walking. You're going to have better use of your hands and your speech. And a few months after that, you'll be even better."

"I'm so tired of your pep talks already. Are you ever going to let me just pout?"

"No, because you don't pout. You never have. I'm not going to let you start now."

He stared at her for a moment before she grinned.

"Fine," she said. "I guess I'll keep you around, then."

"You'd better. I brought sweet-and-sour chicken."

"I love sweet-and-sour chicken."

"I know."

She put her hand on his arm when he started to reach for the bag waiting for him to look at her. "Do you remember when I asked you not to give up on me?"

"Yeah."

"I'm asking again. Please. Don't give up on me."

"Never," he whispered. "I'll never give up on you."

sh

"Hey," Mallory said softly. "Why don't you go home?"

Marcus looked up from the pile of papers on Annie's desk. "No, I'm okay."

Mal sat in the chair that he'd always occupied when coming in to have the exact same conversation about working too hard with Annie. "You can't keep this up, Marcus. You're going to make yourself sick. Mom wouldn't want that."

He gathered the scattered papers and tapped them into a neat stack, more to avoid Mallory's gaze than to organize them. "She wouldn't want me falling behind on contracts either." He smiled slightly. "I did that once. Damn near missed a deadline to get paperwork to the mortgage company. She ripped me up one side and down the other."

"She's good at that. Still is."

The underlying meaning of her words was clear.

"She's going to need time to adjust to her new reality, Mallory. Don't take her short temper personally."

"She told the doctor she didn't want to see me."

"She told the doctor she didn't want to see *anyone*. You know how independent she is, kid. Imagine, just for a moment, what it must be like for her to wake up and be so completely limited in her ability to do anything. She is a mover and a shaker. She takes the bull by the horns and makes it do what *she* wants. She can't do that right now. She may never be able to do that again. This is terrifying for her."

"It's not so great for me either."

"I know. But at this particular point in time, we have to put your mom's feelings above our own. Just a little. She's going to lash out and say things she doesn't mean, partly because she's scared, partly because she's frustrated, and partly because she's got a brain injury that isn't going to always let her think before saying or doing. She didn't mean that she doesn't want to see you. She meant she doesn't want *you* to see *her* in that condition."

Mallory sniffed, and Marcus's heart ached for her. For all of them. This was a hell of a situation.

"I'm supposed to be grateful that she's alive. I *am* grateful that she's alive. But even with all the warnings the doctors gave us, I really thought that when she woke up—if she woke up— she'd still be Mom."

"It was what we all hoped for. But she has damage to crucial parts of her brain. She's not going to be the same. We have to take it easy on her and ourselves."

Drying her cheeks, she took a shuddering breath before meeting his gaze. "Is that what you're doing right now? Taking it easy on yourself? You bounce between the office, meeting clients, and taking care of Mom all day, Marcus. And then you sit in this office half the night. You think we don't know? We do. And we're all worried about you."

"I'm doing what I need to do to keep things going so when Annie is ready, she has a business to come back to."

Mallory stared at him. "Do you think she'll ever come back? Do you think she'll ever recover enough to work again?"

"Well, if she doesn't, this is still her business. It's still her source of income, so we have to stay on top of things."

"Are you sure you're not just..."

"What?"

"Evading?"

He laughed softly. "I'm definitely evading." He toyed with a pen for a moment. "You know, I spent an awful long time waiting for your mom to come around. She finally did, and this happened. It isn't fair, and sometimes I let that eat away at me."

"Did something happen?" She scoffed at her question. "Something *else*?"

He flashed to the memory of the first time he and Annie had eaten dinner in bed compared to earlier that evening. She'd struggled with everything from picking up her eggroll to trying to hold a fork. She'd very nearly given up eating dinner altogether, until he tossed his fork over his shoulder and started eating with his fingers. She'd laughed at him, but after some encouragement, she did the same and was finally able to eat her dinner. She'd been embarrassed. He could tell by the way she grew quiet and her cheeks turned red, but at least she'd eaten.

He shook his head slowly in answer to Mallory's question. "I'm just trying to adjust, too."

"How is she? When it's just the two of you? I know she puts on a front for me. How is she with you?"

He exhaled loudly as he tossed the pen aside. "Terrified. She's terrified, Mal. And it's killing me that I can't do anything to help her." He cleared his throat and shifted. "Did you eat dinner?"

"If you call leftover pizza dinner."

"Want to go to the café? You're right. I need to get out of here. I already ate, but I could go for some pie."

She stood and waited as he rounded the desk and grabbed his coat. Once they slid into the car, he started it and rubbed his hands together.

"Damn, it's getting cold."

"Fall is coming on quick this year," Mallory said.

He pulled from the office and drove the short distance to the square, parking in front of Stonehill Café. There weren't many cars parked there, which suited him just fine. He wanted his sister's business to succeed, but he hated people asking about Annie and giving him that sad look.

Holding the door for Mallory, he shook off the cold as they

sat at a table. He didn't frequent the restaurant these days. It reminded him of dinners with Annie. Being here with Mallory didn't help, either. Now he just thought of the night that he'd pissed Annie off and she'd stormed out before their dinner had even arrived.

Jenna slid a cup of coffee in front of Marcus, and he inhaled deeply. He hadn't let himself think about how much he missed her coffee. He loved her coffee.

"This smells delicious."

After filling a mug for Mallory, she sat next to the girl. "So? Any improvement?"

Marcus frowned. "She started physical therapy today. It was rough."

"What do the doctors say?"

He shook his head as he blew on the hot brew. "The same. Hope, but don't expect."

"I'm sorry," she said softly.

He stared at her for a moment. "Don't, Jenna."

"Don't what?"

"Give me that look. Annie is going to fight her way back."

"Hey," she said gently. "That look isn't doubting Annie's ability to recover. I'm worried about my brother. Annie is in good hands, Marcus. She's being taken care of. But who is taking care of you? You look like hell."

"Told him that," Mallory muttered.

"You've shut me out. You've shut everyone out."

"Told him that, too."

Marcus glared at Mallory. She toasted him with her mug in response.

"I feel like I'm letting you down," Jenna said, "but I can't be at the hospital or at your office every minute of the day, and you never leave."

"I'm here now."

"You know what I mean."

He sighed as he looked at his sister. "You're not letting me down, Jen. Don't think that. Please. I'm where I need to be."

Jenna shook her head. "Marcus, you have to take care of yourself, too."

"Jenna," he said quietly.

"You didn't do this to her."

He lifted his gaze to her. "What?"

"I know you. I know what you're thinking. That somehow you should have stopped this. Somehow you should have protected her."

"I should have."

"You *couldn't* have. There is nothing you could have done to stop that kid from doing what he did. And you certainly can't do anything about the fact that the police haven't caught him."

He raked his fingers through his hair and clenched his jaw. "How about getting us some menus, Jenna? We came for food, not absolution."

She stared at him for a moment before pushing herself up. A moment later, she slapped two menus down. "Snap your fingers when you're ready to order. I'll come running like a good little waitress."

"Jenna," he called, but she marched off. "Brat."

"What do you think you could have done?" Mallory asked quietly.

"What?"

"The shooting," she said. "What do you think you could have done to protect Mom?"

"I don't know."

She stared into her mug. "Maybe if you'd been in the room with her that asshole would have turned around and walked out. Maybe if you hadn't scared him, he wouldn't have pulled the trigger."

He stared at her, startled that she was throwing his guilt back at him.

"But if you had been there, in the room when he came in, maybe he would have shot you, too. Maybe if you hadn't walked in, he would have made sure she was dead before he left. You saved her life, Marcus. You were there to call for help. You were with her when she slipped away. You made sure she wasn't alone." She blinked her eyes as they filled with tears. "We all know you did the best you could. Mom would tell you that you did the best you could if she knew you were torturing yourself."

"Do us both a favor and don't tell her. She doesn't need worrying about me added to her plate."

"I won't. But I'll worry about you for her. Jenna is right. You look like shit, man. You have got to get some sleep."

He laughed quietly. "God, you're so much like your mother."

"I know. That's how I know she wouldn't want you blaming yourself for this. She would hate that you're blaming yourself."

He nodded. "I know. But that doesn't mean I can stop. I was there. And she got hurt anyway. It's a lot to deal with sometimes." He pushed himself up before she could respond. "Figure out what you want, Mal. I need to go apologize to my sister so she doesn't intentionally burn my food."

sh

Annie blinked several times. She never quite trusted her brain these days, but when the vision of the little girl standing over her hospital bed didn't fade, she tilted her head and narrowed her eyes a little.

The girl smiled a toothy grin, and Annie smiled back.

"Remember me?"

Annie nodded at Kara's granddaughter. The little brunette was impossible to forget. She'd walked down the aisle at Paul and Dianna's wedding, proud as she could be, dropping petals and very nearly stealing the day from the bride.

"Jessica Martinson-Canton," she said. "It used to just be Martinson, but then my grandparents got married and Daddy wanted his daddy's name but didn't want to drop his mommy's name. Now, when I put my name on my homework, I have to remember both names and a hyphen. It's *so* confusing."

Annie nodded again.

Jessica's smile fell. "Grandma said you have trouble talking, but she didn't say you *couldn't* talk."

"I can talk," Annie said. "Just not very well."

"Me either. I have Down syndrome."

"I know."

"You got shot."

Annie almost laughed. "I know."

Jessica touched Annie's forehead. "Is that where?"

"Yeah."

"Grandma said you must have really good karma because you should be dead."

Annie looked around the room. "Are you alone?"

"Grandma is outside. Grandpa is visiting his mom. She slipped on a letter that was on the floor in front of her mail slot and broke her ankle. Grandma said that was karma, too, because his mom stole his mail a long time ago so he didn't know Grandma had my daddy. You don't want bad karma." She shuddered as if she were terrified.

Annie laughed at Jessica's dramatic summary. Dianna had told her all about how Kara's mother-in-law had kept Kara's pregnancy a secret from Harry for almost thirty years.

Annie might get confused about some things, but at least she could remember her life and the lives of those around her. At least she hadn't been robbed of her memories as well. "Why are you in here?"

"I'm supposed to be sitting in the chair while Grandma talks to Dianna about things they don't want me to hear. But I did hear. Dianna said you don't want people to see you. Grandma is worried that you're depressed."

"I am depressed."

"They have medicine for that."

Annie wasn't sure if she succeeded or not, but she tried to lift her brows in surprise.

"I know all about this stuff because I spent so much time as a kid in the hospital."

"And how old are you now?"

"I'm in fourth grade."

"Oh."

"You shouldn't be upset that people don't understand you. Sometimes people don't understand me either. Grandma says I have to be patient because they just aren't used to me. When they don't understand me, I just take a breath and slow down." She demonstrated by inhaling slowly and hesitating between each word. "I talk slower and try to say each word so they can hear." She shrugged and returned to her normal pace, which was about five miles a minute. "It can be a pain sometimes, but once they get used to me, they understand. They'll understand you, too. So don't be sad. Or mad. Or think they're stupid. Grandma gets mad when I say people are stupid for not wanting to talk to me, but she thinks the same thing. She just doesn't say it because she's trying to be a good influence on me. Daddy lectures her when she says bad things. He says he's raising me better than that and he needs her to work with him since she's the closest thing to a mother figure I have." Jessica leaned on the bed and looked at Annie curiously. "Do you have a mom?"

"No."

"Me either. Mine left because I'm not normal. Dad says it's because she was scared. But I know better. If I'd been normal she would have stayed."

Annie stared at her for a moment, her heart aching for the kid. "No, she wouldn't have, Jessica. My daughter's perfectly healthy and her dad left. It wasn't because of her. And your mom didn't leave because of you. Your dad is right. Brave people don't leave."

"Dad thinks I'm brave because I don't let people make me feel bad about myself. I think if they don't like me because I have Down, then I don't like them either because they are mean. Is your family mean?"

"No."

"Then why don't you want to see them? Is it because you're embarrassed? Because I get embarrassed sometimes. It's hard not being like everyone else."

Annie nodded and swallowed hard. Damn it. She was not going to cry in front of a fourth grader.

"I have to have help sometimes. I can't always do things that other kids can do. It used to make me mad."

"Not anymore?"

She shrugged. "I can still do other stuff. My grandma taught me to paint. I'm the best artist in fourth grade. And that's no lie. I'll make you something. Do you like rainbows?

Rainbows are my favorite. They make anything prettier. Whenever I get upset, I draw a rainbow and it makes me better."

Annie and Jessica looked at the door when it opened.

A moment later Kara poked her head in. "Oh, Annie, I'm sorry. She wasn't supposed to wake you."

"She didn't."

"She woke up and we had a nice chat," Jessica said as Kara and Dianna walked in. "Well, *I* had a nice chat. She isn't much of a talker."

Annie laughed quietly, but Kara and Dianna looked concerned. "Stop. That look is the reason I didn't want to see you."

"We don't like to be treated differently," Jessica said, sounding defensive. "It hurts our feelings."

Annie looked at her, wondering how the kid had gotten so damned wise. But then she realized she'd been dealing with this kid-glove treatment her entire life. Annie couldn't imagine how frustrating that had to be, even for a kid.

Kara moved to the foot of the bed. "It's good to see you, Annie. How are you feeling?"

"Incompetent."

She smiled. "It'll get better. I promise. Come on, Jess. Grandpa's ready to go home."

Jessica looked at Annie. "Remember. Deep breath. Talk slow. And when you get mad, draw a rainbow."

"I'll remember. Thanks, Jessica."

She trotted off, grabbed Kara's hand, and started her nonstop chatter again as they left the room.

Dianna waited until the door closed before facing Annie. "Sorry about that."

"It's okay." She drew a breath and talked slowly. "I just got schooled on life by a fourth grader."

Dianna smiled. "She's a cool kid."

"Talkative."

"Oh, yes, she is that. But she's ten, so that's a given."

"I remember. Mal talked all the time." Annie tried to contain it, but her freaking emotions bubbled up and tears filled her eyes. "I'm sorry I've been so difficult. I just don't know what to do."

"Oh, Annie, I know." She sat in the chair next to the bed and took Annie's hand. "You don't have to apologize."

"I'm so scared, Di. I don't know how to not be in control."

"I know," she whispered. "This is a scary time for all of us. You just have to know that we're here. We're all right here with you, and we're just as scared and just as frustrated as you are. You can't shut us out. We need you as much as you need us. We're family. And we're going through this together. Don't turn away from us."

"What am I going to do? How am I supposed to go through the rest of my life like this?"

Dianna snagged a tissue from the box on the table and wiped Annie's cheeks. "Let's not worry about the rest of your life today, okay? Let's worry about right now. Let's worry about the first step. And then we'll worry about the second step. And the step after that."

Annie inhaled deeply and blinked away more tears. "I hate your sunny disposition sometimes."

Dianna grinned. "I'm right. You know I'm right."

Annie exhaled heavily. "Know what really pisses me off?"

"What?"

"I'm going to have to learn how to draw rainbows."

CHAPTER TWELVE

*A*nnie stared at her reflection. She hated the short haircut. She hated the loose-fitting dress Mallory had brought her to go home in. She hated the way the features on the left side of her face sagged just a bit. She hated the purple scar on her forehead. She hated that she couldn't put on makeup without looking like a preschooler had taken markers to her face.

She hated everything.

At least that hadn't changed.

Closing her eyes, she sat on the edge of her hospital bed and tried to find a way to be thankful. After weeks of physical therapy she could finally walk, albeit slowly. She was told her speech had improved, and she had regained minimal control over her hands. One day she might even be able to button a blouse so she didn't have to either let someone else dress her or dress herself in ugly, unfitted clothes that she'd never have worn before taking a shot to the brain.

She sat a bit higher at the sound of a knock on the door. Before she could answer, Dianna poked her head in and smiled.

"Oh, darn it. I was hoping to catch you before you got dressed."

"You had plenty of time. I'm slow."

Dianna smiled and stepped in, holding the door for someone else. Kara came in behind her.

"Hey, Annie. I hear you're going home today."

"That's the rumor."

"You must be pretty excited." She sat in the chair next to the bed.

"Yeah." She was finally getting to go home. All she wanted was to crawl into her bed and enjoy some peace—real peace. She wasn't in the mood for one more challenge to get there, yet she sensed Dianna hadn't brought Kara by for a random visit.

"You made quite the impression on Jessica. She's been worried about you."

"That's sweet."

"She keeps asking about your recovery. When I told her you still couldn't use your hands very well, she asked me to help you."

"Help? How?"

"Because of her Down syndrome, she had a very difficult time with fine motor skills when she was younger. When she was old enough to start dressing herself, we realized she couldn't do buttons and zippers because her fingers didn't want to cooperate. Just like what you're dealing with now."

At least Kara didn't use an *I can fix this* tone. She spoke to

Annie as if Annie were still Annie, and that was not something she got a lot of these days. She appreciated the non-sugar-coated approach Kara was taking with whatever she was getting at.

"Dianna bought an outfit that she thought you'd like. I modified it to make it a little easier for you to dress yourself. If this works for you, I can do the same to some of your other clothes. Then you can dress yourself and take back a little bit of your independence. Which, I'm told, is important to you."

She held up a cornflower blue blouse and a pair of black slacks that had been tucked inside a bag.

"I sewed the buttons onto another flap of material so they are fastened properly, but"—she opened the blouse front and revealed a hidden row of Velcro—"you just have to press the front closed. You don't have to try to work the buttons. On the slacks, I did the same. The zipper and button are real, but they're just for show. Oh, and let us not forget..." She held up two bras, both hanging open in the front. "For the girls."

"Yes," Annie said dryly, "let's not forget the girls." She sighed, actually moved by the gesture. She didn't used to be so soft. "Thank you. Mallory has already caged the beasts for today, but I'd like to try these clothes instead of this." She tugged at the dress she hated so much.

"Okay," Dianna said far too cheerfully. "We'll step outside. Let us know if you need any help."

Kara put the clothes on the bed beside Annie, and they left. Annie stared at them for several moments before standing and struggling to get the dress over her head. Starting with the shirt, she slipped her arms in and shrugged it onto her shoulders. Pinching the material between her hands, she managed to get the pieces of Velcro to close with minimal misalignment. A gentle tug assured her the closures were strong enough that her clothing wouldn't spontaneously fall open.

She sat on the edge of the chair and put first one leg, then the other, in the slacks. She'd just managed to pull them up and close the altered fly when Dianna knocked.

"Come on in." Annie stood, barefoot but dressed in real clothes—clothes she would choose to wear. She didn't want to act like doing so was such a big deal, but her eyes started to burn and her chest grew heavy with emotion. "I'm dressed."

Dianna made a cooing maternal sound, and Annie crumbled. Sitting in the chair, she brought her hands to her face to hide her tears. A moment later, arms were around her and she didn't even care that she was being hugged. She turned her face into Dianna's shoulder and sobbed.

"What's going on?" Marcus asked, coming into Annie's room.

Dianna stood, wiped her eyes, and laughed softly. "My fault. I started crying first."

Annie shook her head and took Dianna's hand. "I'm always crying now, too. I hate it."

Dianna put a kiss on her head, something Annie was getting used to. "I'll see you at home."

She was gone before her words sank in. "Why is she going to my house?"

"Did you really think you'd get out of this place without an O'Connell family get-together? She and Donna have been planning this for weeks."

"I just want some quiet."

"Oh, honey, you'll never have quiet again." He brushed his hand over her cheek. "Why were you upset?"

She looked down. "Kara fixed these clothes for me. So I could dress myself."

He lifted his brows. "You dressed yourself?"

That damned bubble of emotion started to rise again as she nodded. "They're altered." She tugged the top of her shirt open to show him the Velcro then closed it again. "But, yes. I dressed myself."

He smirked as he leaned in and kissed her. "I'm going to like these easy-off clothes of yours."

She laughed softly. "I'm sure."

sh

"It feels so odd," Annie said as Marcus drove her home.

"What's that?"

"Seeing the trees bare. It should be spring."

"You slept through spring, honey."

"And was locked up for what was left of the summer."

"Locked up isn't quite accurate."

"Says the man who could come and go from the hospital as he pleased."

He glanced at her, letting the debate drop. "Fall is coming early this year. It'll be snowing soon."

"I don't like the heat anyway." She turned a bit in her seat as they passed a sign with her company name on it. That was it. No photo or agent name. "You changed our signs?"

"Yes. Mallory designed them."

"Mal?"

"Yeah." He smiled. "She gets pretty excited when she sees them around town."

"Why? Did you change them, I mean?"

He sighed heavily. "Paul hired a security consulting team after...the shooting. We both wanted to know what we could do to be safer. Obviously we'll never be one hundred percent safe when we're going out meeting strangers, but there were some things we could do to increase security. The first thing they suggested was that we change to generic signs so the bad guys can't profile an agent before even showing up."

She looked at him, and her brow creased. "You mean...like target women?"

"Yeah."

"Do they think I was targeted?"

"Well, since we never found the guy who did this to you, there's no way to know that, but they said having pictures could make an agent vulnerable. Say a rapist has a thing for women with a specific hair color or a thief is looking for someone of a certain age or gender. We were giving them everything they needed to know right on our signs. They didn't even have to go online to figure out which agent would be where. We did alter our website, as well. No more photos. Names but no photos. Clients have to come in-office to meet the agent and fill out the background forms. No more exceptions."

She closed her eyes. "God. I never thought."

He put his hand on her knee. "Because your mind doesn't work like that, Annie. None of our minds work like that. But the security guys are trained to. They made some suggestions, and Paul and I implemented them. One of them is having security around during open houses now. It's just safer. We can't protect ourselves all the time, but we can at least take measures to deter would-be assailants."

She sighed and put her hand on his. He glanced at her as she stared out the window. He still hadn't quite gotten use to how she had a tendency to fade.

"What's on your mind, Annie?"

She blinked heavily and looked at him for a moment, but then she fell back into the conversation. "Tell me more about the new agent."

"Megumi Tanoka. Mallory's friend from college. Remember her?"

Annie thought for a moment before nodding. "Yes. She never stops talking and is completely disorganized."

"But she's great at sales. Excellent, in fact."

Annie squeezed his hand as tightly as she could, which still wasn't very impressive. "Thank you. For taking care of my business."

He glanced at her. "You don't have to thank me."

"I do. Dianna said you stepped up and took charge without hesitation."

He swallowed, thinking back on all the nights he'd sat in her office with the door closed, remembering every snarky conversation they'd ever had, and hating himself for not protecting her. He cleared his throat. "Well, you weren't really up for the task, so..."

"Which also meant quitting your new job before you started."

"I wasn't really looking forward to it anyway. You know I only took that other job to get in your pants, right?"

She smiled. "I suspected as much." She looked out the window. "I know you've told me, but I can't seem to hold on to it. How did Mallory end up being an agent?"

"She wanted to help out around the office. She started with little things, moved on to reviewing contracts, and when she was ready, she got her license."

"She never wanted that."

"Well, if it doesn't stick, it doesn't stick. I think she just needed to feel like she was helping you, and there was nothing we could do while you were in a coma. This was her way."

She faded but not completely. She was thinking, not blank. "I hate that she gave up California."

"California is still there, Annie. And from what she said, her boss was completely understanding of her decision to stay here.

Maybe, if another position opens up and Mallory is ready, she can try again."

"I feel…"

"If you say guilty, I'm going to pull the car over and spank you."

"Wouldn't you? Feel guilty, I mean. You all gave up so much, and I just…vegged out for three months."

"None of us did anything for you that you wouldn't have done for us."

"You keep saying that as if it makes it okay."

She faded again but only for a moment. He patted her knee and pointed as he neared her house.

"Oh, we're here." She immediately sighed as he pulled into her driveway and revealed a row of cars. "So is everyone else."

He parked beside Paul's car. "They wanted to welcome you home. As soon as you're ready for them to go, I'll kick them out."

She looked at him and her face sagged. "You must think I'm terrible."

"Not at all. You've gone through a lot. It's okay to want downtime."

Marcus hopped out and rushed around the car. He unhooked her seat belt, and after helping her out, he kissed her head.

"You didn't used to do that so much," she said.

"You didn't used to have a bullet hole in your forehead."

"Never going to let me live that down, are you?"

"Not anytime soon." Walking with her, quite a bit slower than his usual stride, he opened the front door. "We're here!"

Excited chatter filtered from the living room. Marcus and Annie turned the corner into a room filled with balloons, flowers, and people. Marcus didn't doubt for a second that Annie hated it, but she smiled and accepted hugs and even a few kisses. The bond between her and her brothers had never been so clear to him as since she'd gotten hurt. They'd always been protective of her, always spent time with her, but the last three months had been hell on them.

Seeing them now, Paul with his arm over her shoulder and Matt with his arm around her waist, reminded him how much they'd always needed her. He'd been so caught up in his own sense of loss and helping Mallory through hers, he didn't think he had really considered how deeply Paul and Matt must have been hurting the last three months. He looked around the room now at Mallory playing a game with Matt and Donna's daughters, Paul's sons hovering over the snacks that had been set out, and Dianna and Donna sitting on the love seat while the three O'Connell siblings sat on the couch.

He didn't feel out of place, exactly, but he didn't feel one hundred percent in place either. At the office, at work, he knew where he fit into Annie's life. Even hovering around her hospital room, he'd felt that he was where he should be. Standing in her house, surrounded by her family, he suddenly wasn't so sure.

"I need to check the ham." Donna started to get up.

"I got it," Marcus said, happy for an excuse to do something besides stare. Shaking the discontent from his head, he walked into the kitchen and grabbed the oven mitt off the counter. Opening the oven, he pulled the rack out enough to lift the foil from the ham, wondering what, exactly, he was looking for.

Dianna came in behind him. "Do you have a clue what you're doing?"

"Nope."

She grinned and shooed him back from the oven. "How are you doing, Marcus?"

"I'm fine, Di." He moved back and let her do whatever it was that he'd volunteered to do.

"Really? Because you look a little out of sorts right now."

Leaning against the counter, he shrugged. "Just trying to...whatever."

She put the foil back on the meat, closed the oven, and turned on the burner beneath a pot of potatoes before turning to him. "Whatever?"

"When she was in the coma, I knew what needed to be done. When she was in the hospital recovering, I knew what needed to be done. I just...haven't figured out what she needs done right now."

She put her hand on his arm and gave him that supportive smile of hers that drove Annie nuts. Marcus didn't get why it was a trigger for her. He thought it was nice—maternally comforting. "You're doing great, Marcus. So is she. We all are given the circumstances."

"One day at a time, right?"

"Right."

"It was great what you and Kara did. She really appreciated that."

"Good. I'm glad. I'll take her shopping to get a few outfits she won't mind having altered. Kara said she'd be more than happy to fix them for her."

"I'll pay her—"

"Kara doesn't work that way. She did this because she wanted to help. If you want to do something for her, get her some material or art supplies. She won't take your money."

He nodded. "Well, when Annie is feeling up to it, we'll go get her something."

"That'd be nice."

Marcus jerked around when a loud bang exploded from the living room. His heart kicked into double time as he broke into a full run, pushing the swinging door so hard it bounced back and nearly bashed him in the face. "Annie?"

She looked up, her eyes wide, as Paul and Matt both reassured her that she was okay.

"The boys popped a balloon," Donna quickly explained. "Scared the hell out of all of us."

Her words did little to slow the pounding of Marcus's heart or stop the tear that fell from Annie's eye.

Paul loudly forced the air out of his lungs, his anger evident as he shook his head at his sons. He pushed himself up. "That was stupid, Sean."

"I'm sorry."

Marcus kneeled in front of Annie and put his hands to her

face. He stared at her for a moment, reassuring himself she was okay. She wasn't shot. She was fine. Well, not exactly. She was trembling like an arachnophobe holding a tarantula. She might not have remembered being shot, but some level of her subconscious clearly had a memory of something from that day. She was visibly terrified. But she was looking at him. *At* him, not *through* him. There was no blood. No need for an ambulance.

"Hey, you're okay."

She nodded and another tear slid down her cheek. The fact that she didn't wipe it away with frustration told Marcus so much. Physically she was fine, but she was far from okay. She was shaken down to her bones. He didn't blame her. The sound had set off a panic in him that he'd hoped to never feel again.

"Want to take a few minutes of quiet time?" he whispered.

She nodded again, and he helped her stand. She leaned into him as he walked her toward the back of the house.

"I'm sorry, Aunt Annie," Sean said in a rare show of humility. The kid was a prankster to the nth degree; little took the laughter out of him, but he obviously realized the effect of what he'd done. "I meant to scare the girls. I didn't think."

She offered him a slight smile. "It's okay."

Marcus patted his shoulder. "She's fine, Sean. We're just going to rest for a few minutes. You guys start dinner without us. We'll be back."

He closed the bedroom door behind them and helped her sit on the bed.

"I feel stupid," she whispered. This time she did wipe the tears from her face.

Marcus exhaled loudly, still trying to get control of his agitated nerves. "Don't. My heart dropped through the floor, too." He ran his hand over her hair. The strands were still short and shapeless, but it was growing out. She'd mentioned more than once that she was going to have to get it styled. Actually, she tended to mention everything more than once. Forgetting what she'd already said and telling him again was a part of their regular conversation now. He didn't mind nearly as much as she did. She'd start to tell him something and then stop as frustration filled her face, and she'd ask if she'd said that before.

Brushing another tear from her cheek, Marcus gave her a soft smile. "He just didn't think."

She lowered her face as her brow scrunched and her lip started to quiver.

"Okay," he breathed, wrapping his arm around her and pulling her to his chest. "You're okay."

She said something, but between her crying and the now-natural slur to her voice, he couldn't understand her. The last thing he wanted to do was upset her by asking her to repeat herself. Instead, he hugged her closer as she sobbed.

This was actually long overdue. She'd shed some tears—either from fear or frustration—but she'd yet to let go of what Marcus had known she'd been bottling up. No one could go through what she had without having at least one or two good cries, and as far as he knew, this was her first. So he didn't ask her to repeat herself. He just held on as she let go. After a few minutes, she leaned back and sniffed. Marcus stretched to the nightstand and grabbed a tissue.

She tried to take it, but it slipped from her hand. She choked out a sound and shook her head. Marcus picked the tissue up from her lap and held it out again. She took her time gripping it the next time, pinching it between her thumb and the knuckle of her pointer finger. "I'm a fucking disaster."

"Nah. I've seen drunk guys in way worse shape."

She chuckled through her tears then took a moment to focus on drying her cheeks. "I hate this. I hate feeling so scared. So broken."

"I know."

"He's still out there, Marcus. I've lost months of my life. I can't even blow my nose, and he's still out there. It's not fair."

"No, it's not fair. But we can't focus on that, sweetheart. We have to focus on getting you stronger and moving on so you don't lose anything else to that coward."

She snuffled, swiped at her face, and then crumpled up the tissue and sighed heavily. "I'm such a mess. I can't go back out there."

"So don't."

"I have to."

"No, you don't." Kicking his shoes off, he scooted to the top of the bed and leaned against the headboard.

She frowned. "I think I snotted on you."

He looked down at the numerous wet spots on his shirt.

"That's okay. I have clean ones." He jerked his head toward the closet.

She looked at the door then back at him. "I seem to recall you threatening to move in when I wasn't looking. I didn't think you'd sink so low as to do it while I was in a coma."

"Hell yes I did. You weren't out five minutes before I was pushing your shoes aside."

He patted the bed beside him, and she smiled before slipping her shoes off and sliding up next to him. She rested her head on his shoulder, and he wrapped his arms around her.

"I only have a handful of clothes in there. Enough to get me through a few days. I wanted to make sure you got settled in okay. I'll stay longer if you want. Or leave sooner. Or just move in. It's up to you."

"Maybe I wanted to hire a cute little male nurse to give me sponge baths."

"Maybe I already hired a cute little female nurse to give you sponge baths. While I watch."

She chuckled and snuggled closer to him. "How did this happen?"

"What?"

"How did you become the one who makes everything okay?"

He grinned. "Oh, I've always been the one. You just didn't want to admit it."

"I was trying to be a good boss."

"A good boss would have let me grab her butt years ago."

"That's sexual harassment."

His smile widened at the clear amusement in her stuffy voice. "What's a little predatory behavior between consenting adults, hmm?"

She exhaled loudly. "I wasted so much time."

He pressed his lips to her head. The teasing had left her tone. "No, you were right. We were co-workers first. I respected your choice, Annie. Don't ever regret that you did what was right for you."

"Look at me now."

"I have. And I love you more than ever."

"You have to say that."

"No, I don't."

She lifted her head. "You'd be a jerk if you didn't."

"I'd rather be a jerk than a liar."

She looked into his eyes, as if searching for some sign that he was hiding the truth, and then kissed him gently. "I love you."

"I love you."

Resting her head on his shoulder again, she relaxed into him. "Let's never leave this room again."

"I can deal with that."

sh

Unfortunately for Annie, they did leave the room. When she and Marcus reappeared at the family gathering, the O'Connells were all sitting around the table, quietly eating. Usually their family dinners were filled with loud voices talking over each other. The discomfort in the room was palpable, even to her in her confused state.

Walking behind Sean, she kissed his head in that annoying way people kept doing to her and ruffled his shaggy brown hair.

"I'm okay," she whispered in his ear before taking her seat at the head of the table. He still didn't look at her, and she figured the lecture he'd gotten from his dad was far worse than the scare she'd gotten from the popped balloon.

Marcus sat next to her and filled her glass from the pitcher of water on the table while she reached for the spoon sticking out of the mashed potatoes. She had to grab at it like a toddler—closed-fisted and awkward—but she finally managed to drop a scoop onto her plate. The green beans were another matter. They didn't stick to the spoon the way potatoes did. They rolled off and spilled whenever she inadvertently tipped the spoon one way or another. Finally, she gave up. If she couldn't get them onto her plate, she probably wouldn't be able to get them into her mouth.

She pretended that everyone at the table wasn't staring as she tried to stab a slice of ham.

"I've got it," she said when Marcus tried to help. But she didn't. The meat wouldn't stay on the fork any more than the beans had stayed on the spoon. After several tries, she frowned and gave up getting meat, reaching for a roll instead. *That* she could handle. The scowl on her face deepened when Marcus scooped green beans on her plate, followed by ham.

"You going to eat it for me, too?" she quietly asked when he started cutting her food.

"If it'll make it easier for you, smartass, I'll feed you like a mama bird."

She winced at the image his words conjured. "You're nasty."

He squawked like a bird, and she laughed while everyone else stopped talking to see what the hell he was doing.

"Ignore him. He's trying to be clever."

"I am clever."

"In your mind."

He went to work on cutting his food, and she stared at her plate. She'd been very careful not to eat in front of her family, and now there she was, at the head of the table while everyone continually cast glances her way. Using her left hand, she managed to hold the fork properly, but actually using it was another story. She had better luck getting the food from fork to mouth with her right hand, but she had to hold the utensil like a little kid just learning to feed herself—which, in a way, she was.

Neither was very dignified. So, left-handed, she scooped up some potatoes and slowly lifted the bite to her mouth. She chewed slowly and swallowed with determination. She was so focused on eating that she apparently missed the conversation happening around her. Marcus put his hand on her arm, and she looked at him.

"Donna asked if you wanted ice cream after dinner."

Annie laughed softly. Clearly Donna hadn't noticed how much time it was taking for her to eat food that *didn't* melt. "No.

Thanks." She looked around the table, listening to the conversation and trying to decipher the overlapping voices and keep up with the chatter, until Marcus put his hand on her arm again.

He gestured toward her plate. "Not hungry?"

She looked down. She'd forgotten about her food. Something so basic as having dinner was far too challenging for her now. Pushing her plate away, she gave him a weak smile. "Listen or eat. Can't do both."

"Eat," he said, sliding her plate back to her.

She shook her head. "Listen. Less work."

He didn't laugh at her joke. He set his plate aside and took her hand. "We'll eat later, then."

She smiled, touched that he'd wait for her.

"You okay, Mom?" Mallory asked from her other side.

"Yeah. Fine."

"Why aren't you eating?"

A bit of shame touched her. Why could she let Marcus in on this but was so embarrassed to tell her daughter? Actually, she knew why. The last thing in the world she ever wanted was for Mallory to see her as weak. She needed to be strong for her child. She needed to be the protector, not the one who needed protecting.

"It takes some effort, Mal. I will."

Mallory looked at Annie's food. "Do you want me to...feed you?"

Annie laughed quietly. "No."

"I don't mind—" She reached for Annie's fork.

"Don't. You. Dare." Any amusement Annie felt left her. "My God, Mallory. I'm not an invalid."

"I just... I thought..."

Annie exhaled, realizing she'd come across harsher than she'd intended as silence fell heavy over the table. "I know. I'm sorry."

"No," Mallory said. "I'm sorry."

Annie lowered her face. Her homecoming was just one disaster after another. Kind of like her life right now.

"I'm tired, Mal. I didn't mean to snap." Looking at Marcus, she frowned then looked around the table. "Thank you all for coming, but I need to lie down." She lifted her hand to stop Marcus when he started to stand. "No. Please. I'd like some quiet time."

Standing, she walked away without looking back at her family. After closing her bedroom door behind her, she leaned against it and closed her eyes.

It'll get better, she told herself. *It has to get better.*

CHAPTER THIRTEEN

*M*arcus jolted awake. Sweat rolled down his brow as he panted from the fear that had made his heart race.

Damn it. He thought he'd be over this by now. Rolling over, he felt some relief to find Annie sleeping next to him. For too long, his only comfort when he woke up from these nightmares was the steady beeping of machines to let him know she was still alive. But she was really there, lying next to him, breathing on her own, sleeping—actually sleeping, not comatose.

He put his hand on her stomach. The rhythm of her breathing soothed him but didn't stop his mind from replaying his dream. Scooting closer, he wrapped his arm farther around her and kissed her temple.

She shifted and moaned, and he closed his eyes.

"Get help," he'd screamed, pressing his hand to her head. *"Hurry! She's been shot!"*

He'd alternated between screaming for help and assuring her she was going to be okay, even though he thought she was already dead—her eyes had been empty, her breath so shallow he couldn't tell if her chest was moving—until he was pulled away from her by a paramedic. He'd sat back, watching them work on her, answering their questions, and asking if she was going to be okay.

"I've got a pulse," one said.

Marcus closed his eyes tightly, trying to stop the replay, but it continued on.

"Her blood pressure is dropping."

Rolling away from Annie, Marcus tossed the covers aside and sat up. Putting his elbows on his knees, he leaned forward and dug his fingers into his hair. "Stop," he hissed.

"Call it in. Make sure they're prepared to handle this."

"Goddamn it." He jumped to his feet and started pacing as he pressed the heels of his hands into his eyes.

"You okay?" Annie asked quietly.

He stopped at the foot of the bed and took a breath so his voice didn't tremble when he answered. "Yeah, just...can't sleep. I'm going to get up so I don't keep you awake."

"Marcus."

"Go back to sleep. I'm fine."

"Wait." She sat up. "Come here. Please."

A moment later, the bedside lamp came on, and he blinked. She faced him, her eyes squinted as well.

She stared at him for a minute. "What's wrong?"

He faked a smile. "Just restless. That's all."

"It's more than that. Isn't it?"

He shook his head. "No. This week has just been a whirlwind, you know?"

She looked down for a moment. "Don't. Please."

"What?"

Meeting his gaze, she practically begged him with her eyes. "You are the only one who doesn't treat me like I'm a house of cards. Please don't start now. This"—she gestured to her arm and face—"might not be the same, but this is." She tapped her head. "For the most part anyway." She laughed uneasily. "I forget what I'm trying to say sometimes. I space out sometimes. But I can still think. I can see when something is wrong or someone is upset."

"I know that, Annie."

"So talk to me. Please. What's wrong?"

He sat on the edge of the bed and grabbed her hand. "I don't want to add more to your plate."

She closed her eyes. "Please. Don't shut me out. That doesn't help me. I want you to talk to me."

He stared at her hand in his. Her fingers were always slightly curled now from the lack of control she had. It probably wasn't obvious to someone who didn't know, but he knew.

He'd never forget.

"I had a dream."

"Nightmare? Of that day?"

He shifted, squeezed her hand, and then kissed it as a way to reassure himself that she was okay. "I was in the kitchen with a couple who was interested in the house. You were in the living room waiting in case someone else showed up. I heard a crash—something getting knocked over. I went to check on you. I called out your name as I entered the living room. I think I scared the guy, because he shot the gun as soon as I called out. I only saw him for a split second, but he looked as shocked as I was. You stumbled back, and I knew you'd been hit."

She creased her brow as she put her other hand on top of his, creating a hand sandwich.

"I ran to you." He cleared his throat when emotion tugged at his voice. "You fell back in my arms, and I eased you down onto the floor." He closed his eyes as the vision filled his mind as clearly as if it were happening in that moment instead of five months before. "There was a hole...just a small hole. But it was in your head, and I... Damn it," he said as his voice cracked.

"Shh," she soothed, scooting closer to him. She wrapped her arms around him. "I'm okay. Kind of."

He laughed softly at her joke but then shook his head. Sniffing, he pulled away and met her gaze. "You were staring. Just staring. There was nothing in your eyes. I thought you were dead. The blood...it was the strangest thing. You'd think it would gush, but it just trickled. I put my hand on your head and screamed for help. God, I must have screamed and screamed. It seemed like forever before the paramedics came. I sat there. Watching. Helpless."

"No, not helpless. You were there. You were with me."

He sighed and closed his eyes. "I dream about that moment.

Every night, it seems. Sometimes it's worse than others. Sometimes I wake up and realize it was a dream and it goes away. Sometimes I can't get the memories to stop."

"Like tonight?"

He nodded. "Sometimes the guilt—"

"Guilt? For what?"

He looked at her. "I got you shot, Annie. If I hadn't walked in and scared him, he would have left."

Her gaze went from confused to sympathetic. "No. No. You don't know that."

"I saw his face. He didn't mean to shoot you."

"He had a loaded gun aimed at me, Marcus. He is the *only* one to blame."

He lowered his face. She scooted closer and kissed his head.

"You can't blame yourself," she whispered as he wrapped his arms around her. "You can't."

"Because you say?"

"Damn straight. Look, I don't remember being shot. I never will. But I know"—she put her hand to his cheek and lifted his face so he was looking into her eyes—"I *know* that having you there made it better. Knowing you were there made me less scared. Just like having you here now makes me less scared. I know I get mad and I want to be left alone, but you have to know I can't do this without you. I can't be strong right now. Not without you."

She kissed him, once, twice, and the third time lingered. Pulling back, she put her forehead to his, cupped his face with her left hand, and stroked her thumb over his lips. "I love you, Marcus."

"I love you, too."

"I'm sorry you had to see that. But I'm not sorry you were there, because in my heart I knew you were there. I knew you were taking care of me. I believe that, and I believe it saved me."

Her words soothed something in him that he hadn't realized was hurting. A sob worked its way up his throat. She hushed him as she pulled him closer. Lying back, she held him against her as everything he'd kept buried came to the surface. She'd had a fairly good cry earlier in the day after being startled. Apparently he was taking his turn now.

"And you accuse me of bottling things up," she whispered after a few minutes.

He laughed quietly and reached for a tissue. "We're a matched pair, you and I. Snotting on each other."

"Hopefully you didn't get rid of all my clothes when you moved in."

"I left a few."

She hugged him back to her. "You should talk to someone."

"I'm talking to you."

"I'm serious."

"So am I."

She sighed. "Marcus. You're clearly having a difficult time processing what happened."

"Yes, but like you, I just need some time to fully recover. Then I'll be fine."

"You've had five months." She dragged her hand over his back. "If not a professional, then Jenna—or maybe Paul or Matt. They've been here, too."

"I didn't want to dump on them. We were all going through so much."

"Well, maybe now's the time to do that, hmm?"

Tilting his head back, he kissed her. "Maybe."

She kissed him again. Then again. The third time, she slid her tongue over his lips, and his nerves jumped to life. It'd been a long time, too damn long, since she'd kissed him like that. His body reacted, came to life, but he pulled back, brushed his nose to hers, and sighed. God, he wanted her, but he didn't feel like it was appropriate to take her. Not now. Not yet. She was still recovering.

Instead, he hugged her close and rolled them over so they were in the middle of the bed, with him back on his side. Kissing her forehead, he exhaled loudly. "Thank you for listening."

"Always."

He pulled her to him and closed his eyes. "Let's get some sleep, hmm?"

"Yeah," she said quietly. "Let's get some sleep."

Normally, Annie would hate the whole girly day thing, but her first trip to the salon after having her head shaved seemed like a big deal, and she couldn't quite face it alone. Dianna and Donna were all over it. They helped her pick out a pixie cut with highlights and a few outfits for Kara to alter.

They'd wanted to make a whole day of it and go out for dinner as well, but Annie had other plans. She never had been very domestic, but even she could see that Marcus needed someone to take care of him. He'd been putting up a strong front for far too long. She suspected last night was just the tip of the emotional turmoil he was hiding.

Instead of spending time with Dianna and Donna, she asked them to invite Mallory out so she could have quiet time. Her real motive, however, was to surprise Marcus with dinner. Granted, she wasn't the most accomplished chef even before the shooting, but standing in the kitchen with chicken burning in one skillet and foamy pasta water boiling over in another pan while sauce splattered in yet another was an all-time low for her culinary attempts. Opening the oven, she pulled burned garlic bread out and tossed the cookie sheet and all into the sink.

Seconds later, the smoke alarm blared, startling her. A wave of panic, not unlike what had rolled through her at the sound of Sean popping the balloon, consumed her. Putting her hands to her ears, she sank to the floor, taking slow breaths, trying to regain some semblance of control.

She should know how to handle this. She should know what to do, but it was all so overwhelming. The smells. The smoke. The shrill beeping assaulting her ears. It was like a whirlwind of colors, making it impossible to know where to look first. Her panic wasn't easing. Instead, it seemed to be increasing with each deafening blare of the smoke alarm. She sat, hands over ears, trying to focus, trying to remember what to do.

"What the hell is going on?"

Annie looked up from where she was sitting against the cabinet in front of the sink. Marcus was turning off burners and moving pans.

"Watch out," he called.

She scooted out of the way as he carried the skillet to the sink. Then he had the broom, waving it in front of the smoke alarm. After several seconds, he tossed the broom aside and grabbed a chair. Climbing up, he jerked the alarm free and tore the battery out. Silence filled the room, and Annie suddenly remembered how to breathe.

Hopping off the chair, he squatted in front of her, pulling her hands from her ears. "You okay?"

She bit her lip and inhaled slowly. "I cooked for you."

He chuckled. "Is that what this is? I thought maybe you were practicing your arson techniques for houses that won't sell."

She closed her eyes and laughed. "I could probably get away with that right now. Plead brain damage and constant confusion."

"Come here." He pulled her from the floor and into his arms. Holding her, he kissed her head before leaning back. "Sit at the table. Let me open some windows."

Once the airflow was pushing the smoke outside, he sat next to her at the kitchen table and took her hands. "Where's Mallory?"

"I sent her to dinner with Donna and Dianna. I told them I wanted to be with you."

"Honey, I-I don't think you're ready to be left on your own yet."

"I'm not a child, Marcus."

"I know, but... Want to tell me what happened?"

"I just..." She sat up straight but then sagged again. "I couldn't remember what to do. I started out okay, but then... I was overwhelmed. I couldn't remember what I was doing or how to do it, and then the alarm went off and... I froze." She closed her eyes. "God, I can't even cook."

"Well, honey, you never could."

"Jerk," she said but couldn't help smiling. "Not funny."

"Jenna sent over plenty of food that just needs to be reheated. Why didn't you make some of that?"

Sitting back in the chair, she pulled her hands from his and twisted them in her lap as she looked at them. "I wanted to do something nice for you."

"Oh yeah?"

She nodded. "I ruined it."

"No, you didn't." He brushed his hand over her hair. "You didn't. Let's check." He pulled her to the sink. "Okay, the chicken and the bread are toast." He grinned at her. "See what I did there? The bread is *toast*."

She rolled her eyes, despite her amused grin. "You should have gone into stand-up."

"Let's check the pasta." He scooped out a few noodles and

blew on them before putting them into his mouth. "A little soft but not ruined. The sauce?" He stirred it then licked the spoon. "Tastes like it came straight from a jar. Grab me a strainer."

She did. He poured the pasta in and then served two plates and covered the overdone noodles in alfredo sauce before carrying them to the table. She sat as he put a bowl of salad in front of her and squirted it with French dressing. He dug into dinner, making a show of how much he was enjoying it. She wasn't buying his act, though. He was trying too hard.

"You don't have to eat it."

"I want to. I like it. I like your hair, too. Very sexy."

She gave him a weak smile as she touched the short strands at her temple. She still wasn't used to the cut. "Thanks."

He stopped before adding more fettuccine to his mouth. "You don't?"

"I liked it long."

"Well, if you hadn't made the doctors remove a chunk of your skull, they wouldn't have had to shave it."

"They could have just taken my face off to get the bullet out."

"I suggested that. Asked if they could get rid of some of those wrinkles while they were at it, but they said it would cost extra."

She playfully glared at him. "You are so rotten."

He leaned forward and kissed her. "You love that about me. Thanks for dinner."

"Sure."

"I notice you're not eating."

She frowned and shrugged. "I really just wanted the bread."

Marcus laughed. So did Annie.

"I'm such a mess," she said after a minute.

He nodded. "But a conscious mess. Which is a step in the right direction."

Picking up her fork, she twisted pasta onto the prongs and managed to get food into her mouth with some effort. For a moment, as she chewed her food and Marcus smiled at her, she almost felt normal. Which was *also* a step in the right direction.

CHAPTER FOURTEEN

"*W*hat are you doing?" Mallory asked cautiously.

Annie hesitated in turning her attention away from the pan on the stove. "Cooking."

"You've been staring at that pan for like three minutes, Mom."

She sighed. "Well, you missed my attempt at dinner the other night. It was a disaster."

"Marcus said it wasn't that bad."

She frowned and turned her attention back to the chicken in the pan. "I can't multitask anymore. I completely freaked out. My occupational therapist wants me to try again. But only do one thing at a time. Then two. Then three. And so on. Until I can cook a meal without curling up in a ball and crying like a toddler."

Mallory stared at her with that damned sorrow filling her

eyes. Annie didn't want to see pity in her daughter's eyes, so she returned her attention to the pan.

"Mom, I can—"

Annie put up her hand when Mallory started to reach for the pan. "Stop. Mallory, I have to learn how to do this."

"But I can help."

"Not always. Not forever. You're not going to live with me the rest of your life, cooking my dinner and cutting my food. No. I have to learn. You and Marcus. You have to let me learn."

She lifted her hands in defeat. "Okay."

Annie gestured to the table. "You can put the plates out. God knows I've broken enough of those since I've been home." Turning her attention to the chicken, she poked at a breast with a fork and frowned. "I'm not going to lie. This is a bit like watching paint dry. I used to be all over the place when I was cooking."

She turned when Mallory didn't respond. Annie's heart sagged when she noticed her wiping a tear from her face. She tried to remember what she'd said, tried to pinpoint what she'd done wrong, but she couldn't recall snapping at Mallory.

Setting her fork down, she moved to the table, her brow creased with concern. "What'd I say?"

Mallory offered her a weak smile. "Nothing."

"You're crying."

"I know. I just... You didn't do anything. I was thinking. That's all."

"About?"

She lowered her face, and her cheeks turned bright red.

"About when I didn't have to stare at chicken to cook it?"

Mallory's face scrunched, and she nodded. "I'm sorry. That's really shitty of me."

"No, it's not. I think about it all the time. I used to be able to cut my own food, Mallory. I used to be able to articulate my words. I used to be able to cook a simple pasta dinner without fear of burning down the house. It's okay to miss those things. I sure as hell do."

"It's not right of me to think like that. You're here, and that's what matters."

"For the most part. But it'd be great if I were here and could still do all the things I used to do. It's okay to miss the old me, honey. I do, too. And I cry for what I've lost. So can you."

"I feel like an ass doing that, Mom."

"Don't. But understand that jumping in and rescuing me from every little thing isn't going to help me. If I'm ever going to be anything like I was before, you have to let me struggle."

Mallory sniffed as she wiped her cheeks. "Remember when I was dating Tommy Ballard in high school?"

Annie moaned. "I hated that kid."

"I was convinced that he was the love of my life and we could overcome whatever came our way. No matter how many times you told me I deserved better, I had to learn on my own. When I came home from the prom crying because I caught him kissing another girl and I finally broke up with him, you said the hardest thing you ever had to do was stand back and watch me get hurt."

Annie nodded.

"I totally get that now. Because I just want to make things right for you. I see you struggling, and I just want to make it better."

"But you can't. You can't protect me from having to relearn basic things any more than I could protect you from getting your heart broken. The only thing you can do is be there for me when I need your support."

Mallory smiled. "Well, that's a given." Her lips fell and her eyes widened. "Oh, no. Your chicken."

Annie gasped and rushed to the stove. Using the fork, she flipped the meat over and frowned at the black surface. "This time, the burned chicken is on you."

"I completely take the blame."

Turning off the burner, Annie moved the skillet and grasped the handle of a saucepan between both palms.

"What now?"

"Now I'm going to fill this with water and watch it until it boils so I can make mashed potatoes. Don't you dare distract me this time."

"You just stand there and stare at that pot, Mom. Let me know if you need anything."

Annie nodded as she set the water on the stove. Taking a breath, she focused all her attention on waiting for it to boil, determined that she wasn't going to let the boxed potatoes get ruined.

8h

Marcus lifted his gaze from the book he was reading when the bathroom door opened. He'd given up trying to help Annie get ready for bed. It just made her mad, and that wasn't his intent. She was right; she had to do things on her own, but just like Mallory, he wanted to jump in and help with every little thing. Not because he didn't think she could handle it but because he could make it easier for her, and at this moment in his life, that seemed to be all he could do.

Even so, he was doing his best to step back and let her do things on her own—even if it did take her twice as long to get ready for bed.

He smiled as she walked to bed in the satin two-piece pajamas that had been altered to make it easier for her to get into.

"You know," she said, pulling the covers back on her side of the bed, "that isn't the same look you used to give me in the bedroom."

"Oh, no?"

She shook her head. "I liked the other look better."

"What's wrong with this look?"

"With the thank-God-she's-still-alive look?" She eased into the bed and leaned against the headboard. "Everybody gives me that look. It's old, Marcus."

"Well, we are very thankful that you're still alive."

She nodded. "I know. Me too. But it'd be nice if you could get over it and start looking at me like you used to."

"Just in the bedroom or everywhere?"

She smirked. "Everywhere would be good."

"You've only been out of the hospital for two weeks, Annie. We still need some time to stop being amazed by your incredible awesomeness."

"Well, that will never happen. But at least Donna and Dianna have stopped crying all the time, and Mallory almost knows how to act around me."

"And your brothers?"

She laughed softly. "They still hover."

"And how are you feeling? You made some progress today, I think. Cooking dinner."

"And with minimal incident. One of these days, I'm going to be able to cook two things at once without being a serious hazard to my own safety."

"Don't get ahead of yourself."

She laughed, and his heart swelled with love for her. The sound of her laughter wasn't quite the same as it used to be, but he still thought it sounded like beautiful music. She tilted her head, and her smile softened. It was her way of letting him know he was staring at her—something that wasn't new but seemed to hold a different meaning these days.

He used to get caught up in the magic of her, mesmerized by her. Now it was more amazement that she was there. Sitting with him, talking to him, laughing. It was less a feeling of awe at his love for her and more a feeling of awe that he hadn't lost her. He tended to get lost in those thoughts as easily as she got lost in whatever thoughts made her eyes glaze over.

"Stop," she said.

"What?"

"You always get that sad look in your eyes whenever we have a moment of normalcy. I know what you're thinking."

"Do you?"

"That you're lucky I'm still alive."

He smiled. "I do think that quite a bit."

Reaching for his hand, she covered it with hers. "I feel like we've switched roles."

"No, you're still the cranky one."

She grinned. "You always told me to talk about my feelings, and I always evaded. Now I tell you to talk to me, and you shrug everything off and make a stupid joke. That's my trick."

"You taught me well."

"Marcus."

Closing his book, he set it aside and lifted his arm, signaling for her to scoot closer. She did, and he cuddled her against him, putting what was now his customary kiss on the top of her head.

"I want to talk," she said quietly. "A real conversation, Marcus. Not you reassuring me that I'm going to get better and us making lame jokes to skim the surface. Nobody *talks* to me anymore."

"Okay. What do you want to talk about?"

"Us."

His heart skipped a few beats. "We're fine, Annie."

Sitting back, she turned to look up at him. "We were just getting started before this happened. We don't have years' worth of foundation to build on, Marcus."

"Stop right there. We may not have spent the last five years dating, Annie, but we were friends, and I loved you for a hell of a long time before you finally realized I was the best thing that ever happened to you." He chuckled when she smiled. "I like to believe that you loved me, too. So maybe we weren't together in the traditional sense, but we do have a foundation. A damned strong one."

"But we only spent one week of that as a couple."

"And now we've got the rest of our lives."

She stared at him, as if trying to figure out how to say what was on her mind. "Is this what you want, Marcus? Me? Like this?"

Damn it. He'd known this was coming. Eventually—if not tonight then another night—she was going to try to give him an out, and it pissed him the hell off. "Yes, it is."

"You didn't sign on for this."

"No, I didn't. But neither did you. Did you ask that asshole to shoot you in the head? Did you ask to stay in a coma for three months or to wake up and have to spend months in speech and physical therapy?"

"If you want to leave—"

"Don't—"

"I won't blame you, and I won't be angry. I promise, I won't be angry."

"Well, you know what, Annie? *I'm* getting angry." Tossing the blankets off, he stood and raked his hand through his hair. He paced, trying to tamp down his knee-jerk reaction so he didn't take his frustration out on her. Finally, he faced her. "We've been over this. Before you got shot, we went over this a hundred times. I'm not abandoning you. I'm not like Mallory's dad. I'm not going to walk away the first time life throws us a curveball. Stop lumping me in with that son of a bitch."

"This is different—"

"No, it's not. Goddamn it." Sighing, he sat back on the bed and looked at her. "I know this isn't going to be easy. For either one of us. I know we have a rough road ahead. But I'm not going to turn back now. I don't know what to say or do to make you understand how much I love you. You are everything to me. You and Mallory are my family, Annie. I felt that way long before you ever gave me permission to. I'm not giving up on you, and I wish to hell you'd stop trying to give up on me."

"I'm not—"

"You are. Every time you tell me that you think I'm going to leave you, that's you giving up on me. That's you thinking that I'm not strong enough or that I don't love you enough, and that hurts me. I'm not leaving you, so stop trying to give me an out."

"I'm never going to be the same, Marcus. We can pretend that maybe someday, but the truth is, I won't ever be like I was before."

He nodded. "I know."

"And you really can live with that?"

"I really can live with that." He brushed his hand over her hair. "Honey, the only thing I couldn't live with was if I'd had to say goodbye to you."

She blinked a few times before nodding. "I'm trying so hard to make things normal."

"This *is* our new normal. We've got to take the time to figure out what that means. All of us."

"I just want you to be happy."

"I am happy, Annie. Things are tough right now, but I'm happy. How are you?"

"Honestly?"

"Honestly."

"I'm terrified. And frustrated. And…maybe a little lonely."

"Lonely?"

"I always kept everyone at arm's length because I didn't want to be attached if they left me. Now… Now I feel like I make everyone so sad, and I don't want them to be sad, so it's better to stay away from them."

"You don't make them sad. The situation does. But again, we've all just got to start working on accepting and moving forward."

"I want to wake up and have this all be a dream, but that isn't going to happen, is it?"

"No. This is our reality. Ours and the family's. Don't push

them away. Don't keep them at arm's length. They're your family. They love you and want to help you."

Pulling her knees up, she hugged them and her eyes glazed over in that way that still spooked him.

Finally, she blinked and sighed. "I'm going to call my brothers tomorrow. We're going to have lunch. Like we used to. And...and if I spill food all over me, then...so be it, right?"

He smiled. "Just...wear a bib."

She looked at him for a moment before giggling. Leaning forward, she wrapped her arms around his neck. He hugged her to him and kissed her cheek. She leaned back, pressed her lips to his, and rested her forehead to his for a moment before kissing him again. Desire flared through him as Annie leaned back, pulling him with her as she continued to kiss him.

He broke the kiss and sat back enough to look down at her, intending to ask if she was sure she was ready, but his heart seized in his chest. Leaning over her, staring into her eyes, he was suddenly back in that house. He nearly forgot how to breathe until she touched his cheek.

"Marcus?"

He gasped quickly as his lungs kicked back into action. Smiling, he took the fingers lightly brushing his cheek and brought them to his lips. "Come on," he whispered. "Let's get some sleep."

Confusion lit her eyes for a moment, but he looked away, turning his attention to stretching out and turning off the bedside lamp. Once he was settled under the covers, her hand brushed over his chest then slid around him. He closed his eyes and tried not to picture her dead on the floor, but the images assaulted him.

"You okay?" she asked quietly.

He exhaled slowly. "Yeah, of course." He kissed her head. "Good night, Annie."

"Yeah," she said, sounding hurt. "Good night."

CHAPTER FIFTEEN

*I*t had taken Annie nearly a month after her release to decide to go into the office. Now that she was there, she looked around the space where she'd once spent so much time and felt like she didn't belong. Things had been moved. Her monitor. Her keyboard. Her electronic coffee-warming coaster. The photo of her and Mallory from their vacation several years ago.

Marcus had effectively taken over her space.

"We ran out of office space when we hired Meg and Mallory as agents," he said from behind her. "Someone had to move in here. It made the most sense for that someone to be me."

She faked a smile. "Of course."

He stopped gathering papers for the meeting and looked at her. "You can tell me how offended you are. It's okay."

"I was"—where was the pen holder? It was a gift from Matt's daughters—"hibernating."

"I will put everything back exactly as it was. I just needed this space to be functional for me while I was in here."

"Well, I..." Had he changed her chair out for another? "I can't exactly come back to work yet anyway." He had. He'd changed her chair. This wasn't even her office anymore.

He stepped around her desk and picked up the framed photo that was sitting in the space her candy dish used to occupy.

"From the wedding," he said, showing her the picture.

It wasn't the one she'd seen before. This image was snapped candidly, when neither was posing. Marcus had his arm around her shoulder, pulling her to him as he laughed. She was smiling, and her cheeks were blushed. He'd likely just said something completely inappropriate that she should have been offended by.

Warmth spread through her chest, and some of her irritation at him for moving her things smoothed over. She grinned. "I like it."

"Me too." He looked at the image. "It suits us."

Her smile faded a bit. "I remember."

"What?"

"Being here. Before the open house. You kissed me."

Marcus smiled. "You let me."

She focused on the flash of a memory, trying to regain more, but it was gone. "I'm never going to remember what he looked like, am I?"

"Probably not."

"They'll never catch him."

He shook his head. "I don't think so."

She closed her eyes. "After what he did to me..."

Putting his hands on her shoulders, he lightly kissed her forehead. "You're still with us. We have to focus on that."

"So you keep saying."

"Because it's true."

Slipping into his arms, she completely disregarded her own rule about keeping romance out of the office. She needed to feel the security of his embrace.

"Hey, boss, I need you to sign off on... Oh, sorry."

Annie turned and smiled at the young woman who had walked into her office—Marcus's office. "Hey, Meg."

"Annie, it's so good to see you."

"Thanks for stepping in while I was recovering." Her smiled faltered when Meg's did.

Meg looked to Marcus, and Annie realized she hadn't understood her. Her family had gotten adept at translating her apparent gibberish. She'd forgotten that she wasn't speaking as clearly as she thought.

"Thank you. For helping," she said more slowly.

Meg's smile returned. "Of course." She looked at Marcus again. "If you have time before the meeting, I needed you to sign off on this purchase order."

Annie creased her brow at Marcus. Since when did agents make purchases?

Marcus took the paper from Meg. "I'll get to it. Go on in. We'll be there in a few minutes."

Meg left, and Annie took the paper from Marcus, skimming it. "What is all this?"

"Some new marketing materials. Meg and Mallory took this on for me. Remember? Mal designed the new signs. We're going to get our business cards and website and all that in line with the new look. I've been busy, so she and Meg worked on it." He took the paper from her. "It's all right, Annie. We've spread out the expenses to have the least impact on our immediate budget."

"That's great, but...new marketing materials? New signs? New security company? Yet you said sales were down. Spreading the impact out is great, but at the end of the day, where is this money coming from?"

"Paul and I reworked the budget."

Her mouth fell open a bit. "Even a reworked budget has a limit. The money has to come from somewhere. I don't want the safety net I've built over the years to go to marketing."

"Annie," he soothed, "we have to change some things for the security of the staff, as well as to try to get sales up. Yes, it cost more than what you had originally budgeted, but it was necessary."

"But if sales are down—"

"Hey," he said calmly, "I'm taking care of it. Don't worry." He added the paper to the stack on the corner of his desk.

"No, Marcus. I am worried. I may not remember everything, but I know what my finances were, and there wasn't room for all these additional expenses. I appreciate you taking care of things while I was gone, but you can't just do all this without anyone's permission."

The muscles in his jaw tightened. "I had Mallory's and Paul's permission, Annie. Someone had to manage your business. They agreed that someone was me. I've been mindful of the budget in light of the unplanned expenses. That's why Paul and I reworked things *before* we made any major purchases. I'm not running your business into the ground, but I am *not* going to put our staff in a position where they could get hurt. Steps had to be taken."

"Can I see the new budget? Or do you need to confer with Mallory and Paul first?"

Reaching into a desk drawer, he grabbed a folder and held it out to her with a scowl. "We know how much your company means to you. We were far from reckless with your finances. Paul and I took everything into consideration and came to the same conclusion every time. Safety first. His wife, his sister, his niece. You all work here now. He's not going to let anything happen to any of you. None of us are going to let anything like that happen again."

"Marcus," she said as he stepped around her.

"I need some coffee."

She sighed heavily. She certainly had a way of screwing things up these days. Her frown deepened when the pages inside the folder fell out and scattered across the floor as she lowered her hand. Easing to her knees, she tried to pick up the papers, but her inability to properly use her fingers made the action nearly impossible.

"Damn it," she whispered harshly.

"Everything okay?" Dianna asked, kneeling beside Annie and gathering the papers.

A humorless laugh left her. "You thought I was rough around the edges before... Just wait until you get to know me now."

"Give yourself a break, Annie. You were—"

"Shot. In a coma. Yeah, I know." She closed her eyes and sighed. "See? That right there. I don't mean to snap. It just comes out."

Dianna stood, helping Annie up as she did. "I'm guessing by the way Marcus marched out of here, he got a good snapping, too. Why? What happened?"

"Because I just found out he threw my well-planned budget in a blender."

She nodded. "He and Paul really scrutinized things. They didn't just toss your plans aside. They weighed everything and had a lot of discussions over what was best for the agency."

She took the papers from Dianna. "I know. I know they wouldn't be careless. It's just..." She inhaled slowly and looked around. "Everything is different. You guys have a few months of adjustment time on me. I need to catch up." Sitting in a chair in front of her desk—*Marcus's* desk—she dropped the folder on the surface and frowned. "I want my life back, Di, but this"—she gestured toward her head—"won't let me. I can't think. I can't... censor myself."

"You're pushing yourself too hard. It's barely been a month since you've been home from the hospital. Nobody expects you to come back to work or to even be your old self. You've been through an incredibly traumatic experience."

"And it takes time and there's no telling how long or how far I'll progress. Yes, the therapists tell me this over and over."

"And it's still not sinking in, is it?"

Annie smiled sadly. "I always did have a thick skull. Good thing, huh?"

"Yeah, good thing."

She exhaled heavily. "I just want to pick up the pieces and put them back together, but they're so broken. I'm so broken."

"Not broken," Dianna whispered. "You're not broken, Annie. Stop thinking of yourself as damaged."

"I *am* damaged."

"No. You're *recovering*. You're *surviving*."

"And you're a goddamned Pollyanna."

Dianna chuckled. "Someone around here has to look at the bright side. It sure as hell isn't you."

"Hard to see the bright side when I'm so easily distracted by the lights that I can't remember what I was looking for in the first place."

"So be distracted. Take time to look at the lights. They're beautiful."

"Jesus," Annie sighed, "how does Paul stand your sunshine bullshit?"

Di giggled. "Come on. Staff meeting is about to start."

She shook her head. "No. I, um, I'm going to pass."

"You came for the staff meeting."

"I think… Marcus is… He should just keep doing what he's doing."

"Don't let this beat you, Annie."

She drew a breath. "I'm not. I'm just going to sit this one out. For now."

"But—"

"Dianna." She closed her eyes for a moment before looking at her sister-in-law. "I know you're trying to help, but I'm feeling completely incompetent at the moment, and walking into a meeting where I have no idea what is going on is just going to make it worse. So no, I'm not going. I need to… I don't know what I need, but it isn't sitting in there being reminded that I've lost so much. I'll be ready soon, but that time isn't now."

"You know, they don't need me in there. Why don't we go—"

"No. Please. I'm fine."

Dianna's face sagged a bit. "I don't want to leave you when you're so upset."

"I'm not upset. I'm…facing a very hard truth. I lived for this company for so long, and now…now I have to stand on the outside and let someone else take it, and that hurts. Just one more thing I can't do."

Dianna put her hand on Annie's. "It will take time, but you will get back into the swing of things. You *will* get back on your feet."

Annie nodded. "Yeah. Just not today, huh?"

"You two ready?" Marcus asked, sticking his head in the door.

"Go," Annie whispered. "I'm fine."

Dianna hesitated a few more seconds before standing. She quietly ushered Marcus from the room, thankfully fielding his questions and stopping him from pressing Annie to go to the meeting. She didn't need to say again how unprepared she was to attend a staff meeting. Hearing voices filtering from the conference room, she reached for the photo that Marcus had shown her earlier, sighing when she nearly dropped it.

She stared at her image for a long time. That had been a week—just seven days—before her life had changed forever. And that week had probably been one of the happiest of her life. She'd finally stopped running from her feelings. She'd finally stopped being scared of being left and let Marcus in. And then, just like that, it was over.

Her therapists tried to be encouraging. Her family and Marcus kept telling her to give herself more time. Be more patient. She'd even told herself that from time to time, but saying and doing it were two different things. She'd never been patient, and that hadn't changed.

She wanted her goddamned life back. She wanted her confidence back. She wanted to feel like herself again. She wanted to walk into that conference room and take charge and know that was her place. Know that she belonged there.

Her life had been altered so much, and she hadn't been there to see it. She was an outsider, and a fairly bewildered one at that. She was tired and frustrated and scared and pissed off, and she couldn't seem to sort it all out and make sense of it. Everything seemed to jumble up when she tried to work it out. The more she thought about it, the more confusing it became. She didn't used to stumble like this. She didn't used to trip up on her own thoughts.

Staring at the image, she rubbed her fingertips over the raised scar on her forehead. One moment. One stupid kid. And everything was different. Nothing would ever be the same.

"Hey," Paul said gently from the door.

She looked up, puzzled for a moment. "Hi."

"What's up?"

She lowered her hand and the picture. "What are you doing here?"

"I was going to take my wife to lunch. I forgot about the staff meeting."

Annie frowned at him. "Liar. She called you."

He gave her a slight shrug. "She's worried about you."

"And you just dropped everything to run over here?"

He nodded as he sat in the chair next to her. "I did. And before you blame that scar you were fondling, I'd have done the same before that happened. I'd always drop everything and come running for you, Annie. That's what we do for each other."

She smiled. "Yeah."

"That's a good picture, huh?"

She looked at it again, but the image blurred as tears filled her eyes. She tried to blink them away, but one fell and splattered on the glass. "I can't stand this, Pauly," she whispered. "I have no control of my mind or my mouth...my life."

"I know it's hard. But you can and you will get through this."

"What if I never get better than this? I don't want to be so perplexed all the time. Everything seems so difficult. I don't want to talk to people and have them look at me like I'm speaking a foreign language. My job is sales. I can't sell a house if the buyer can't understand me."

"Your speech is getting better."

She shook her head. "No, you're just getting more used to my pattern. I talked to Meg earlier, and she didn't have a clue what I said." She lowered her face. "I get so mad at you guys, and you're just trying to help. I don't mean it, but I can't help it. I'm so angry."

"You have a right to be angry."

"Not at you."

"Well, if we ever find the asshole who did this to you, we'll all take turns taking our anger out on him, okay? Until then, you use us as your emotional punching bags as much as you need. We're here for you, and we understand how difficult this is for you."

Tears welled, and she shook her head. "I thought...I thought I could just be me again, but everything I do reminds me that I'm not. The more I try to be the old me, the more I prove to myself that she's gone. I came in here today, determined to integrate myself back into work, and all I managed to do was confuse Meg and get pissed at Marcus for trying to save my business while I was in a coma."

He frowned as he took her hand. "Come on. Put your coat on. Let's go for a drive."

She started to protest, but he pulled her to her feet and grabbed her coat from the rack in the corner. Holding it open for her, he helped her slip her arms in then pulled it up to her shoulders. He walked her out to his car and opened the passenger door.

"Are you hungry?" he asked, backing out of his parking spot.

"No."

"Coffee?"

She sighed. "Know what happened to my coffee this morning?"

"What?"

"I dropped it. All over me and the kitchen floor."

He chuckled. "You say that like you've never dropped anything before in your life."

"I do it more frequently now."

"Well, you are getting older. More frail."

She grinned as he laughed. He reached over and took her hand, squeezing it as he reassured her he was just teasing.

"I'm a certifiable klutz these days."

"Damn, you really are being hard on yourself."

"I'm starting to feel pretty sorry for myself."

He glanced at her. "How are things with Marcus?"

She looked out the window and frowned. "Fine. How are things with Dianna?"

"Amazingly well. I got lucky this time."

"You did."

"Now, you want to be honest with me? How are things with Marcus?"

"He, um... He's been supportive. Understanding. Patient. Perfect."

"You say that like it's a bad thing."

She swallowed as she debated voicing the fear that had been nagging at her for weeks. "It feels fake. Forced. Like he's doing what he's supposed to be doing, not what he wants to be doing."

Paul was quiet for a moment. "You're projecting your fear onto him, Annie."

"My fear?"

"The same fear you've always had. You think he's going to leave you. He's not."

"I didn't say that."

"You didn't have to. I know you."

"No, I'm beyond that. I trust him when he says he doesn't want to leave."

He glanced at her. "Then why are you convinced he doesn't want to help you?"

She could actually feel her face heating. "I don't want to talk to you about this."

"Why?"

"Because it's...private."

"It's just you and me here."

Annie shook her head. "It's *private*."

He chuckled. "It's about sex?"

She closed her eyes and sighed. "You're my brother."

"Who happens to have sex with his wife on occasion. I learned all about the birds and the bees a long time ago, big sister. I'm fairly certain I can have this conversation without being grossed out."

She rolled her head back. "Every time we get close to being intimate, he...shuts down. Rolls over. Goes to sleep. I think..." She lowered her face, surprised at the tears that stung her eyes. "I think... I don't think Marcus wants me...like this." She looked out the window as she sniffed and wiped her tears away. "It's stupid."

"No, it's not." He handed her a handkerchief. "Have you talked to him about this?"

"No."

"You should."

She sighed loudly. "It's pathetic. To be so upset about sex."

"No, Annie, it's not. You're in a relationship, and that is part of being a couple. If he has issues—which, by the way, I don't believe for a minute that he does—you need to talk about it."

"He's trying."

"But if he doesn't know that this is hurting you, he can't fix it."

"I don't want him to fix it, Paul. I mean...if he isn't attracted to me anymore, then the last thing I want is to guilt him into bed."

"There has to be more to this. You are beyond the point in your relationship where physical attraction is the number-one trigger for sex. It's about the intimacy. It's about the emotion."

"So he just doesn't love me anymore?"

"That is definitely not true. That man would not have put himself through the hell of sticking with you through your coma if he didn't love you. Don't ever question whether or not he loves you. He's proven that time and time again."

"So what is it?"

"I don't know. Ask him. But I'd venture to guess it's something he's feeling about himself, not about you."

She frowned at her hands curled in her lap. She didn't look up again until he parked the car. When she did, she noticed they were sitting in front of the house where they'd grown up.

Sometime between the time Annie had sold it—one of her first sales—and now, it had had a major overhaul. The siding was no longer broken and mildewed, and the shutters weren't hanging haphazardly off the second-story window that had been her bedroom. The gardens were trimmed instead of overrun with weeds. Even so, she could see the house as it was when they were kids, and her heart started pounding.

"What are we doing here?" she demanded.

Paul looked at the house. "That night. When you were shot. The doctor told us to prepare for the worst. She said the chances of you surviving until morning were minimal. We all went in and said our goodbyes to you." He lowered his face and took a shaky breath. "Man, that was…that was the hardest damn thing I've ever been through. Seeing you like that, with your head wrapped up in gauze and your face so swollen you didn't even look like yourself. Never in all my life had I seen you so still. I'd never seen you so empty. And that's how you looked. Like you—the essence of you—was already gone. You've always had this presence, this way of making the world know you were there, but in that room, that night, Annie, you were gone. And one thing kept popping into my mind, one memory."

He shook his head. "The night Mom died. I remember you sitting with Matty and me and explaining that she had been in an accident and was gone. I remember us crying and you promising that you'd take care of us. You tucked us into bed, like Mom had always done, and then you sat with us until you thought we were asleep. After you left, I stared at the ceiling for a long time, thinking about how it wasn't fair that you had to take care of us because Dad was too drunk. I was so mad, I threw the covers off and stormed downstairs to tell him that. When I got to the living room, he was passed out, and there you were, taking care of him. Just like Mom used to do. I watched you take his shoes off and cover him with a blanket then clean up all his beer cans. All of a sudden, I wasn't angry anymore. I was sad. I was sad for you because you were the only one left to take care of us and that wasn't fair to you. Even as a kid I knew that wasn't fair."

Annie sniffed and wiped her face. "I was the oldest."

"Yeah, but that wasn't the only reason. You took care of us

because that's who you are. That's what you do. You always did that. There has never been a moment in my life when I ever doubted that you were there. Not until that night in the hospital, and it tore me in two, Annie. I swear to God, part of me wanted to die with you because I can't..." He stopped when his voice cracked. "I can't even begin to imagine what I would do without you."

"Stop," she whispered as she gripped his hand as hard as she could—which still wasn't very hard.

"You are my rock. You always have been. I know this recovery process is hard for you. I know it's frustrating because you've always been so strong, but believe me when I tell you that having you here is something that I never thought would happen. So you get mad, and you get upset, and you take it out on me all you want, because it's my turn to be your rock. And I'm not the only one who feels that way. None of us will ever walk away from you, Annie. And none of us would ever think less of you because of something you can't control."

"I know that, Paul. I just—"

"Think less of yourself."

Her lip trembled as she lowered her face.

"I don't know why I started coming here," he said quietly. "I felt compelled for some reason. When that one night turned into a week and that week turned into a month, I'd come here and stare at the house and remember how you kept us together. I'm surprised I haven't been arrested for stalking whoever lives here, actually."

She chuckled. "Try to explain that one. I come here to remember how my sister was a real bitch before she went into a coma."

"You weren't. Well..."

She laughed again. "My bitchiness got you through some really bad teenage years."

He put the car in drive and pulled away from the curb. "Yes, it did. And it's going to get you through this."

"Oh, Paul. This...this is different."

"No, it's not."

"It is. There are things here I can't control."

"And that is driving you insane."

"Do you have any idea how hard it is for me to know what the problem is and not be able to fix it? This stupid hand. I go to therapy, and I try and I try, and it does nothing. They ask me to lift two pounds, and you'd think I were trying to move a building. I do all their speech exercises, and I still sound like Dad on any given Saturday night."

Paul snorted. "You're much clearer than that. Trust me."

"I can't live my life like this. I can't go back to work and not be articulate. I can't take care of my properties when I can't even manage to cook dinner. What am I going to do?"

"Focus on getting better. That's all you can do right now. The rest will come. For once in your life, just take a break and let everyone else do the worrying for you. You focus on your therapy and let Marcus worry about the business. He's doing a great job. I'm keeping an eye on everything. Let Mallory help around the house. That's why she moved in with you."

"I don't want to be dependent."

"You're not. You're letting us help, but you are far from being dependent. It's okay to accept help when you need it."

She sighed and leaned her head back against the headrest. "I never cried for her. I couldn't. I wanted to. I knew I should. But I couldn't. I've cried more in the last few weeks than I have in the last —how long has it been?—thirty-four years. I never realized how numb I'd gotten until Marcus. I was just starting to figure out how to be...normal, when this happened. I was just starting to feel, *really* feel. The shooter took that from me. He took everything from me. I know there are people who have it worse than me, Paul. I know that. But I was just starting to feel alive for the first time ever. He took more than my voice and my clarity and my hands. He took the life I'd been wanting for so long. Now I look at Marcus, and I feel like he's stuck with this broken-down woman who can't even dress herself without altered clothing. This isn't what he expected."

"This isn't what any of us expected, Annie, but when you love someone, you love them through all of life's ups and downs. This is a down time. But it won't always be this hard. You'll either get better or you'll come to terms with your limitations and learn to work around them. Marcus loves you no matter what. He just wants to make your life as good as it can be—the same as before the shooting."

"I'm not making that easy on him, I'm afraid."

"Well, you didn't before, either. So that hasn't changed."

She laughed quietly. "I should have let him in sooner."

"You can't look back. Looking back doesn't help anybody. You let him in. That's what matters. He isn't going anywhere, if that's what you're afraid of."

"No. He was stupid enough to love me before; he's sure as hell not smart enough to run now. I guess this whole situation is my comeuppance, hmm? I refused to give in to my feelings for so long, and now I'm the one on the outside wishing he'd let me in."

"He barely left your side, you know? We had to kick him out a few times so we could sit with you, too. That man loves you. He'd do anything for you."

"I know."

"Talk to him. Tell him you know that he doesn't mean to, but he's hurting you and you just need to understand his hesitancy at being with you. And as for the business, trust him. He is doing what is best for your company. If you need to be a part of things, let him help you. He's not trying to take anything from you."

"I didn't think he was. I just... That's my life. That's my... everything. And I can't be a part of it, and it's killing me inside."

"You can be a part of it, Annie. Just not like you were before, at least not yet. You'll get there. I promise you, we'll find a way to get you there. Take it one step at a time, and you'll get where you want to be soon enough."

She closed her eyes. "Stop being so goddamned logical. Logic has no comforting qualities, whatsoever."

He laughed. "Now you know how I felt every time you tried to fix my last marriage."

"Oh, there was no fixing that marriage. I just wanted you to wake up and realize how hideous she was." She smiled as she reached for his hand. "We had it all for a few minutes, didn't we? Us messed-up O'Connell kids. For a little bit, we had it all figured out."

"We still do. We're all happy, and we have good people in our lives."

She looked out the window when he slowed and turned on his blinker. "Paul, what are you—"

"When's the last time you were here?"

She sighed as he pulled into the cemetery. "Dad's funeral."

"That's what I thought." Parking the car, he turned off the ignition. "You're so damned emotional these days, I figure now's the time."

"For what?"

"You've been bottling it up for thirty-four years, Annie. It's time to grieve for Mom. It's time to feel the pain of losing her."

Tears blurred her vision. "Oh, you little jerk."

"Yeah, I know." He climbed out as she sat frozen in her seat. He opened the passenger door and nodded toward the graves behind him. "Come on."

Wrapping her arm around his, she walked with him to two flat markers. They hadn't been able to afford anything better for their mother, and their father didn't deserve more. She inhaled the crisp November air, feeling it sting her lungs before letting it out slowly and finally looking down. She was certain an arrow had been shot through her heart the moment she saw her mother's name written in raised lettering on the plaque at her feet. She pictured her, smiling despite the bags under her eyes and the shadow that always seemed to be hanging over her soul.

Her voice echoed through Annie's memory. *You're my brave girl, Annie. Mama loves you.*

The pain spread from Annie's chest until she was clinging to her brother as she cried for her mother and her lost childhood and her wasted life and everything she'd lost in that one moment when a bullet ripped through her.

CHAPTER SIXTEEN

*M*arcus tried to act casual when Annie walked in the front door well beyond dinnertime, but the fact was, there was a panic settling in his heart and he was barely controlling it. Paul had texted him, let him know they were fine and that they were going to have dinner before coming home. That had done little to ease Marcus's anxiety. In fact, it increased it. She hated when people saw her eat. Where was he going to take her? What was she going to order that didn't require his assistance? Had Paul considered any of that before taking her out to eat?

On top of all that, Marcus didn't like her being out on her own. Not that she was on her own. She was with Paul. But she wasn't with Marcus, and that triggered a kind of fear in him he couldn't explain any more than he could explain the relief he felt at seeing her.

Setting the papers he was looking over onto the end table, he smiled as she walked into the living room. She'd been crying. Why the hell had she been crying?

"Hey," he said as lightly as he could.

"Hi."

"You okay?"

"Yeah." She sat next to him. "I'm sorry about today."

"You don't have to apologize."

"I do. I got testy, and you didn't deserve that. You've done so much to help me."

He ran his hand over her hair. "I never thought for a moment that you'd appreciate all the changes that were made without your consent. I knew you'd be frustrated that we made decisions without you. But they had to be made."

"I know. Safety first. I've always preached it. And you were right. I couldn't stomach it if something happened to one of our agents because of the budget. They are so much more important than that."

He nodded. "We knew you'd feel that way; that's why we moved forward with the new signs."

"And the rest of the marketing has to reflect that to have the strongest impact. I know. You're right."

Grabbing the papers he'd been looking over, he held them out to her. "Dianna said you didn't really look at this. Let's do it now. I'll explain what we've done, and you make whatever changes you feel are necessary. I didn't sign off on the order for new marketing materials. You should do that."

She pulled her lips between her teeth and bit them gently for a moment. "I want you to know that I trust you to take care of my company. I wasn't trying to imply that I didn't."

"I know that."

"I don't want you to think I don't appreciate you. I know I don't show it well, but I do."

His smile widened. "You may think you're complex, Annie O'Connell, but I've got your number. I know how your mind works."

She scoffed. "I'm glad one of us does."

He wrapped his arm around her shoulders and kissed her temple. "Are you okay? Really?"

"It was a rough day. Paul brought up some things I didn't really want to talk about."

"Such as?"

"Mom's death. Dad's drinking." She sighed. "We went to the cemetery. I hadn't been there in years."

"How'd that go?"

"Oh, I cried. A lot." She smiled sadly.

"That's good."

"Is it?"

He nodded. "You need to get it out. You can't keep bottling all this up, honey. You'll explode."

"Yes, I should talk about what's troubling me. Like you do."

She cocked her brow at him, and he chuckled.

"Let's not make this about me."

"Paul said you didn't reach out to him about your dreams. He didn't know anything about them."

"I never said I was going to reach out to Paul."

"Did you reach out to anyone?"

He sighed loudly. "They're getting better."

"No, they're not."

"They are."

"Marcus—"

"Don't argue with me about what's going on inside my head."

She frowned at him. "You argue with me about what's in my head all the time."

"That's because I can read your mind. Mine is still a mystery."

She scoffed. "Right. You want to know why you are having nightmares?"

His heart started to race, and he shifted beside her. "I don't want to talk about it."

"Because you blame yourself for what happened to me."

He sighed as he looked at her. "I just said I don't want to talk about it."

"It's not your fault some stupid kid thought he'd try a life of crime."

"Annie."

"I got shot, Marcus, and there wasn't a damn thing you could do about it."

He closed his eyes and lowered his face. Damn, she really wasn't going to let it go. "Do you want to look over the budget with me?"

"I want you to talk to me."

He clenched his jaw and took a slow, deep breath. "Not about this."

"Why is it okay for you to try to dig into my head, but as soon as I try to do the same to you, you shut me down?"

"I don't shut you down."

"You don't touch me."

Her words made him pause. "What?"

She licked her lips, and her cheeks turned red. "Before I got hurt, you were always touching me. You never touch me now."

"Are you... You mean..."

The heavy exhale that escaped her let him know she wasn't exactly comfortable either. "I thought it was just the sex. I thought..." She blinked as her already red and puffy eyes filled with tears. "I thought that you didn't want me because...I'm not...because you...you weren't attracted to me anymore."

His heart ached. "Annie—"

"Paul thinks—"

"You talked to Paul about this?"

She frowned at him, and he clamped his mouth shut.

"He dragged it out of me. He thinks you can't be intimate with me because of something that you are going through, not because of me. And I realized, because of your bullheadedness, you haven't gotten over feeling guilty that I got hurt on your watch."

He stared at her for several moments. Initially he wanted to tell her how silly this whole thing was, but then he realized she was right. He hadn't been able to be intimate with her, but it wasn't guilt. Not exactly.

"You were my backup, Marcus. You were the second agent on site to deter any would-be trouble. But our plan failed. We fooled ourselves into believing that we were safe in pairs. That's not your fault. You aren't to blame. And you have to find a way to accept that you couldn't have stopped this. You couldn't have prevented what happened to me. It is not your fault."

Clasping his hands together, he looked at them and sighed. "It seems like whenever I let my guard down, whenever I stop moving, I see you lying dead on the floor. I can't get that image out of my head. When we're in bed and you try to get close to me, not just like that—*anytime* we get close, it makes me think how much I love you. And thinking about how much I love you reminds me how close I came to losing you, and this fear just... God, Annie, it's so strong and so real and so deep. It consumes me."

"You have to talk about it."

"Talking about it doesn't help, honey. It makes it worse. It makes it so much worse. The only thing that helps is this..." He grabbed the papers. "Doing something to help you. I know it makes you crazy that I'm constantly in your face, taking over and trying to make things better for you, but helping you is the only thing that makes me think of something besides your death."

"I didn't die, Marcus."

He shook his head as the image of her on the floor hit him.

"You were closer to death than anyone has any right to come back from, Annie."

Gently stroking her hand over his head, she tilted a bit to see his face. "Hey. I *didn't* die. I'm right here."

Dropping the papers again, he rubbed his eyes. "I know. But you don't understand. You'll never understand. I was there. I saw you. I watched you fade away until you were just a body lying motionless on the floor. There was nothing inside of you. You were gone."

"I'm here now, but in a way, I feel like that's not enough. I feel like you are missing something that used to be here. I wish I could give that back to you, Marcus, but I can't. I can't be what I was before. I'm trying, but it's just not working."

"No." Putting his arms around her, he kissed her head half a dozen times before putting his cheek to her head. "Don't ever feel like that. Please don't feel like that. This is my problem, Annie. It isn't you. I swear it isn't you." He kissed her head again, and she chuckled. "What?"

"I should make you pay me a quarter every time you do that," she said. "I'd be rich."

"I can't help it."

Her smile faded. "I don't remember getting shot. I don't remember much about that day at all. But I remember we were happy. We were about to have everything we'd denied ourselves for so long. When I woke up, it took a long time to understand how much time had gone by. It felt like I'd just taken a nap. You know how you doze off when you don't mean to, and when you wake up, you can't believe hours have gone by? That's how it felt but on a much larger scale. Then it took so long to get my strength back and get my head to start working somewhat right. When I did, I just wanted to jump right back into my life, and it's taken me a while to realize I can't do that. But the one thing I can do, that never changed, was how much I love you and how much I want that life we said we were going to have. But I can't have that, Marcus, if you push me away. And I don't mean sex—please don't think this is about sex. This is about the intimacy we had before that we don't have now. We're just living each day like it's something to get through, one more obstacle to overcome. I feel like this is it. This is what we've got. No more jokes about running off to elope. No more Chinese food in bed. No more...anything. I need those things back because those things were *us*. That was who we were, but that's not who we are now. I need something more in our lives than you taking care of me."

He held himself together pretty well until she brought up the memory of eating in bed. He'd told her those were the moments that would make up their life. And she was right. Those moments were missing. Everything they were now was getting her through the day. Marcus swallowed hard, trying to control his emotions. "I get that. I do. You're right. We're still trying to find our footing, Annie."

"No, you're still bottling up your fears. You know I did that for most of my life. Just pushed my hurt away so I could move on and do what needed to be done. You know what happens when you do that for too long? You get cold. Aloof. And your employee has to sexually harass you to snap you out of it."

He laughed quietly. "Well, I don't have any employees. I guess I'm shit out of luck."

She ran her hand over his back. "Please, Marcus. I am begging you. Get help. Reach out to someone. I don't care who. Talk to someone before this completely destroys you."

Inhaling slowly, he closed his eyes. "It was my job to protect you, Annie. I failed you. Never in my life have I failed someone as much as I failed you that day."

"You didn't fail me. You've never failed me."

"I did."

She pressed her cheek to his shoulder. "Do you remember that night after Paul's wedding when we were talking on the couch? You said you could make me promises all night, but that didn't make them true. I just had to trust you. The same applies here. I can sit here and tell you all night that this wasn't your fault, but that won't make you believe me. That kid brought the gun, Marcus. He chose to pull it out and aim it at me. Now, whether or not he meant to pull the trigger is irrelevant because he did. He shot me, and in a split second the damage was done, our lives were different. I can't begin to imagine what you went through seeing me like that, but when you look at me now, I don't want you to see that. I want you to see *me*. I want you to see that I love you. That I trust you and believe in you. That you never have and you never will fail me. I couldn't have made it this far without you. Please believe that you haven't failed me. I need you to find a way to forgive yourself for whatever you think you didn't do. We can't move on until you do. We can't have our life until you do."

Marcus closed his eyes. The image hit him. Annie shot. Annie bleeding. Annie dying. He choked on the emotion. She hugged him closer, whispered in his ear that she was right there. He tried to push the image from his mind, but it wouldn't budge.

"Look at me," she said softly. She put her hand to his cheek. "Marcus. Look at me."

He swallowed hard as he met her gaze. The look in her eyes was concerned. Not blank. Not empty.

She was right there, and she was okay.

Pulling her against him, he hugged her tight and closed his eyes again. It took some effort, but instead of seeing her lying dead on the floor, he saw Annie smiling.

CHAPTER SEVENTEEN

*S*itting in the conference room staring at a screen wasn't the same as being the lead agent of her business, but it was something. Annie had to put all her concentration into what she was doing, but the large touchscreen tablet let her drag images around and make flyers for the office. Sure, any one of the other staff members could do it faster, but she was contributing, and that was more than she had thought she'd be able to do weeks ago.

"How's it going?" Mallory asked, coming into the room.

Annie finished adding the number of bedrooms to the house description she was working on before looking up. "Slow but steady. Just like your old mom."

"Old?"

Annie chuckled, but she sensed her daughter had something else on her mind as she sat at the table. "What's up, Mal?"

"The company from California called. The position they'd

hired me for just came open again. The guy they replaced me with didn't work out. They asked if I was ready to come out now."

"And you told them yes."

"I told them I'd think about it."

"Do it, Mallory. Go. It's what you want."

She stared at Annie for a few seconds. "It was. I don't know if I want it now, Mom. I've kind of settled in here. I was just starting to think that you're improved enough that you don't need me living there with you and Marcus. You can be on your own more."

"All the more reason you should go."

"No, all the more reason I should buy a house of my own. In Stonehill. Close enough that I'm here, but far enough that you and Marcus can have your privacy."

Annie shook her head. "No. Listen to me. I love you. I love that you want to be here, but I'm fine, Mallory. I'm still getting better. You can go to California without worrying about me. And listen," she said before Mal could argue. "If you go and you hate it, you come home and you pick right up where you left off. I'll never tell you that you can't come back here. O'Connell Realty isn't going anywhere. Marcus is seeing to that."

Mallory sighed. "The last time I tried to move away, you got shot."

"Well"—Annie shrugged—"maybe this time I'll just get the flu."

They both smiled, but Mallory's didn't last long.

"I feel badly leaving you, Mom."

Annie shook her head. "You know what I hate more than all the pity I get? The guilt. You are allowed to live your life. I *want* you to live your life. I want to live *my* life. I want us all to start living again."

"I can put off starting until after Thanksgiving, but I'd be gone before Christmas."

Annie smiled. "Maybe Marcus and I will come to you? That'd be fun."

"It would be fun." Her grin widened. "Remember when you said maybe you'd come to San Diego to elope? A Christmas wedding in California would be lovely."

She laughed. "I don't know that we're quite ready for that, but maybe someday."

"I'm glad you guys are doing better."

"I didn't realize we were doing badly."

"Come on, Mom. Up until a few days ago, you were more like friends than a couple."

Annie nodded. "He had some guilt, and I had some insecurities. I think we're moving past them. I hope we are."

"Well, once I'm gone, that should help."

"You aren't in the way, Mallory. You've been wonderful."

"Yeah. Except when I'm trying to feed you."

They both laughed.

"I put you to work," Marcus said, coming into the conference room, "and here you are goofing off with our girl."

Annie smiled up at him. She no longer felt put out by him

calling Mallory their girl. How could she be when it always made Mal smile? To be honest, knowing Marcus cared so much about her daughter made Annie smile, too. They really had started to feel like a family.

"Has she told you the big news, or did I actually get to hear it first this time?" Annie asked.

"You heard it first," Mallory said. She looked at Marcus and took a deep breath. "California is calling. They've offered me a position again."

"Well, you must have really wowed them, kid."

"She is my daughter," Annie said.

"When do you leave?"

"After Thanksgiving. But you and Mom are coming out for a visit as soon as I get settled." She stood and hugged Marcus then came around the table and hugged Annie. "I'm going to go call them and set a start date. Thanks, Mom."

"I'm proud of you, Mal." When they were alone, Annie smiled at Marcus. "Sorry. I committed you to a trip to California without asking."

He shook his head as he leaned down and kissed hers. "I wouldn't miss it. We'll have to plan it in advance, though. We don't want to wait until the last minute to fly out, and we should go in the middle of the week. It will be mayhem at the airport on a weekend."

She sighed. "I'm not going to lie. I'm a little scared at the thought of flying. All the lights and the people. I think it would be overwhelming for me. I'm afraid I'd freeze."

"So we drive."

"In the winter?"

"Whatever it takes." Sitting next to her, he ran his hand over her back. "Show me what you've done here."

She frowned as she looked at the tablet. "Not much, but I'll get the hang of it." She swiped the screen and showed him the flyer she was putting together. It wasn't overly impressive in the scheme of things, but considering how much effort she'd had to put into it, she was pretty proud of herself.

He brushed her bangs from her forehead. "Good job, sweetheart. You'll get better at this the more you do it. Once you get the hang of this, we'll see what else we can dump on you...I mean, have you help with." He winked at her. "I've been thinking about something. You were right. When you said I needed to reach out to someone. I'm going to have lunch with Paul and Matt. I hadn't wanted to burden them with this, but I'm not sure anyone else will fully understand. They've been with me through this whole thing. They felt the same fears. They'll get it."

She put her hand on his face. "Thank you. Maybe I can stop worrying about you so much now."

He put his hand over hers and turned his face to kiss her palm. "Why are you worrying about me? Hmm?"

"Because you aren't as tough as you try to be."

He sat back and widened his eyes, playfully shocked. "Oh, is that so?"

"That's so. I've been telling you that for years."

"I'll show you tough." He cupped the back of her head, pulled her to him, and kissed her square on the lips. "Now. What do you have to say about that?"

The thinly veiled lust on his face made her heart do a little flip. "Oh my, Marcus. That's a look I haven't seen in a while."

"I watched you sleep for a long time last night. I was just thinking. Remembering. Every time the guilt and the fear started creeping in, I pushed those feelings away and focused on something good. That helped. Focusing on the good memories helped."

"Good."

He dragged his thumb over her lips as his eyes scanned her face. Her heart did more than a flip. It picked up double time as her body started tingling. He smiled sexily, and she returned it. Running her hand up the length of his forearm, she gripped his wrist.

"We're at work," she whispered.

"I know." He leaned in and lightly pressed his lips below her ear. "That's what makes it so fun."

She wanted to tell him no, but then he kissed her neck again and her body nearly melted where she sat. "What, exactly, is it about being in the office that turns you on so much?"

He chuckled seductively. "You are one seriously sexy boss."

A throat clearing loudly made Marcus lean back.

"So, sorry to interrupt your completely inappropriate work meeting," Mallory said with a grin, "but thought you'd like to know I confirmed my start date for December second. I'm going to go book a flight while you get back to, um, making flyers. Shall I close the door?"

"Yes," Marcus said, while Annie said, "No" at the exact same time.

Annie tried to glare at Marcus, but she couldn't. Her heart was too light. Putting her hands to his face, she leaned forward and put her lips to his.

Marcus sighed as he ran out of small talk to make with Annie's brothers. They all knew they were there for heavier conversation. He had started to doubt if he wanted to talk to them about this, but it was important to Annie, so he had to try.

"I told Matt about your dreams," Paul said.

Marcus chuckled. "You O'Connells. Nothing is sacred with you, is it?"

"Family is sacred," Matt said. "And for all intents and purposes, you're family."

Marcus nodded. "Thanks."

"Are the dreams any better? After talking things out with Annie, I mean."

"A bit. I'm working on pushing out the bad thoughts and letting in the good, but... That day," he said quietly. "It's never going to leave me. Not completely."

"I still see her like that," Matt said. "With the bandages and her face so distorted. Scared the hell out of me."

"Me too," Paul admitted. "Did she tell you how I coped?" He glanced at his little brother. "Whenever it'd get to be too much, I'd go sit in front of the old house and think about when we were kids."

Matt scoffed. "Why'd you want to think about that?"

"Because that's how I remember her. You were pretty young when Mom died, Matty, but I remember Annie before she turned into a mother hen—always fussing and pushing and reminding us to keep trying."

Matt dropped his sandwich. "I would go to the baseball park. Sit on the bleachers and remember how she used to always find a way for us to play. I hated having to wear secondhand pants and shoes, but I always got to be on the team, and that's what mattered. Not back then. Back then I was pissed I didn't have the best of the best. But now I know playing is what mattered. Man, I gave her a hard time when I was a kid."

"You didn't know better," Paul said. He looked across the table. "How'd you cope, Marcus?"

He drew a breath. "I didn't. I guess that's the problem. That's...that's why she's pushing me to talk to you guys now. Because I haven't coped. I just pushed it down and got through the day and did what I had to do."

Paul nodded. "And now it's catching up to you."

Marcus picked up a fry but then tossed it down. "I relive that day every time I close my eyes. When I look at her, when I look into her eyes, I see them as they were when she was shot. Blank." He ran his hand over his face. "I try to push it away, but it's there.

When we try to get close..." He stopped and looked at them. "You really want me to talk to you about this?"

"Yes," Paul said, and Matt nodded.

"When I caught her, when I eased her onto the floor and I was leaning over her, I thought she was dead. She *looked* dead. She wasn't talking, and her eyes were just flat. Empty. I thought —" He stopped when the emotion caused his chest to tighten. "I thought she was already gone. I kept begging her to hold on, but I really thought she was already dead. I don't think I understood that she was still alive until the paramedics got there and found a pulse. I can see her lying there as clearly now as the day it happened. Whenever we're close, when I'm holding her... That all comes flooding back, and I can't... How am I supposed to..." He closed his eyes and shook his head. "I know she's hurting because she thinks this is about her disabilities, but it's not. It's not Annie. It's me. How am I supposed to make love to her when every time I get close to her, I think about her dying in my arms?"

Silence hung over the table long enough that Marcus scoffed. "She thinks talking to you guys will help. I was worried I'd just add to what you are already going through."

"Stop," Paul said. "You aren't adding to what we're going through. You think we don't have the same thoughts? You think I don't look at her and see her like she was after surgery? Bruised and bandaged. We thought she was dead, too, Marcus. I know it's not the same because we weren't there, but the doctors all but said she was going to die. We lost her, too. What you are going through isn't that different than what we have gone through. The thing to remember is that she is still alive. She's still with us. When you're holding her now, she isn't dying in your arms, Marcus. She's living. As much as she can given what happened."

"I can't imagine what you went through," Matt said. "Seeing her get shot like that had to have been horrifying. How often have you asked yourself what you could have done differently?"

"About ten times every minute since that day."

"Have you realized yet that you couldn't have done anything differently?"

He lowered his face and sniffed, trying to stop his grief from surfacing. It didn't help. He had to clear his throat and push the tightness in his chest down so he could breathe again. "Logically, I know that. I walked into the room, said her name, and he pulled the trigger. I didn't even know what was happening until it was too late. But in my heart?" There was that damn emotion again. He bit his lip, almost controlling himself until Paul put his hand on his shoulder. Marcus choked out a quiet sob. "I was there to protect her. I was there to keep her safe. And I didn't."

"You couldn't have," Paul said softly. "Marcus. You couldn't have. I don't know what to say to help you ease your guilt. But I do want you to know that none of us, not even for a moment, blamed you for what happened to Annie. We know you would have taken that bullet for her. I don't doubt that for a second, but that's not how it played out. She got shot, but she beat the odds, and that's what we have to focus on."

"It should have been me," Marcus said quietly. "She should

have been trying to get the sale. She should have been safe in the kitchen. Not me."

"Does Annie feel that way?" Matt asked. "Does she wish it had been you?"

Marcus scoffed. "You know better. She doesn't think like that."

"She'd take a thousand hits before she let anyone she cares about take *one*," Paul said. "And she loves you, Marcus. She would never want to see you hurt."

"I know that. That's why I'm here. Dumping this shit on you guys. Because she can see that I'm hurting, and that's hurting her, and the last thing I want is to make things more difficult for her. She's going through enough already."

Paul shook his head. "You aren't dumping."

"Here's the thing," Marcus said. "My brain knows I did everything I could, but that doesn't stop me from feeling like I should have done more. The guilt is eating me alive. Every time she takes a step forward in her recovery, the happiness I feel for her is overshadowed by this feeling that we wouldn't be celebrating her"—he waved his hand—"opening a fucking ketchup bottle if I'd done what I was there to do. I shouldn't have been off trying to lock down a sale. I should have been with her. I was there to look out for her."

"And *why* were you off trying to lock down a sale?" Matt asked.

Marcus sighed and shook his head.

"Because *Annie* wanted you to. *She* sent you into the

other room. Because she never thought for a moment that some punk-ass kid was going to walk in with a gun. Because nobody ever thinks that is going to happen, Marcus. Neither of you were being lax in security. You both did what you had done hundreds of times before. Hell, I've run a quick errand when I was supposed to be there to deter this kind of shit from happening. Nothing that you or Annie or anybody else could have done would have stopped this from happening."

Marcus nodded. "Yeah, Matt. I have this same pep talk with myself all the time."

"His point," Paul intervened, "is that your guilt is unfounded. Did you think, even once, when she was in a coma that she'd ever open a ketchup bottle again?"

Marcus looked at him and scoffed at the absurdity of the question. "No."

"Did you think, even once, that she was going to die like that?"

The heaviness in his chest returned. He nodded. "Every day for almost three months."

"Me too. Every time I walked out of that hospital, part of me thought it was going to be the last time I'd see her alive. So the fact that she opened a ketchup bottle *is* worth celebrating. The fact that she can still tell us all to go to hell is worth celebrating. That's what you need to think about when you're holding her. She's still here."

"I've tried. Don't you think I've tried? It's not that easy."

It was Matt's turn to put a supportive hand on Marcus's shoulder.

"Paul's right. Nothing we say is going to flip a switch for you, but we do need you to know that there is no one else in the world we'd want looking out for our sister right now, Marcus. We know how much you love her and how protective you are of her. We trust you. If that means anything at all."

Marcus laughed. "Actually, that means a lot. I know you O'Connells don't trust easy, especially an outsider."

"You're not an outsider," Paul said. "No matter what happens between you and Annie, you've proven yourself to us. You stood by her during the worst time in all of our lives."

He shook his head. "This isn't going to end us. I'm not going to let that happen. We've been through too damn much. I just have to get my head around some things."

"I wish we could be more help," Matt said.

"You have helped. More than you know. Then again"—he lifted his near-empty bottle—"maybe that's the beer talking."

They chuckled quietly, and Paul waved over a waitress, ordering refills all around. Marcus used the distraction to take a few deep breaths and put his despair back in check.

Paul tapped his fingers on the table a few times before saying, "Sometimes, when I think too hard about what she's been through, I wonder how she survived it. How the hell did she survive taking a bullet to the brain? Then I think about how damned stubborn that woman is."

They all laughed.

"But that's what got her through," he said with a nod. "That's what got her through raising us. That's what got her through being a single mom and building a business from the ground up. That's what got her through being shot. And that's what's going to get her through recovering."

Marcus nodded in agreement then lifted his beer. "To Annie's stubbornness."

They all chuckled and clinked their beers before taking long drinks.

"I still haven't decided if you're a saint or a fool," Paul said, "but I'm glad she has you."

Marcus laughed. "Pretty sure I'm a fool. That's what she's always telling me anyway."

sh

Annie smiled brightly when Marcus came in the front door. She didn't usually do the giddy welcome-home thing, but she was so impressed with him for meeting her brothers and herself for what she'd been able to accomplish while he was gone that she couldn't wait to see him.

He'd barely hung his coat up before she hugged him and planted a kiss on his cheek.

"How was your day?" she asked.

"Good. And yours?"

She drew a breath and put her arm through his. "Come with me. I have something very important to show you."

He laughed quietly. "Okay."

She led him to the kitchen and pushed him toward the table. "Sit." As he sat, she peeled the foil off the pan she'd used to bake a cake. She bit her lip as she fiddled with the knife until she was finally able to cut a piece and put it on a plate. She carried it to him and set it in front of him. "Ta-da. Granted, it's out of a box, but I baked a cake."

Marcus stared at it for a moment before looking up at her. "Very nice."

"I'm impressed. I didn't burn it or anything."

"Good job, sweetheart." Grabbing her wrist, he tugged until she sat in his lap.

She wrapped her arms around his neck. "If you bite into an eggshell, I fully expect you to smile and swallow it down."

"I will certainly do that."

She dragged her hand over his jaw, and her smile faded. "I thought you might need it after your dinner with my brothers. How'd it go?"

"It went really well, actually."

She lifted her brows. "Really?"

"Yes, really."

"Do you feel like it helped?"

He shrugged. "I don't know, Annie. I still have a hard time talking about what happened. I think we all do, but we did manage to discuss it a little. I guess I got so caught up in what I was going through that I never really let myself think about what Matt and Paul must have been thinking. I knew they were going through hell, but I never thought about how much."

She frowned. "I need to have some one-on-one time with Matty. I haven't done that yet."

"He'd like that." He chuckled. "We toasted your stubbornness."

"My stubbornness?"

"We credit your survival on your inability to relinquish control to anyone else."

She chuckled. "That very well could be true. And in that line of thinking, because we both know that I'm a beast without caffeine, I also managed to re-teach myself how to make coffee. Would you like some with your cake?"

"I would love some."

She started to stand, but he tightened his hold on her. "Thank you for being patient with me."

She sighed. "I think you've earned it. You've taken an awful lot of crap from me, and not just since the shooting." She traced his jaw again. "I just want *us* back. I know that we didn't have much of an *us* before, but I really liked what we did have."

"We had plenty of us before. And I really liked it, too. I miss it, Annie. I don't mean you the way you were. Because underneath all this, you are still you. I mean the comfort level between us. The banter. The fun. You've been taking steps to get back to that, and tonight I feel like I took my first step, too." He smiled up at her as he ran his hand over her hair. "We're going to get there. We're going to find a way to put all this behind us and move forward, and when we do, our life is going to be so beautiful you're going to want to scream."

She chuckled but then shook her head. "I have a little different perspective on all this now, you know. I can't hang on to the past anymore. I can't be so scared that I don't live anymore. I know you'll never hurt me, and that has given me so much freedom, Marcus. You can't even begin to imagine how much you have given me."

He smiled and nodded. "I hope so."

She dipped her head but waited for him to close the distance. He did, and the kiss lingered. It wasn't passionate or an invitation for more, simply a soft kiss, but it still stirred something inside her, and when she leaned back, she chuckled. "I forgot what I was going to do."

Marcus grinned.

"Don't look so cocky," she whispered. "I have brain damage. I forget a lot of things."

He laughed as he lifted her from his lap. "Coffee, you shrew. You were making me coffee."

"Right." Leaning down, she kissed his head. "I remember now."

CHAPTER EIGHTEEN

*S*tonehill Café wasn't usually quite so busy. It was good for Jenna that the restaurant was bustling, but Marcus had picked it expecting it to be slower. He put his hand on Annie's back, trying to gauge her comfort level. She offered him a smile, clearly to reassure him, but she looked uneasy. She still couldn't wrap her head around all the noises and movements of a crowd.

"Shall we leave?"

She shook her head. "If we are going to take steps to get back the things that make us *us*, then I need to work on this."

"We can find someplace quieter."

"No. This is what you wanted. This is what we're having. I'll be fine."

He hesitated, still uncertain, but when Jenna smiled and gestured for them to have a seat wherever they wanted, he led Annie to a booth that sat away from most of the diners.

"It's so good to see you, Annie," Jenna said.

Annie smiled. "You, too."

"How are you?"

"Doing better every day."

She slid the menus onto the table, and Annie turned her attention to scanning the options. Marcus didn't know why. They both knew she'd get the grilled chicken sandwich with no vegetables—they slid off and made the sandwich more difficult for her to hold—and fries—she could eat those with her hands without feeling awkward about it.

When Jenna returned, he ordered the same, just to show Annie a bit of solidarity in their meal. He watched her closely as the noise in the restaurant surrounded them. She was getting better—being around a houseful of O'Connells once a week was turning into great practice for being in larger groups—but she was still clearly uncomfortable with the volume and confusion that too many things happening at once caused.

Reaching across the table, he took her hand, trying to get her to focus on him. He smiled when she met his gaze. "Between lunch and dinner, we used to come here several times a week. I think this is a great place to get back into our habit of dining out."

She nodded. "I came here for lunch with Paul and Matt last week. Remember?"

"You guys came early to avoid the crowd, though. I think it's safe to say, this is more like what we should expect when we go to restaurants. How is it?"

She squeezed his hand lightly. "I'm okay, Marcus. Stop worrying about every little thing."

"I love worrying about every little thing."

"Yes, I know. To add to that, I wanted to talk about the trip to San Diego. Are you sure about driving?"

"Yeah. And you know, that's the perfect time to take Mallory her stuff. We'll take a moving van out, attach my car to the back, and haul it with us then drive back in it."

"It's a long way."

"Are you concerned about the drive?"

"No. I'm not allowed to drive anymore. I'm concerned about you driving. And the weather turning."

He glanced at a group of teens headed toward a booth close to theirs. He wasn't exactly going to ask them not to take the free table, but he was hoping they'd move on and sit elsewhere. They were loud coming in, and he expected they'd be just as loud sitting around a table. The added noise was sure to disturb Annie.

His spine stiffened when one of the kids turned and adjusted his cap. The hat—white with a Harley Davidson logo—flashed into Marcus's mind. The shaggy hair was longer now. But the square jaw was the same. His build was the same.

"Marcus?" Annie tugged at his hands.

The kid smiled at something one of his friends said as his gaze met Marcus's. It should have only been for a split second, but the way he stopped and his eyes grew wide told Marcus what his gut already knew. That was the bastard who'd shot Annie.

"Don't move," Marcus said to Annie as he stood.

"Where are you going?"

Marcus had just taken a step when the kid turned and ran, just like he'd done from the scene of the shooting. This time, however, Marcus was right behind him.

"What the fuck, man?" one of the other teens asked as Marcus pushed through the group.

The kid was almost to the door when Jenna inadvertently stepped in his way. He plowed into her, knocking her down. The tray she was holding crashed to the floor, and glasses broke as sodas mixed and ice cubes scattered with the shards of glass. The kid jumped over her, stumbled, and tried to steady himself, but Marcus was on him a second later, slamming him to the floor. First he'd shot Annie, and then he'd knocked Jen to the ground. There was no way in hell this kid was getting away again.

Marcus grabbed a fistful of his shirt, flipped him over, and slapped the hat off his head.

"I didn't mean it," the kid said. "I swear, I didn't mean it."

Slamming his back to the ground, Marcus glared at the young man who couldn't have been older than twenty. "You shot her."

"It was an accident."

Marcus wouldn't ever consider himself a violent man, but the rage inside him took over, and he pulled his fist back and punched the kid when he struggled to get free. "It's not an accident when you aim a loaded gun at someone's head."

Hands pulled at Marcus's shoulder, but he clung to the kid.

He wasn't letting him go again. He grabbed his shirt and shook him. "Do you have any idea what you've put her through? What you've done to her family?"

"Sir," someone said firmly, "I need you to back down."

Looking over his shoulder, he realized one of the cops who had been sitting at the counter was behind him. Hand on the butt of the gun at his hip as he pulled at Marcus. Annie was standing with Jenna, holding her hand as the other officer who had been waiting for dinner looked Jenna over. The wide-eyed fear on their faces made him ease his hold. He was pulled back, and the officer put himself between Marcus and the kid.

Annie was immediately at Marcus's side.

Her lips trembled as she looked into his eyes. "He shot me?"

He nodded and pulled her to him. She buried her face in his chest, and he held her tightly as he answered the officer's demand to know what was going on.

Annie rolled over when Marcus sighed. He'd been making that sorrowful sound about every two minutes if her calculations were correct. Putting her hand on his back, she rubbed gently. "You okay?"

"Am I keeping you awake?"

"Not really. I can't sleep either." She scooted closer, spooning him from behind, and slid her arm around his waist and up his chest.

His hand instantly covered hers, and he sighed again. "I'm so sorry."

"About what?"

"Losing my temper."

She kissed his back and pressed her cheek against his warm skin. "I told you not to apologize for that anymore. If you hadn't gone after him, he would have gotten away again."

"I shouldn't have hit him like that."

"Well, since the police wouldn't let me have a go at him, I'm glad you got your hit in." She smiled, but he didn't respond. "Marcus, he deserved it. Look what he's done to us."

"But I upset you."

"No." She leaned back and pulled at him. "Roll over. Please."

After a moment, he turned onto his back so she could look down at him in the dimly lit room.

"You didn't upset me. I was confused at first, but once I realized what was going on, I got it. I *get* it. He got away with what he'd done to us for too long."

"I was almost arrested for assault. If you hadn't called Paul..."

"Hey," she gently teased. "What good is it having a criminal defense attorney in the family if I don't get to use him every now and then?"

He sighed and sat up, leaning against the headboard. "I've never lost control like that before. I just...I saw that damned hat he was wearing, and that moment came back. I remembered how he had it down on his face, like it was going to disguise him. His eyes. I remembered his eyes. He had that same shocked look, like he couldn't believe what was happening."

"He's ruined the rest of his life."

Marcus's face tensed. "He ruined the rest of *your* life."

Annie frowned and pushed herself to sit. She pulled her knees under her and kneeled beside him as she stared into his eyes. "I felt that way for a while. For too long. It took a lot of time to realize that you were right when you told me that I needed to be thankful to be alive. I finally am. I finally get what you were saying. My life is different. My life is more difficult. But my life *isn't* ruined." After stroking her hand over his hair, she rested her palms on his cheeks. "My life would be ruined if I lost you. If he'd shot you instead of running, *then* my life would have been ruined. But we're both here. We're both alive." Tracing his laugh lines with her thumbs, she smiled softly. "He's going to get what is owed to him. And so are we. Because from this point on, we're not looking back. We're just going forward. We're going to focus on us and the life we said we were going to have."

"You amaze me," he whispered. "Every single day I am amazed by you."

She grinned. "Well, I'm amazing."

"Yes, you are."

"You're pretty great yourself." Leaning in, she kissed him lightly before resting her forehead against his. She considered only for a moment before kissing him again, this time letting it linger. She waited for the inevitable moment when he shut down, but instead, he put his hands to her hips and lifted her to his lap. She straddled his thighs and wrapped her arms around his neck as she parted her lips and let his tongue in. His fingers pressed into her, pulling her closer. Fire lit inside her at the feel of his body reacting to hers. Grinding into him, her breath caught as he moaned.

Breaking the kiss, Marcus exhaled slowly, warming her face with his breath. "Annie."

"I'm not going to break," she whispered. "I promise."

He brushed his nose against hers, and she kissed him lightly.

"I promise."

"If you start to feel overwhelmed..."

"Oh, honey. You're good, but—"

He gently bit her lip, causing her to giggle.

"You're a smartass," he said.

"You love that about me."

He ran his hand over her hair, and the teasing left his gaze. "I love everything about you. I really do."

She softened her smile as well. "I love you. We've made it this far down the path. We're going to make it to the end. Together. Like we said."

Pulling her to him, he kissed her, and this time, she knew he wouldn't stop.

CHAPTER NINETEEN

*I*t wasn't easy for Annie, but she sat at her kitchen table while her daughter, sisters-in-law, and Jenna took control of Thanksgiving dinner. They bustled about the room, mixing, spilling, and laughing as they went. She used to be in the mix, but now that she was sitting on the outside, she had to admit she kind of enjoyed it. It was nice to be able to watch and actually see the happiness her family felt. Seeing them together like this filled her with her own sense of pride.

This was her family and after so many years of emotional turmoil and hardships, they were finally coming into their own. Matt and Donna were as happy as ever. Paul and Dianna were content with their lives, and she and Marcus were settling in as a couple. Mallory would be leaving for California over the weekend. Once she got to San Diego, she'd find a home and officially be on her own. Everything was growing and changing, but unlike before the shooting, Annie didn't feel a sense of loss at the changes. Life wasn't being lived if it wasn't changing. She understood that now. She embraced it now.

Hands on her shoulders pulled her from her thoughts. She smiled when Marcus bent down to kiss her head. Funny how seven months before, she would have hated how he constantly did that. Now it was one of the most comforting things in her life. He never missed a chance to press his lips to her head, and she'd come to expect, and appreciate, it.

"Okay?"

"Better than okay," she said.

He kneeled in front of her and took her hands. "You were a million miles away."

"No, I was focusing on that." She nodded toward the women.

He glanced over his shoulder. "Making sure they don't mess up dinner?"

"Soaking in the happiness."

He lifted his brows. "Oh?"

"Can we take a walk?"

"Do we have time?"

"They won't eat without us."

He stood, held his hand out, and pulled her to her feet. "We'll be back," he said to the three women cooking. Leading Annie through the living room, he made the same declaration to Paul and Matt.

Paul looked up from the newspaper he was reading. "Where you headed?"

"I need some air," Annie said.

"Everything okay?"

"Everything's perfect." And she meant it. Bundling in her scarf and coat, she struggled with her gloves until Marcus reached for her hands and helped her pull them up. She'd figure it out, she'd learn how to put them on without him, but until then, she'd learned to accept his help.

The cold air bit at her cheeks when they stepped outside. "It's going to snow."

"Supposed to start anytime now."

She drew a deep breath as he took her hand. "It's still beautiful out."

"Was it getting to be too much noise?" he asked as they started down the sidewalk.

"No, actually, I was just thinking about how lucky I am. Funny how it took a bullet in the head for me to finally start to get what you've been telling me for so long."

"Everybody needs a wake-up call sometime."

"I was sitting there feeling so happy, so complete. That's a good way to put it. My life is finally complete. And I realized there is one thing that will make it better."

"What?"

"I want to do it."

He lifted his brows and looked around. "Right here?"

She laughed as she tugged at his hand. Pulling him to a stop, she drew a deep breath and looked into his eyes. "I want us to get married."

The surprise on his face made her giggle.

"I know this isn't the most traditional marriage proposal, but when have we ever been traditional?" she asked. "I don't want the fuss, and not just because I'm not about all that, but honestly"—she touched her head—"I couldn't handle it. If it's okay, I thought maybe we could just elope, like said we would. Just a quiet ceremony in San Diego when we visit our girl. Like we joked about."

He smiled. "You called her *our* girl."

"She is *our* girl. You're the closest thing to a dad she's ever had. That she'll ever have. And we're a family, right?"

"Damn straight we are." He put his gloved hands to her face and kissed her. "Don't move."

"Hey," she called as he started back toward the house. "The last time you told me that, you punched a guy."

"There will be no hitting this time," he said. "I promise. Just don't move."

She watched him trot to the house then looked up at the sky as snowflakes started to fall around her. Holding her hand out, she used the strength she'd been gaining to almost—but not quite —straighten her fingers so she could catch a few pieces of the white dusting. She grinned as the snow rested in her palm for a few seconds before melting.

A moment later, the front door closed, and she looked back to the house. Marcus was running back to her. By the time he reached her, the front door opened again and a flock of curious family members were peering outside.

"I have been wanting to do this for so long," he said before kissing her again.

Annie creased her brow, confused until he opened his hand and revealed a silver band with a single diamond sitting atop. It was simple, but it was beautiful. It was perfect.

He eased down on one knee before her, and Annie laughed at the sound of gasps coming from the house.

"Annie O'Connell, will you do me the immense honor of becoming my wife?"

She forced a scowl. "You always have to outdo me, don't you?"

"Always have. Always will. Forever." His smile widened. "Now say yes."

She took a moment to pretend to ponder. "Fine. Okay. Yes. Yes, I'll marry you."

He tugged her glove off, slipped the ring onto her finger, and then stood and scooped her against him. She barely heard the squeals of the women on the porch over the pounding of her heart as he kissed her.

sh

Marcus smiled at his bride as she scrunched her face with frustration. She'd been expecting a simple ceremony, but then Mallory got ahold of her, put her in a knee-length lacy dress and pearls, primped her hair, and was now adding a light application of makeup.

"I don't need all this," Annie said as Mallory dabbed on a bit of what used to be Annie's favorite eye shadow. She didn't wear much makeup these days. She had better control of her hands but still had too much difficulty with tasks that required such fine detail.

Marcus didn't mind. He thought she was beautiful without all the fuss makeup added. Even so, he couldn't help but come to Mallory's defense. "Leave her be, Annie. It's the only time she's going to see her mother get married."

Mallory smiled. "I just want everything to be perfect for you, Mom."

"It will be." She pulled Mallory's hand away. "Hey. You and Marcus are here. That makes it perfect."

Mallory smiled. "I'm so happy for you. You have no idea how much it means to me to know you and Marcus are taking care of each other."

"Don't get soft on me, kid," she said, closing her eyes. "I'll ruin the face paint you just put on me."

"No running mascara. I don't want her to look like a hooker in our wedding photos," Marcus said, putting his hands on Annie's shoulders. He chuckled as she nudged her elbow into his ribs. He assured her he was kidding and kissed the back of her head. "Are we about to get this show on the road?"

"You have the license?" Annie asked.

He patted one pocket then the other. Her eyes widened and her mouth dropped, but he smiled and pulled the paper from his inside pocket.

"Of course I have the license."

She narrowed her eyes at him. "Is this how things are going to be once we're married?"

"This is how things have always been." He kissed her cheek before walking to the clerk and handing her the paper. "I tried to talk her out of it, but she still wants to get married."

The woman smiled. "The judge is ready. Come with me, please."

Marcus could barely contain his excitement as they followed her to a courtroom. He grabbed Annie's hand. It was trembling. "Okay?"

"I can't believe I'm about to get married." She smiled up at him with tears in her eyes. "Never thought this would happen."

He kissed her forehead. "Me either. You sure didn't make this easy for me."

"Never will."

The clerk opened the door, and Annie squeezed his hand as her smile spread."Ready?"

"Ready." His heart filled to damn near overflowing when they stepped into the room and she gasped.

"What the hell?" she demanded but didn't sound the least bit upset. Instead, she pulled away from Marcus and went straight into Paul's arms.

"Did you really think we'd miss this?" he asked, hugging his sister.

"This was supposed to be small."

"It is." Matt opened his arms, and she practically threw herself at him. "Just the family."

Annie laughed. "Yeah, like I said. Jenna," she whispered before hugging Marcus's sister.

"We had to be here," she said.

Marcus shook Paul's hand and then Matt's as Annie greeted their wives.

"I can't believe we managed to surprise her," Paul said.

"I'm glad you guys could make it," Marcus said. "I know it was a bit inconvenient coming all this way."

"We wouldn't miss this," Matt said. He looked at his sister, and Marcus saw emotion brewing.

He cleared his throat, not wanting to break down. He'd managed to hold himself together so far; he intended to make it through the ceremony.

Dianna hugged Annie tightly. "You look so beautiful."

"I'm glad you let Mal dress you up," Donna said.

Mallory beamed. "I didn't give her a choice."

"No, she didn't. If I'd known you guys were going to be here, I might have reconsidered."

"Oh," Mallory teased, "you'll dress up for them but not for me?"

Annie playfully glared at her. "This makes it a bit more...formal."

Taking her hand, Marcus pulled her from the half circle of family members. "We've got about ten minutes until the judge kicks us out. Are you ready to do this?"

She grinned. "I'm more than ready."

"Okay."

She started to walk with him but then pulled back. He felt his stomach tighten a bit, not sure if she was having second thoughts. She turned to her brothers, and the tears that had been occasionally shimmering in her eyes dripped down her cheeks. She hesitated before hugging them both. Marcus couldn't hear what she whispered, but it did the guys in, which did him in.

Damn it. He lowered his face, sniffed, wiped his eyes, and didn't look up again until she grabbed his hand.

"Come on, you old sap," she said, pulling him toward the judge. "We don't have all day."

Taking a deep breath, he walked with Annie to the judge and smiled as he looked into her eyes and made her his wife.

Mallory was sliding into a booth by the window when she noticed a little girl peeking over the top of the cracked red vinyl seat across from her. She grinned, immediately recognizing her. "Hey, Jessica."

The girl beamed, clearly thrilled that Mal remembered her.

"What's up?" Mallory asked.

"The sky."

Mallory laughed more than the joke required. "Very clever. How are you?"

Jessica rested her folded arms on the back of the seat back and her smile widened. "Jenna added rainbow pancakes to the menu. And guess what?"

Mal didn't have a chance to guess before Jessica told her.

"She named them after me because she didn't have rainbow pancakes until *I* asked her to make them. They are on the kid section, but she'll let you order them. You should. They are *delicious.*"

"I bet they are." Mallory couldn't help but feel excited for the girl. Clearly this was a big accomplishment for her. Then again, who didn't want pancakes named after them?

A few beats passed as Jessica narrowed her eyes thoughtfully. "I thought you moved away."

"I did. But I came home to see my mom."

"I don't have a mom," she said as casually as one might comment on the weather.

Mallory opened her mouth but wasn't quite sure how to respond. She knew that Jessica's mother had bailed when the girl was an infant. Mal understood the hole in Jessica's life—her dad had ducked out before she was even born. Annie had been a single mother from the moment she'd told him she was pregnant.

"I didn't have a dad for a long time," Mallory said, wanting to give the girl hope, "but then my mom got married. To Jenna's brother, actually. I like to think of him as my dad even though he really isn't. And that makes Jenna my aunt."

Jessica rolled her eyes with all the reprehension the rainbow pancake-loving little girl seemed to be able to muster. "My dad will *never* get married. He's too peculiar."

Mallory didn't mean to laugh, but the sound ripped from her chest. She'd met Jessica's father. He was cute. Nice. A bit of a hippie, but he *was* Kara's child and that woman looked like she'd walked out of a Woodstock documentary. Even so, Phil hadn't seemed odd to Mallory. "What do you mean, he's too peculiar?"

"Grandma says that he'll never find a girlfriend if he doesn't stop being so picky."

"Oh. You mean *particular*."

Jess shrugged, as if she didn't care that she'd used the wrong word. "Grandma says it's important that Daddy be choosy, but he can't expect to find someone if he never dates anyone. He says he'll date when he's ready, but I think he is ready because I caught him flirting with my teacher." Jessica looked up and smiled when a throat cleared as someone approached her table. "Hi, Daddy."

Phil seemed to have overheard at least a part of the conversation he'd interrupted. He had an air of disapproval on his face as he drew his mouth tight and lifted his brows at his daughter. "Hey, Punk."

"Did you remember to use a paper towel to open the bathroom door so you don't get germs on your fingers?"

He nodded. "I did. Thanks for checking."

Jessica returned her attention to Mallory. "Some people don't wash their hands after using the bathroom so you should always use a paper towel or your sleeve to open the bathroom door."

"Good tip. Thanks." Mallory tried to hide her smile, but figured her amusement was out there for the world to see. Jessica's father, on the other hand, still didn't appear amused. "Hi, Phil. How are you?" Mallory asked to rescue the girl from his scowl.

He stared, as if not quite sure who she was. Most people who knew Annie immediately recognized Mal as the woman's offspring. From her straight blond hair to her pointed nose and cool gray eyes, Mallory was practically identical to her mother.

"Mallory O'Connell. We met at my uncle Paul's wedding. I'm Annie's daughter."

The light went off in his eyes as he nodded. "Right. How's your mom?"

"She's okay. Getting better every day, so she says."

"I was glad the guy pled so Annie didn't have to go through the trial. My mom said she was really worried about having to testify."

Yet another reason why Mallory had hated being away from home. Anticipating the trial had been nerve-racking for Annie and Marcus. Neither had wanted to relive the moment their lives had changed forever. They hadn't said as much to her, though. Mallory heard from her uncles how choked up Annie still got talking about the moment a bullet ripped through her and how she didn't seem willing to do that in front of the man who had hurt her. Her mother had reluctantly given a statement at the sentencing hearing and only because the prosecution insisted the judge needed to see firsthand how much damage had been done. Mallory knew that alone would have been stressful and was glad Annie hadn't had to sit on the stand and answer detailed questions about the incident and her recovery.

Phil put his hands casually into his pockets. "I thought you were—"

"In California," she finished. "Yes. I was. I just got back, actually."

"For good or just visiting?"

"For good. I felt like a shi—" Her gaze darted to where Jessica was still peering over the booth, hanging on her every word. "Like a jerk not being here for Mom. I know she and Marcus can use my help right now. Even if they won't admit it."

He furrowed his thick brows, as concern filled his dark eyes. Though Kara clearly impacted his taste in attire, his olive skin and dark features were all Harry Canton. "Is she really okay?"

"She doesn't like when people feel sorry for her," Jessica said. "If you feel sorry for her, she's going to be mad at you."

Jessica wasn't wrong. Annie and Marcus both would be furious if they knew the real reason Mallory had given up her dream job and living in SoCal was that she felt so damned guilty living her own life that she couldn't even sleep at night.

While Annie had been in the hospital recovering, she and Jessica bonded over their disabilities. Jessica had grown up dealing with pity, but that kind of attention was new to Annie, and she hadn't handled it well. Kara had made an effort to bring Jessica around once she saw Annie interacting with the girl. Kara said one of Jessica's natural talents was helping people who didn't know they needed it. She was right. Without even being aware of what she was doing, Jessica was able to guide Annie to the inner strength she needed to stop being angry about her situation and to start recovering. The two had forged a strong bond, one that was evident in Jessica's defense of Annie now.

"I'm not feeling sorry for her," Mal said. "I just want to be here for her."

Phil gestured to the table that Jessica hadn't faced since Mallory sat down. "Finish your pancakes, Punk."

Jessica huffed but turned and disappeared behind the booth.

Phil sank into the seat across from Mallory. The concern in his brown eyes was almost enough to make Mallory cry, though she didn't understand why. She wasn't the one who needed the help. She was the one who had come home to help.

"I know worrying and family go hand in hand," Phil said, "but your mom really does seem to be doing okay. She and Marcus came to Jessica's birthday party last weekend. She smiled and laughed and seemed to enjoy herself. Marcus had to help her a little bit, sure, but she really was okay."

"Good to hear."

Jenna set a cup of coffee in front of Mallory and smiled at the little face poking over the seat. "How are your pancakes, Miss Jess?"

"Fine," Jessica said with a pout to her voice.

Mallory tried not to chuckle, but a giggle escaped. "Can I get some of those rainbow pancakes she was telling me about?" she asked to atone for the slip.

"The Jessica Special? Coming right up. Phil, you need anything?" She glanced between the two adults, clearly trying to gauge what was going on.

"No, thanks, Jen. I'm good." Phil waited for Jenna to disappear before looking at Mallory again. "You didn't answer me before—and feel free to tell me it's none of my business—but is Annie okay?"

"Yeah, she's fine. I mean, she's not *fine*, she's...got residual issues, but..." She laughed awkwardly. "She's not in a coma anymore, right?" Her smile faded, and she sipped her coffee as he scrutinized her from across the table. Finally, she sat the cup down and fell back in the booth. "Sorry. I tend to make inappropriate jokes when I'm upset."

"I don't mean to upset you."

She frowned as he gave her an encouraging smile. His mother had that same look. The one that made the words want to pour out of Mallory. When Annie was in the hospital and no one knew if she'd live, let alone recover, Kara had a way about her that made Mallory want to break down and let out some of her fear. She never had. She'd been too terrified that the reality of her mother's condition would consume her. That fear still lingered in the back of her mind.

Even though Annie was on the road to recovery, she'd never be the same. Nothing would ever be the same. That was terrifying. Mallory had never let the horror of what she felt really touch her. She attributed that trait to Annie. The woman was stronger than granite. But even granite cracked sometimes, and the way Phil was looking at her now made Mallory want to crumble. He apparently practiced the same emotional voodoo as his mother.

Mallory took a deep breath to brace herself against his dark powers. "Mom's probably handling her disabilities better than I am," she confessed. "No. She's definitely handling her disabilities better than I am. She was always the strongest person I knew, completely unshakable. Seeing her… God, I sound like an ass."

"No, you don't," Phil reassured her. "You sound like someone who is struggling with a drastically changed reality. Maybe I should be asking if you're okay."

"I felt guilty not being here." She stared at him hard. "And if you *ever* repeat that, I will deny it to my dying breath."

He crossed his heart. "Your secret's safe with me."

"I stayed in California as long as I could. I wanted to come home so many times."

"What was the final push?"

"Uncle Paul slipped. He said she was having a hard time coping with this brick wall she's hit in her recovery. The therapist doesn't think her speech will get any better and regaining full use of her hands is taking longer than they thought. She's struggling with that. I realized it was time. I need to be here. I need to help her, even if she doesn't want me to."

"I don't think that's the issue, Mallory. Of course she wants you home and close. She talked about you so much at Jessica's party. She's incredibly proud of you. I think she just wants you to be happy and worries that taking time out of your life to care for her isn't going to make you happy. My unsolicited advice would be that since you've made the decision to come home, make a point to have a life outside of looking after Annie. Or you'll both regret your decision."

Phil gave her that damned comforting smile again. He had a

little dimple in his left cheek that drew her attention until she forced her focus back to her coffee cup. She'd talked to her family and friends about this, but something about the understanding in Phil's eyes made her feel that coming home simply because she needed to be closer to Annie didn't make her a baby. She appreciated that more than he could ever know, and apparently more than she could say since she couldn't seem to find the words to thank him for being sympathetic. Or figure out why all of a sudden her eyes burned with unshed tears.

"Sorry," she whispered, snagging a napkin from the dispenser on the table.

"Parents can be a handful, huh?" he asked softly.

She laughed quietly as she dabbed her tears before they could fall. "Sometimes."

"Speaking of which"—he jerked his head back to the booth behind him—"I wasn't flirting with her teacher. Just so you know."

"Yes, you were," Jessica called.

He rolled his eyes and shook his head.

ABOUT THE AUTHOR

As a teen, Marci Bolden skipped over young adult books and jumped right into reading romance novels. She never left.

Marci lives in the Midwest with her husband, kiddos, and numerous rescue pets. If she had an ounce of willpower, Marci would embrace healthy living, but until cupcakes and wine are no longer available at the local market, she will appease her guilt by reading self-help books and promising to join a gym "soon."

Visit her here:
www.marcibolden.com

 facebook.com/MarciBoldenAuthor
 twitter.com/BoldenMarci
 instagram.com/marciboldenauthor

CPSIA information can be obtained
at www.ICGtesting.com
Printed in the USA
LVHW050308041121
702414LV00004B/66